PRAISE FOR S*

"Malfi's descriptive writing captures the cold and desperate scene in a way that will lure new fans to the genre." —*Las Vegas Review-Journal*

"An absolutely top notch horror novel."   —HorrorNews.net

"*Snow* is an impressive work that leaves the reader eager to see more from this talented writer."   —*Dark Scribe Magazine*

"An impressively atmospheric novel with a wicked streak."
             —*Dread Central*

"A genuine page turner that grabs you from the very first word and doesn't stop cranking until the very last."   —*House of Horrors*

"Some 'old school' horror storytelling of the highest degree."
             —*Bloody Disgusting*

"Absolutely brilliant . . . A must read for every lover of horror fiction and . . . very highly recommended, you really don't want to pass this one by."   —*Horror World & Reviews*

SNOW

SNOW

RONALD MALFI

OPEN ROAD
INTEGRATED MEDIA
NEW YORK

For Deb, my shelter in the storm.

Copyright © 2010 by Ronald Malfi

ISBN: 978-1-5040-7562-6

This edition published in 2022 by Open Road Integrated Media, Inc.
180 Maiden Lane
New York, NY 10038
www.openroadmedia.com

SNOW

PROLOGUE

M r. Farmer? Is that you?"
But she knew it wasn't George Farmer. Even if it looked like him, it wasn't George Farmer.

Wiping strands of sweat-slicked hair from her face, Shawna Dupree crouched below the counter inside the deserted Pack-N-Go. Too frightened to sit up and peer over the countertop, she managed to survey the store in the reflection of the tortoiseshell antitheft mirror above her head. The blood on her hands was starting to freeze to the rifle's cold steel.

The lights were out and the store itself was a mess. Aisles were cluttered with fallen, rotting goods. Bottles of soda had burst, leaving behind sticky puddles of molasses on the linoleum. Someone—one of the others?—had knocked over a metal shelving unit, driving it into the glass doors of the industrial refrigerator that lined one wall; despite the freezing temperatures outside, the ice cream had begun to melt in the freezer. Worst of all, Jared's body lay somewhere amongst the junkfood and girlie magazines. She'd had no choice with Jared.

"George Farmer?" she called again, her voice a pathetic squeal that reminded her of weathervanes twisting noisily in the wind. She winced, held her breath, counted silently to ten. When she spoke again, she tried desperately to sound more in control: "If that's you, goddamn it, you better answer me! I've got a gun!"

Daylight fell through the plate glass windows, one of which was decorated with a bull's-eye webbing of cracks. The light was pale, ghostly blue, casting an eerie glow over the otherwise darkened store. Beyond the windows, the town square was blanketed in snow, the roofs of the nearby shops nearly bowing under the weight. She could make out the whole downtown area in distorted miniature in the antitheft mirror above the register. The spire of St. John's remained a solitary reminder of what the town had been only a short time ago. At the horizon, the sky looked like hammered sheet metal.

Something shifted toward the back of the store.

Shawna drew her legs up closer to her chest, her heart jackhammering. A rivulet of fresh blood, dark as chocolate syrup, oozed from her left pant leg and across the floor. She forced her eyes from the antitheft mirror and glanced at the blood soaking through her jeans. Just looking at it caused the pain—at least subconsciously—to intensify, and almost instantly she could feel the burning, jagged laceration along her calf all over again. On the floor, the runnel of blood was temporarily arrested when it reached a rubber WEL-COME mat. Then it grew darker and seeped along the mat's edge, angling around one corner.

Holding her breath, Shawna listened for the sound again, but the store remained silent. It had been a whooshing, shuffling sound—like someone walking in pantyhose, their thighs rubbing together. Miss Brennan, her middle school math teacher (so many years ago now), had sounded like that when she walked—that *shush-shush-shush . . .*

They know I'm here. Somehow, they know I'm here, right here.

Was it possible that this was all a dream? A horrible, hellish dream?

She squeezed her eyes shut . . . but in doing so, the image of Jared jumped up behind her eyelids, his face frozen in a mask of pure terror, his skin gone a horrible milky white, his eyes covered in a film of tallow mucus. There had been a constellation of blood speckling the right side of his face, and more blood—a *lot* more—in the nearby snow bank outside, where she'd shot him the first couple of times. But he'd pursued her across the town square, along with George Farmer and several others. She shot him again in the magazine aisle of the Pack-N-Go. That was finally when he went down. Before he died, he'd managed to lift his head, his voice shredded and nothing more than a croak as he attempted to speak her name: *"Shaw . . . naah . . ."*

A sharp bang echoed from the opposite end of the convenience store. Shawna braced herself, gripping the rifle tighter. *Come on, fucker.* Another bang—louder than the first. Then the rushing sound of ghost-feet or batwings or old Miss Brennan's pantyhose came charging down the aisles. Bags of potato chips and plastic tubs of motor oil exploded up into the air like a shark's dorsal fin cleaving through water.

It was hunting for her.

Shawna executed one final glance in the spotty mirror above the register and saw—or *thought* she saw, for it was there and then gone in a single instant if it was even there in the first place—the flickering visage of something large and thin and so pale she could see the burnt umber of the setting sun shining right through its shimmering, translucent flesh—

Soda bottles burst off the shelves directly behind her and loose coins sprayed the linoleum.

Shawna jumped up, swung the rifle around, and screamed as she pulled the trigger.

PART ONE

THE STORM

CHAPTER ONE

The newscaster with the plastic-looking face and the electric yellow tie spoke of doom. Todd Curry glanced up at the screen just as an HD map of the Midwest replaced the newscaster. A digital white mass blipped across the state, moving in staggered increments across the screen, completely obliterating Chicago and the surrounding suburbs. At Gate 16 of Chicago's O'Hare International Airport, a number of people groaned in unison. For a moment, Todd thought it was in response to the digital snowstorm on the flat-screen television set, but then he looked over to the check-in counter and saw that Flight 218 to Des Moines—his flight—had been delayed another hour.

"Son of a bitch," he whispered to himself.

"The snowstorm will continue through the evening and well into tomorrow afternoon, which is bad news for a number of commuters who are desperately trying to make it home this Christmas Eve," the newscaster said, grinning like a ventriloquist's dummy in high definition despite the bad news. "Downtown Chicago has already been hit with six inches and some of the outlying areas may see as much as fifteen inches before this storm passes. So unfortunately for all you holiday travelers, there appears to be little reprieve in sight. Back to you, Donna."

"This is bullshit," grunted an enormous man in a Chicago Bulls sweatshirt and cargo pants that looked like they were cut from the fabric of a multicolored circus tent. The man was sweating profusely and balancing a triangular Sbarro's pizza box on his left knee. His small, squinty eyes shot over to Todd, who was seated two chairs away. "You believe this? You just watch, buddy. They're gonna cancel this flight."

"Sounds like my luck," he returned. In his lap, his hands wrestled with each other while between his feet his laptop sat in its nylon carrying case. Like someone anticipating a horrible telephone call, Todd's eyes kept shooting back to the flat-screen TV bolted to one of the rafters above the rows of seats. On the screen, a mildly attractive woman in a burgundy pantsuit was shaking her head at the unfortunate weather conditions.

"That's their little trick," the big guy in the Bulls sweatshirt went on, jabbing an index finger roughly the size of a kielbasa at the check-in counter's electronic screen. "Right now they know this flight's been cancelled. Hell, look outside! Doesn't take a meteor-fucking-ologist to see we ain't leaving the ground anytime soon."

The big guy was right: over the past hour, the walls of plate-glass windows had become great sightless cataracts, blinded by twirling, billowing snow. Todd could just barely make out the vague dinosaur shapes of the airplanes out on the tarmac, gray and indistinct beasts fading into the background the longer he looked at them.

"They keep *saying* the flight's delayed just to weed out the more impatient travelers," said the man. He had his pizza box opened now and he was trying to gather up the messy slice inside with his overlarge fingers. "They get a few boneheads going up to the counter, changing their flights and asking point-less questions, before they slink away like dogs who've been beat for nosing around in the kitchen trash."

Indeed, a small line had already formed in front of the check-in counter, though it did not seem to be moving very quickly.

"You just watch," said the man in the Bulls sweatshirt. "Once that line dwindles, they'll put up the cancel sign on the board. It's a lock."

"We could still get lucky."

"Wanna bet?"

Ha, Todd thought morosely. *You have no idea, chubby.*

"They do it this way to stem the flow, know what I mean?" said the man. "They don't wanna get rushed by a hundred people all at once, see?"

Todd ran his hands through his hair and said, "You do a lot of traveling?" With his run of bad luck, he was already thinking this fat bastard would wind up sitting next to him on the flight . . . if there *was* a flight.

"I'm in sales. Medical supplies. Pharmaceuticals." The guy finally man-aged to wrangle the slice of pizza out of the box but not without having a wedge of pepperoni land in his lap. "Shit on a stick." He looked up at Todd with his piggish, squinting little eyes. "How about you?"

"Travel much? No, not really."

"I meant, what do you do for a living?"

"I'm a lawyer."

"No shit? Private practice?"

"Personal injury, DUIs, that sort of thing."

"Gotcha. Ambulance chaser," said the guy in the Bulls sweatshirt, sliding the tip of the pizza into his mouth. He tore a bite out of it that would put the shark from *Jaws* to shame. "I get it. There big money in that?"

"I do okay." He checked his watch: 5:45 p.m. The goddamn flight was sup-posed to have left two hours ago. He envisioned Justin watching television in the living room of the little house on Calabasas Street in Des Moines, wear-ing his *Turbo Dogs* pajamas and sporting his fresh crew-cut, while Brianna—Todd's ex-wife—scampered around the house doing a little last-minute tidying up. She'd been a good sport about all this and Todd silently thanked her for it. After all, it was for Justin's sake.

It had been almost a full year since he'd seen Justin, back in . . . Jesus, was it back in March? For the kid's seventh birthday? That long ago? Of course, he was supposed to have had Justin three weeks this past summer, too, but life had a way of changing plans without fair warning. This past summer had been a mess—a complete fucking wreck, in fact, thank you very much—and, in the end, his only communication with Justin since March had been over the telephone or through handwritten letters in the mail. Justin's teacher had taught his class how to write letters and address envelopes—something the boy had been infatuated with since learning it—and it wasn't long before bulky white envelopes started to appear in Todd Curry's mailbox, the printing done in big childish capitals, usually in Magic Marker, the stamp crooked in the corner like a poorly hung picture. The letters had touched Todd deeply—deeper than he had thought they could—and it wasn't until one morning in late July, after returning from a pitiful and humbling weekend in Atlantic City, that Todd collapsed into tears over a ridiculous crayon drawing of a cat wearing a top hat with arrows for whiskers that Justin had sent him. He'd stuck the drawing to the refrigerator in his tiny Manhattan apartment with a Domino's Pizza magnet . . . but the drawing had been so accusatory and made him feel so guilty that he removed it after only two days. The next time he spoke with his son over the phone, it was all he could do not to crumble apart again like a sandcastle. Something had changed in him. Immediately after the phone call, he scrounged through the kitchen trash to retrieve the stupid drawing of the cat in the top hat, but it had been too late—it had gone out with the trash earlier that week. Gone.

Gone, he thought now, and the word resonated like a ringing gong in the vacant chamber of his mind.

"I usually don't travel on Christmas Eve," the fat guy in the Bulls sweatshirt was saying, his mouth loaded with pizza, "but this was a big client and I didn't want no one getting the jump on me. The pitch went fantastic, too. I really hammered them. Wore a suit and tie, the whole nine. Really did the thing up nice, know what I mean?"

"Sure," he said, snatching up his laptop and standing. The last thing he wanted to do was spend another minute talking to Chunky the Pharmaceutical Rep. "I think I'm gonna grab a coffee."

Chunky looked dejected. "Don't you wanna see how the flight plays out? We got a bet."

"No bets. And besides, I thought you said it's going to be cancelled? That it was a lock?"

The guy shrugged his enormous shoulders. There was nothing but pizza crust left in one grease-streaked hand. "You mark my word, Perry Mason. You just watch and see."

Todd bustled down the corridor, a few fast food joints to his left and his right. Any of these places would serve coffee, but his eyes happened to lock on a small bistro at the end of the gangway called Hemmingson's. Thanks to the delays, it was now well past happy hour. Fuck coffee; what he needed was a stiff goddamn drink.

The place was overpopulated, no doubt due to the multitude of cancellations and delays, yet Todd managed to squeeze his way to one corner of the bar and order a Dewar's on the rocks without taking an elbow to the ribs. A hodgepodge of Christmas decorations and sports paraphernalia hung from the walls and, despite the smoking ban, someone was puffing away on a cigarette. The TV behind the bar was tuned to the Weather Channel. On a steady replay, the television showed clip after clip after clip of Midwesterners in parkas with fur-lined hoods trudging through the blizzard. These clips were replaced by shots from a traffic-cam along the interstate, where it looked like the world was made up of nothing but fender-benders and police lights. Todd felt something cold and wet turn over in his stomach. When his scotch arrived, he gulped down a hefty swallow in hopes of killing whatever angst was squirming around down there.

"Excuse me, excuse me," came a woman's voice somewhere beyond the crowd of bar-goers. Todd turned around and could see a woman in a cream-colored knit wool cap struggling just beyond the wall of broad male shoulders. "Excuse—*shit!*" With that, the woman came bursting through the crowd. Overburdened with luggage and squeezed into a knee-length jacquard coat that was maybe two sizes too small, she looked as though she were about to rebound off the lacquered countertop. Todd reached out and grabbed her forearm, steadying her before she completely lost her balance.

"Whoa," he said. "You okay?"

"Christ," she huffed, and dropped both bags at her feet right in front of him. "It's like Custer's last stand in here. What's a girl gotta do to get a drink, anyway?"

Todd grinned. "I think you made out pretty well, actually. No arrows in the back or anything."

"Although I think some Indian brave back there cupped an ass cheek." She pulled the knit cap off her head and a sprig of red wildfire hair exploded from her scalp. She had a cute face, though, with narrow cheeks and large, beseeching green eyes. A smattering of faint red freckles peppered the saddle of her nose. All of a sudden, what with three days' growth on his face and dark patches beneath his eyes, Todd felt uncharacteristically self-conscious. "I really should have brought my stun gun," she said, her eyes not settling on him for more than a split second. "March through the crowd like a goddamn cattle driver."

"Maybe a stun gun won't be necessary," he said. "What do you want?"

"To drink?" She looked instantly flummoxed. Then: "Oh, yes—uh, do they have Midori?"

He blinked. "I don't know."

"Midori sour, if they have Midori. But do *not* substitute generic melon ball for Midori," she added quickly. "It's not the same and, anyway, I think something in the melon ball makes me break out in hives." She raked stunted fingernails down the length of her neck, as if the simple mention of hives had summoned them into existence.

"Duly noted," Todd said. As it turned out, the bartender had Midori. The drink was mixed and set on the bar posthaste. "Merry Christmas," Todd said, and they clinked glasses.

"So you're a 'merry Christmas' and not a 'happy holidays' kind of guy, huh?"

"I'm sorry, did I offend you?"

"Not at all. It's refreshing. I'm so sick of political correctness. I'm suffocated by it. We're so goddamn politically correct that we lose our individualism, our definition as human beings. Don't you agree?"

"I guess I never thought of it that way."

She downed half the drink in one healthy swallow. Then she set the glass down on the bar and proceeded to pull off her leather gloves. She was sporting a jammer roughly the size of a disco ball on her ring finger. It sparkled like a movie star's smile.

"God," she groaned, "can you believe this weather?"

He nodded, sipping his scotch. "Your flight cancelled or just delayed?"

"I had a dream last night that I was trapped inside a submarine and there were all these people in business suits all trying to climb up the ladder and get out of the sub." She had totally ignored his question. "They started pulling each other off the ladder and fighting and clawing at each other like animals. Women, too, only they were in ball gowns. Just everybody swinging and punching and clawing at each other. I just stood off to one side and watched the whole thing go down. Then, from somewhere deep in the belly of the sub, some big alarm starts going off." When she imitated the alarm sound from her dream—*WEEE-ooh, WEEE-ooh, WEEE-ooh*—several heads turned in her direction. She didn't seem to notice. "So, shit, we're sinking, right? And these assholes are just pawing at each other like children on a playground, grabbing each other in headlocks and rolling around on the floor of the sub." She sighed and looked instantly miserable. And somehow that made her more attractive. "I guess it was a prophetic dream."

"Prophetic? You mean you were on a submarine this afternoon? That actually happened?"

"Lord," she groaned, rolling her eyes playfully. A coy smile overtook her features and he felt something squash that uneasy feeling in the pit of his stomach. She held out one hand—the one flaunting the massive engagement ring—to address the overcrowded barroom. "Are you really that *literal*? I'm talking about here, right here in this airport." She frowned but meant nothing by it. "Where's your sense of symbolism?"

"I guess I'm not very symbolic."

"Well, then," she motored on . . . then paused, her eyes finally settling on him. They were brilliant aquamarine eyes, shimmering like Caribbean water. "Hey," she said, her voice softer, "I'm sorry. I'm going off like a firecracker. I'm Kate Jansen."

"Hey, Kate." They shook hands. "Todd Curry."

"Thanks for the drink, Todd."

"No sweat."

"I guess you're one of the terminal," she said.

"Terminal?"

"A casualty of all these cancellations."

"Oh." He smiled. "Terminal. Very clever. I get it."

"Where're you headed?"

"Well," he said, glancing again at his wristwatch, "I was supposed to be on the four-thirty flight to Des Moines, which is now the *six*-thirty flight . . ."

"Then we're both afflicted with the same ailment." Again, she clinked her glass against his then took another strong swallow.

"So you were on that flight too, huh?"

"Guilty as charged. Was tasked with spending Christmas with my fiancé and his family, but I guess it's in the gods' hands now."

"You say 'tasked' like it's some sort of castigation."

"Oh," she said, nodding fervently, "it is. His family is *atrocious*. They're like the villains in a Charles Dickens novel, all hunched over and swarthy, wrapped in drab, colorless clothing and screaming at peasant children."

"They sound marvelous."

She exhaled and he could smell her perfume—something sweet, like candy—mingled with the Midori on her breath. "But I love the son of a bitch so I put up with them."

She caught him looking at her diamond ring but didn't say anything about it. Todd quickly jerked his eyes away and feigned interest in the newscast on the television. Snow, snow, and more snow. *Damn it,* he thought, still picturing Justin in his *Turbo Dogs* pajamas. *I tried, buddy. I tried.*

"How about you?" she said. "Is Des Moines your final destination?"

"Yes."

"Going home?"

"Visiting my son."

"So you're divorced?"

"Yes. He lives with his mother."

"You two get along? You and the mother, I mean. Not the kid."

"No."

"Your fault or hers?"

"That we don't get along?"

"The divorce in general," she clarified. "Your fault or hers?"

"I . . . it was mutual, I guess."

"Mutual?" She looked skeptical.

"It just didn't take."

She laughed once, sharply. More heads turned in her direction. "You say it like a surgeon who's just botched an operation. 'The transplant didn't take.'"

"What I meant was we both agreed it was for the best."

"So you both equally agreed that she'd keep the kid?"

Her boldness shocked him. "Wow. You go right for the jugular."

"Oh?" She seemed genuinely surprised. "I'm sorry, was that rude? I get weird talking about divorce. My parents went through a messy one when I was eleven and I took turns playing the hostage for each of them. I'm sure it fucked me up in more ways than one, too. You should have seen me in college, boy." She lowered her voice a bit. "I didn't mean anything by it."

"It's okay. I guess there's no such thing as an easy divorce."

Kate Jansen offered up that same coy little grin. "Or an easy childhood."

This made him think again of Justin. What the hell was he doing? It was Christmas Eve and he was drinking scotch in an airport bar while chatting up some stranger. He set his drink on the bar and picked up his laptop. "It was nice meeting you, Kate, but I should go check on my flight."

"Our flight," she corrected.

"That's right. You coming?"

"I think I'll stay here and finish my drink. Hate to break it to you, bub, but I don't think we're going anywhere tonight."

"I hope you're wrong, honey," he said, dumping enough bills onto the bar to account for both drinks. "Guess I'll see you around."

"Save me a bag of peanuts."

He pushed quickly through the crowd, the laptop's carrying case thumping numbly against one knee while he perspired in his coat, hoping against all rationale that the goddamn flight wouldn't be cancelled, wouldn't be cancelled, wouldn't be cancelled.

CHAPTER TWO

The flight was cancelled.

"Fuck me blue," he uttered under his breath. The electronic sign at the check-in desk flashed the word over and over again—CANCELLED. A mob had formed in front of the desk, the timbre of their mingling voices irascible. Somewhere, an infant was screaming.

"Eh?" It was the big guy in the Chicago Bulls sweatshirt, lumbering up beside him while dragging along a carryon with squealing wheels. The intensity of his respiration was nearly frightening, and all too obvious was the Texas-shaped blossom of pepperoni grease on the front of his pants. "What'd I tell you, yeah?"

"You must be psychic."

"They won't even give out hotel vouchers. They only do that if the cancellation is the airline's fault. Shitty weather ain't covered on the insurance plan." The guy dropped a heavy hand on Todd's shoulder. "Think I'm gonna have a seat, catch some shuteye. Happy holidays, bud."

The carryon's wheels moaned as the big guy retreated through the crowd.

It took a good ten minutes for the mob at the check-in counter to disperse. Most of the would-be travelers stormed away looking infuriated; others seemed caught in some suspended combination of shock and boredom. As he watched, he could see all the other gates down the corridor flashing their own CANCELLED signs. Christmas music suddenly spilled out of speakers recessed in the ceiling: a desperate attempt to pacify the distempered crowd.

"Hi," he said at the check-in desk. The woman behind the counter looked utterly drained and Todd felt a pang of compassion for her. "Don't worry. I'm not the yelling type."

"Amen."

"And I know you're probably not the psychic type, but do you think these planes stand a chance of getting up in the air by tomorrow morning?"

"Sir, this storm is supposed to continue straight on through the night and into tomorrow afternoon. They're talking over a foot of snow. We can't even get our guys out there to deice the planes until the snow stops and the temperature climbs up out of freezing." She shifted over to a computer terminal and put her bright pink acrylic nails to work on the keyboard. The sound was like tiny birds pecking on a Frisbee. "You can either wait out the storm or I can go ahead and cancel your flight. If I cancel the flight, though, I'm afraid there's no way to retrieve your checked luggage from the plane until we're able to send a crew out onto the tarmac."

"Wonderful."

"Then what would you like to do, sir?"

He handed over his boarding pass. "Let's go ahead and cancel the flight, please."

The woman went back to work on the keyboard, her startling pink talons hammering away. She glanced at the boarding pass. "This was supposed to be your connecting flight?"

"Yes. I flew in from New York this morning."

"Rotten luck, getting stranded in a strange city. At least some of these folks can just go home. Do you have friends or relatives in the area?"

"No." He checked his watch again. "How far is it to Des Moines, anyway? Mile-wise?"

"You're talking about driving? A little over three hundred miles."

"So about five hours?"

"At least," she said. "And that's in good weather. Sir, you're not planning to actually *drive* in this mess, are you?"

"You don't understand," he said. "I need to get to Des Moines."

The woman cocked her head toward the rows of seats where all the would-be travelers had planted themselves, their luggage corralled around their legs and their winter coats unbuttoned in the stifling heat of the airport. There was an air of dejection hanging heavy all around them. "All those folks need to get to Des Moines, too. We've got a whole airport full of cancelled flights."

The printer beside the computer terminal whirred and spat out a perforated receipt for his cancelled flight. The woman tore the receipt free, folded it down the middle, and extended it to him over the counter. He grabbed it but she didn't immediately let go, drawing him closer in an imitation of tug-of-war.

"And while I'm sure your family would love to have you home for Christmas," she said, almost conspiratorially, "I can bet they wouldn't want you risking your life to get there."

She let go of the receipt and he stuffed it quickly into his jacket pocket. "Thanks," he said. "I mean it."

"I do, too. Think about it."

"I will." But he already knew that was a lie; he had made up his mind before ever approaching this woman and he had no intention of changing his plans now. Too easily he could recall the guilt he'd felt in having that drawing of the cat on his refrigerator, and all the bullshit that had happened over the summer—ridiculous bullshit that was due only to his own carelessness and irresponsibility—which had prevented him from seeing his son. Just the fact that Brianna was amenable to him coming out for a couple of days for Christmas underscored just how important this visit was to their son.

He didn't think he could live with himself if he didn't make it out to see Justin for Christmas.

Surprisingly, there wasn't a very long line at the Rent-A-Ride counter. *That's because no one is crazy enough to drive in this weather,* a small voice spoke up in the back of his head. For a second, he thought the voice sounded very much like Brianna.

"Great minds think alike." It was Kate Jansen, coming up beside him in her too-small jacquard coat and knit cap.

"Or maybe we're a couple of gluttons for punishment," he said.

"Oh," she retorted, "I've always been that."

He waved a hand at the Rent-A-Ride counter. "Be my guest."

"Thank you."

Kate went to the counter and Todd filed in behind her. As if to emphasize the foolishness of driving in such weather, the few other customers at the desk were canceling their orders rather than picking up their vehicles. When the associate behind the counter finally called to Kate, it was already 6:30 p.m. Todd pulled out his cell phone and dialed Brianna's number. It rang a number of times before she answered, sounding out of breath and distracted. Again, he pictured her scampering around the little house, scooping up Justin's toys and stuffing unwashed clothes under the bed. This summoned image then segued into a *real* image—a memory—of lying in bed beside Brianna, the nakedness of her body accentuated by the pearl-colored moonlight pooling in through the bedroom windows. They were back in the old apartment in Greenwich Village, in a time before Justin was born, and they were both much younger and very much in love. He thought of the way she smelled in the sheets and the perfume fragrance of her hair fanned out along the plump pillows. He thought—

"Hello?"

"Hey, Bree." Suddenly, his throat was parched. "It's me. Have you been watching the news?"

"You mean the weather? Because it's coming down pretty hard here, too. Are the flights being held up?"

"They've been cancelled."

"All of them?"

"Yes."

"Well," she said, and that was all she said. He knew she was disappointed for their son but she was not talented enough—nor did she care enough?—to mask the subtle relief in her voice. This had promised to be a difficult weekend for the two of them.

"Listen," he said, running a hand through his hair. The old stress was coming back to him in nauseating waves. "I'm renting a car and driving up. It'll take most of the night but I'll be there for Christmas morning."

"Is that a good idea? The weather's terrible, Todd."

What do you care? he almost said, catching himself at the last minute.

"Unless I want to spend Christmas stranded in O'Hare, it's the only option. And I want to see Justin."

"Well," she said, "he wants to see you, too."

"Is he there? Can I talk to him?"

"He's watching a Christmas special on television."

"Can't you put him on, Bree?"

He heard her expel a rasp of exasperated air. "Hold on," she said, and set the phone down. Distantly, over the line, he could hear Brianna calling Justin's name, followed by the blare of the television set in the background. Brianna came back on the line. "He's coming."

"Thanks, Bree."

"Don't make promises you can't keep, Todd."

There it is, he thought. *Same old Bree, blaming me for the collapse of the world. As if this snowstorm was my own goddamn fault. Fuck you, Brianna.*

But that wasn't exactly fair, either. He'd fucked up enough in their marriage to warrant such accommodation.

"Daddy!" Justin's smallish voice came over the line, a jouncing glee in his voice that shot like an arrow straight into Todd's heart. He felt his knees grow weak.

"Hey, sport."

"It's snowing!"

"It's snowing here, too. Pretty neat, huh?"

"Can we build a snowman when you come?"

"We can build a whole army of them." His voice trembled.

"Are you on the airplane?"

"Not yet, buddy."

"Mommy took me to the mall and we bought you a Christmas present."

"Is that right?"

"But I'm not supposed to tell you what it is. Mommy said it would ruin the surprise."

"Well," he said, "I guess she's right."

"When are you coming, Daddy?"

He closed his eyes and swiped a set of fingers over the lids. "I'll be there in the morning, sport. When you wake up."

"Good," said his son, "because I miss you."

"Miss you too, Justin. And I love you."

"Love you, Dad!"

"Put your mom back on."

"Bye!"

Brianna came back on the line. "He's been talking about this for weeks, you know. We shouldn't have told him beforehand. You should have just surprised him when you got here. This way—"

He cut her off, knowing all too well where she was going. "I won't disappoint him, Brianna. I'll be there. I promise."

Again: that exasperated sigh. "I've told you a million times, Todd," she said. "Don't make promises you can't keep." And before he could respond, she said, "Be careful driving. Goodbye." Then she hung up.

He glanced down at his cell phone, and at the flashing CALL ENDED on the screen. The hand holding the cell phone was shaking.

"Next," said the attendant behind the rental car counter. Kate had taken her paperwork and her small carryon bag and slid down the length of the counter.

"Hi," he said. "I'm gonna need something that can get me to Des Moines."

The attendant—a dark-skinned teenager whose face was peppered in a barrage of pimples—sucked his lower lip. When he spoke, he did so in an indistinct Middle Eastern accent. "Unfortunately, sir, the only thing we have left are economy-size vehicles, none of which—"

"No four-wheel-drives? Jeeps? Anything like that?"

"So sorry, sir. I just gave away our last four-wheel-drive vehicle. And I must advise you, sir, that to drive to Iowa in this weather—"

"What about chains? Do you guys put chains on the tires?"

"We do not have these chains, sir. The weather, you see, is very bad right now and we're—"

"I don't need a lecture," he said, the strains of his son's voice still resonating in his head, "I need a car."

"As I've said, sir—"

"Todd." It was Kate Jansen, holding up her folded rental agreement. "You'll never make it driving a PT Cruiser. Come with me."

Behind the counter, the attendant's eyes looked as large as softballs. *He thinks I'm going to hit him,* Todd thought . . . and felt an odd sense of satisfaction at that.

"Thanks, anyway," he said to the attendant.

"Four-wheel-drive Cherokee," she said as he approached, handing him the rental agreement. "We're both headed in the same direction and, to be honest, I wasn't thrilled with the idea of traveling by myself in this weather. You'd be doing me a favor. I drive like Stevie Wonder."

"All right, but I insist on paying for half."

"Well, I certainly wouldn't want to emasculate you."

"Then it's a deal." He looked down the length of the hallway that led back toward the gates and the baggage claim corrals, toward the shops and fast food joints lining the walk. "Listen, I'm going to grab some supplies—bottled water, snacks, a flashlight—then I'll meet you back here."

"Jesus," she said. "Do you think we'll need that stuff?"

"No, I don't. But it couldn't hurt to have it with us just in case. Is there anything you needed?"

"Books."

"Books?"

"Hey," she said. "If there's a chance we might get stranded for a few days in the middle of nowhere, I gotta do something to pass the time."

"Fair enough." He handed the rental agreement back to her. "And thanks. You saved my butt."

"Consider it repayment for the drink."

He stopped in a Hudson News boutique and loaded up on bottled water, candy bars and potato chips, a roadmap, a flashlight and batteries, aspirin, two pairs of gloves and two knit scarves with the Chicago Bears logo embroidered on them. He grabbed a couple of paperbacks for Kate then, realizing his luggage—along with his gifts for Justin—wasn't going to make the journey with him, he selected the largest stuffed bear he could find, which was roughly the size of a small child. Lastly, he purchased a canvas duffle bag to carry all the items and tucked the bear under one arm. The woman behind the counter looked at him as if he'd lost his mind.

Back at the rental car counter, Kate stood holding two steaming cups of Starbucks coffee.

"Nice bear."

"You're a savior," he said, taking a long swallow of the coffee. It burned his throat but he didn't care.

"This is Fred and Nan Wilkinson," Kate said, stepping aside to reveal a silver-haired couple in their late sixties standing behind her, overburdened in heavy coats and matching carryon bags. The man looked to be in decent shape and the woman still carried with her the vestige of her youth. They both looked more than pleased at the introduction.

Todd nodded at them. "Hi."

"They're coming with us," Kate said.

CHAPTER THREE

The Cherokee was roomy enough for all four of them and their carryon bags, which they tossed in the spacious back section. Todd started out driving, though Fred Wilkinson offered to split the trip with him, and Kate

Jansen sat in the passenger seat and worked the heater and the radio (and, she added with a sly wink, to keep Todd company so he wouldn't fall asleep and run them all off the road).

The Wilkinsons were a pleasant enough couple. Fred was a veterinarian who owned his own practice in Atlanta. Well-groomed and well-spoken, he was the type of man Todd would have hoped his own father might have been, instead of the pathetic societal drain that he was. Fred Wilkinson's wife, Nan, was a grade school teacher who also taught aerobics on the weekends. She possessed the lean, sinewy body of a dancer and, despite her close-cropped silvery hair, looked much younger than her sixty-odd years. They were on their way to spend Christmas with their daughter Rebecca just outside Des Moines—a tradition they'd maintained, according to Nan, for many years. "She's married to a cardiologist," she said, "and they've been hinting at a special Christmas gift this year. Fred and I think they're planning to announce a forthcoming addition to the family." Todd surveyed them both as they climbed into the back seats of the Cherokee, silently thankful that they both seemed to be in exceptional health for their age. The last thing he wanted was for one of them to suffer a heart attack during the excursion to Des Moines.

The driving started out bad and only got worse. The sky was already bruised with oncoming darkness by the time they turned out of the rental car garage, but at least the roadway leading to the interstate had been recently plowed. The snow swirled down in tornado clusters, rushing at the Cherokee's windshield and spiraling in the cones of light issuing from the headlamps. Not surprisingly, they were just about the only vehicle on the road. The interstate narrowed and cut through a vast pine valley, with great heaping snow banks studded with black firs rising up on either side of them. The occasional set of headlights passing them on the opposite side of the road were reminders that civilization was, indeed, still out there.

Two hours into the trip, Fred Wilkinson was sawing wood in the back seat with his head craned back on his neck. Nan was slouched against her husband's chest, sleeping in her own silent way. They had been playing solitaire only twenty minutes earlier, giggling like two schoolchildren while Nan accused her husband of being a dirty old cheater. The cards now lay splayed in their laps, forgotten.

In the passenger seat, Kate was adjusting the radio, hoping to locate a station strong enough to struggle through the storm and make contact. She was having little luck. Finally, she managed to come upon an oldies station and settled for Little Anthony and the Imperials crooning through the static.

"So what's your son's name?" Kate asked, settling back in her seat.

"Justin. He's seven."

"You got a picture of him?"

He propped himself up on one buttock and fished his wallet out from the back pocket of his jeans. "In here," he said, tossing the wallet into Kate's lap.

She opened the wallet and examined the catalogue of tiny pictures housed in their little plastic sleeves. "He's adorable," she said. "Does he look more like you or your wife?"

"Ex-wife," he said automatically. "Most people think he looks like me. But that was when he was younger. He looks like his own person now."

She flipped through more photographs. "And he lives permanently in Des Moines, huh?"

"Permanently. With his mother."

"That must suck, what with you living in New York."

He shot her a curious look then turned back to the highway. "How'd you know I live in New York?"

She held up his wallet. "Driver's license."

"Ah. Very industrious of you."

She turned to the last picture and a folded length of stiff paper eased out of the wallet and into Kate's lap. "Whoops," she said, scooping it up. "Wallet contents abandon ship." She picked up the folded bit of paper and was about to stuff it back into the wallet when she noticed the dried bloodstains on it.

"What's this?"

Todd knew what it was just from glancing at it through the periphery of his vision: a horse racing form. The dried blood on it was his. He reached over and plucked it out of her hand.

"It's a reminder," he said.

"Was that blood?"

He said nothing.

"I'm sorry. It just fell out."

"Don't worry about it." He stuffed the form into the breast pocket of his coat. On the radio, Little Anthony and the Imperials were replaced by The Guess Who. Intermittent bursts of static cut through the song.

Perhaps in an effort to change subjects, Kate turned and looked out the passenger window. "Snow's letting up."

"It's been slowing down for the past twenty minutes or so . . . which is a good thing, because we're making shitty time."

"And the road's beginning to disappear."

"Yeah," he said, a hard lump in his throat.

For the past several minutes, the thin white powder that had covered the blacktop had increased substantially; now, the pavement was completely gone, hidden beneath a hard-packed blanket of pure white snow several inches thick. The driving had become more treacherous and Todd could feel the steering wheel pulling all over the place as the Cherokee advanced through the worsening terrain.

"I don't see any more tire tracks," Kate marveled, peering through the front windshield now. Then, echoing Todd's thoughts from earlier, she added, "We must be the only fools out driving on a night like this."

"Don't remind me," he said back, hoping he sounded more lighthearted than he felt.

The roadway seemed to narrow to one lane just up ahead, the snow encroaching on it from either side. The Cherokee bucked and groaned and, once, scraped its undercarriage against an undulation of packed snow. Todd slowed the vehicle down to a cool forty-five. The tires spun freely then caught and pulled the Cherokee along.

"Check the map," he said to Kate. "Make sure we're still on the main road."

"I never saw a sign to get off," she said, unfolding the map across her thighs. "I can't even see the mile markers out there. They're buried under the snow."

"We've just been going straight. I can't imagine how . . ."

Todd paused. He leaned farther over the steering wheel, squinting at a brief flare of reflective light he thought he caught up ahead in the darkness. But it was a fleeting glare, there and then gone.

"What?" Kate said. "What is it?"

"Thought I saw something."

She leaned forward in her seat, too. "What kind of something?"

"A road sign. At least, I *think* it—"

"There!" Kate said, as excited as a schoolgirl.

"Yeah. I see it, too."

It was one of those standard green roadside signs with the luminous white letters, and it came sliding out of the snow-covered pines like an apparition. The moonlight caused the white letters to glow.

WOODSON
3 miles

"Civilization," Kate breathed, the relief in her voice so evident it was nearly comical. "Thank God."

"No exit number," Todd said.

"There's a Woodson on the map," Kate said. "It looks like it's just off the main highway. Which means we're in Iowa already."

"Christ. I don't remember seeing a sign entering Iowa, either. Do you?"

"No . . . but it was snowing pretty hard until now. Maybe we missed it."

The Cherokee bucked and whined. Todd eased it down to thirty-five. Glancing up in the rearview and beyond the snoring portrait of Fred Wilkinson, the world had vanished into heaps of white snow and, beyond the snow, infinite blackness. The moon was a blazing silver scythe in the sky.

"Todd!" Kate's hand clamped down on his arm. He jerked his eyes back to the road just as a shape—indistinct except for the fact that it had been undeniably human—shuffled into the swell of black pines off the right shoulder of the road. Kate's grip tightened on his arm. "Did you see it?"

"A man," he said.

"Are you—"

Suddenly, the figure was in the middle of the road, only a few yards in front of them as if he had materialized out of thin air. Kate made a sound like a small dog and Todd slammed on the brakes. The brakes locked and the Cherokee plowed forward, sliding effortlessly on the ice-capped snow. The man stood as still as a frightened deer, the vehicle's oncoming headlights seeming to drain all color from the man's face. A man in a black and red checkered flannel coat and high boots, mid-forties, bearded, pale—

"Jesus, Todd!"

He jerked the wheel to the left and felt nothing. Then he overcompensated to the right and instantly knew it was a bad move: the Cherokee fishtailed until it was running perpendicular, the headlights now illuminating the high bank of packed snow along the right shoulder of the road. For two split seconds, the world ceased to make sense. Then, miraculously, the Cherokee somehow righted itself and faced forward again, though not perfectly centered on the roadway as it had been before. Todd could no longer see the man in the red and black coat and was overcome by a sudden, nauseating certainty that he had run over him. Then the right front bumper slammed into a snowdrift, smashing out the right headlamp and causing the Cherokee to shudder to a stop.

White-knuckled, Todd clenched the steering wheel. Beside him, Kate was running her fingers through her hair and repeated "Oh, God," over and over again like a mantra. In the backseat, Fred Wilkinson scrambled to sit up straight, one hand pawing stupidly at the side window.

"Everyone okay?" Todd managed. He sounded like he was talking into an electric fan.

"What the hell happened?" Fred's voice was equally shaken.

"There was a man in the road," he told Fred. "I think . . . I *think* . . ."

"No," Kate said. Her hand had returned to his arm, much more tenderly this time. "You didn't hit him. He moved."

"Did you *see* him move?"

"A *man?*" Fred sounded incredulous.

"You didn't hit him," Kate said again, as if repeating it would make it fact. "We would have . . . would have *felt* it if . . . if you . . ." Amazingly, she uttered a nervous laugh. A sprig of red curls had come loose from under her wool cap and dangled down her left temple.

"We're okay," Nan piped up, speaking for both her and her husband. "You're okay, aren't you, Fred?"

"Sure," Fred said, calming down. "Wish I would have thought to buy some extra undies at the duty free shop, though . . ." He cleared his throat then said, "A *man* out there, did you say?"

"Yeah, Fred. Yeah."

Their nervous, mingled breathing had fogged the windows. Todd could see nothing except the dull tallow glow of the remaining headlamp cutting through the darkness outside. He exchanged a look with Kate then popped open the driver's side door.

The cold attacked him mercilessly the second he stepped from the vehicle. He hugged his coat around himself, stuffing his bare hands beneath his armpits. Something was hissing beneath the Cherokee's hood, causing vapor to billow up in a cloud from the grille where it practically froze into crystals in the freezing night air. Todd afforded it no more than a cursory glance—the right front corner was wedged into the snowdrift, of all luck—before stepping out in the middle of the roadway.

He expected to see a black ribbon of blood snaking through the packed snow, perhaps one of those high forester boots strewn off to one side. Entrails, even. But the road was clear, the snow unblemished except for the double helix carved into it from the Cherokee's fishtailing tires.

"Hello?" he called out . . . though he could hardly muster more than a pitiful croak.

"Todd?" Kate said, coming up behind him. Her breath clouded the air like great bursts of magnolia blossoms. She placed a tentative hand on his right shoulder. "Todd?"

"Hello!" he yelled, much louder this time. His voice boomed and echoed down the canyon of snow.

A shape moved in the darkness up ahead, red in the glow of the Cherokee's taillights.

Kate's hand became a claw digging into Todd's shoulder. He thought he could feel her heartbeat vibrating through it.

The shape staggered out into the middle of the snow-covered roadway, blood-red in the taillights' illumination. He moved like something out of a George Romero film, and although Todd was relieved to see the man unharmed, this relief was instantly followed by an unanchored sense of animal dread. One winter when he was thirteen years old, he'd been skating on a frozen pond behind the church with some friends. Before anyone knew what had happened, one of the kids—a chunky, poorly coordinated boy named Bernie Hambert— had vanished. He'd broken through the ice and plunged straight down into the black, inky water. He'd left only a single glove behind, a five-fingered starfish on the ice. There had been adults nearby who ushered them all off the lake then risked their own lives creeping out toward the hole in the ice in an effort to save poor Bernie. Amazingly, one of the adults had managed to reach in and simply snag a hold of Bernie's ski jacket and yank him up through the hole in the ice. The kid was sopping wet, his skin the color of carbon paper, his teeth rattling like maracas in his head. The second he hit the air, frost began to form on his clothes and even, Todd remembered with horror, on his *skin*. One of the adults draped a coat over the boy's quaking shoulders. When Bernie Hambert followed the adults off the ice and to the safety of solid ground, he'd walked with an uncertain Frankenstein gait, a sort of lumbering toddler walk that conveyed to all the other kids watching from the snowdrift that this had been serious business. That he could have *died* down there, for Christ's sake, under the ice.

Todd thought of Bernie Hambert now as he watched the man in the red and black flannel coat shuffle toward him. He had that same disoriented Frankenstein gait Todd remembered so clearly from that day at the frozen pond.

"Sir?" Despite his unease, Todd approached the man. "Are you hurt?"

The man froze as Todd came up to him. His eyes were as rheumy as a drunkard's, the lower lids rimmed in red, and his complexion was a mottled cobalt hue, networked with delicate spidery veins. His cheeks were deep divots and the lower portion of his face was covered in a lumberjack's beard caked with ice.

"Are you hurt?" Todd repeated.

It seemed to take a few seconds for Todd's words to sink in. Then the man shook his head almost imperceptibly. "No."

"You . . . you came out of nowhere . . ."

"I'm lost."

"How'd you get out here?"

The man lifted his head and scanned his surroundings, including the trees high above the road and the blanket of stars above. As if he were searching for something. Todd caught a glimpse of the man's enormous Adam's apple, protruding like the knot in the bole of an oak tree.

"Todd," Kate called. She hadn't moved from her spot beside the Cherokee. "Is everything okay?"

"Yes." He turned back to the man. "What's your name?"

"Eddie Clement." Then some semblance of coherence seemed to flicker behind his iron-colored eyes. The man reached out and clamped both hands on Todd's forearms, startling him. "You have to help me."

"Sure. We've got—"

"My daughter." The man's breath rushed into Todd's face, reeking like soured milk. "She's lost, too."

"Your daughter is out here?"

"Our car broke down just up the road. Maybe . . . maybe a mile up the road. I don't know. I stopped to have a look under the hood. I was looking for no more than two or three minutes, tops. But when I got back inside the car, she was gone." The man's hands tightened on Todd's forearms. "You have to fucking *help* me!"

"Okay, okay. Calm down." He turned and waved Kate over.

"I've been looking for her, calling out to her," the man went on, his fingers digging into Todd's arms. "At first I thought she was playing a game. Sometimes we play those kinds of games. But it's too cold to play games out here. And she never came out of hiding after I called her name over and over, and after I told her that it was not a game. I started cursing and yelling and telling her to come out. But she never came out."

"What's going on?" Kate said, rubbing her gloved hands together.

"His name's Eddie Clement. He's got a daughter out here somewhere, too."

"Jesus."

"What's her name?" Todd asked.

"Emily."

"How old is she?"

"Eight."

"Jesus Christ," Kate said, her voice seemingly dropped an octave. "How could she . . . I mean, how long has she been out here?"

The man—Eddie—narrowed his eyes in concentration. He was a heavy guy, short and stocky, with hands that felt like bear traps on Todd's arms. "Half hour, I guess. Or maybe an hour." Frustrated, Eddie shook his wooly, white-powdered head. Chunks of ice dropped off his beard. "I don't know. I can't . . . I can't really be sure. I can't remember."

"What's going on, Todd?" It was Fred Wilkinson now, standing outside the Cherokee. He blew into his hands. "Everything all right?"

Todd gave Fred a thumbs-up then turned to Kate. "Get Mr. Clement into the car before he freezes to death."

"What about my daughter?"

"We'll find her," he promised the man. "But you need to get yourself warm right now. This is Kate Jansen. Follow her to the car."

Finally—blessedly—Eddie Clement dropped his big meaty hands from Todd's forearms, leaving behind dull aches in their wake. The son of a bitch probably bruised him down to the muscle by the feel of things, and Todd was almost certain there were red finger-shaped splotches impressed on his flesh.

Kate put a hand on Eddie's broad flannel back and led him back to the

Cherokee. Todd noticed two rips in the fabric of Eddie Clement's flannel coat, one at each shoulder blade, each one perhaps five inches long. The fabric around each slit looked frayed. As they reached the Cherokee, Kate peered back at Todd from over her shoulder as if to shoot him her thoughts through invisible magic rays. Vaguely, Todd wondered if Eddie Clement made her feel as uneasy as he had felt when Eddie had had his wide, stumpy fingers digging into his arms.

Still blowing into his hands, Fred Wilkinson came up alongside him. "What's the story?"

"Guy's been wandering out here for God knows how long. Says his car broke down a mile or so down the highway." He rubbed his hands down his face, suddenly aware that his nose was growing numb. "He says his eight-year-old daughter is out here somewhere. Lost."

"Are you serious?" Fred Wilkinson looked instantly ill.

"Well, that's what he *says* . . ."

"But you don't believe him?"

In truth, it hadn't occurred to him that maybe Eddie Clement wasn't being completely truthful until just now. "I don't think so, no."

"Why would he lie?"

Todd shrugged and stuffed his hands back beneath his armpits for warmth. "I have no clue. But he said he's been out here walking around for maybe an hour."

The skepticism on Fred's face only reinforced Todd's own. "In these temperatures? He'd be a popsicle in under thirty minutes."

"That's what I'm thinking, too."

"Then of course, if there *is* a little girl out here somewhere . . ." Fred's voice trailed off. He turned and looked out over the vast terrain—the mounds of snow rising up on either side of the highway and the looming forest of pine trees all around them, so tall they looked capable of poking holes in the sky. "So what's the game plan?"

Todd considered. "Well, hoping the goddamn car's not fucked from running into that snow bank, I say we keep driving until we find Mr. Clement's car. If a little girl disappeared from it, there may be some sign, some clue."

"Footprints in the snow," Fred suggested.

"Right. Or maybe she'll be there when we find her." But this last thought had caused something hideous to surface in his mind: the little girl's body stripped naked and disemboweled, blood soaking into the seats and pooling on the floor, constellations of blood spattered in frozen gems across the windshield, a sodden pair of panties partially buried in the snow.

Perhaps Fred Wilkinson was thinking this, too; his eyes shifted haltingly in Todd's direction then retreated back to the canopy of stars high above the treetops.

Both men began trudging back to the Cherokee.

"Fred," Todd said. "Just help me keep an eye on this guy, all right?"

Fred clapped him on the back, his eyes streaming tears from the cold; they froze before they reached the swells of his cheeks.

"You bet," he told Todd. "You bet."

CHAPTER FOUR

It took Todd, Fred, and Kate leaning against the front grille of the Cherokee while Nan Wilkinson gunned the accelerator in reverse to excavate the vehicle from the snow bank. It withdrew with a desperate crunching sound, broken bits of glass and metal showering to the icy roadway. The tires squealed and Fred held up one hand to instruct his wife to let up off the accelerator.

Todd dropped to his knees and swiped two fingers through a spill of green liquid glistening on the surface of the ice.

"Radiator fluid," Fred said from over his shoulder.

Kate, who was already shivering from the cold, said, "That's bad, isn't it?"

"Ain't good," Fred replied, noncommittal.

"There's a town about three miles up the road," Todd said, standing up and wiping his fingers down the length of his jeans. "If it's not leaking too badly we can make it there and assess the damage."

"And what if it *is* leaking too badly?" said Kate.

Todd was at a loss for words. Thankfully, Fred Wilkinson intervened, putting a fatherly arm around each of them. "We'll deal with that when we come to it. I think we'll be all right."

"Let's go," Todd said, and they all climbed back into the Jeep.

Nan volunteered to sit in the roomy hatchback compartment with their bags. She rested her head on the oversized stuffed bear Todd had bought back at the airport and hugged herself for warmth. Todd eased the Cherokee along the roadway, his line of sight cockeyed now due to the missing headlight. In the passenger seat beside him, Kate sat facing the backseat where Fred Wilkinson was attempting to examine Eddie Clement's vital signs. Fred pressed a thumb beneath each of Eddie's eyes and pulled the reddened lids down.

"Look up," Fred instructed him.

Eddie Clement looked up. "You a doctor?"

"A veterinarian."

"I look like a cocker spaniel to you?"

"He's trying to help you," Kate interjected. Todd thought she'd been offended by the stranger's inconsideration.

Fred ignored the comment completely. "Let me see your hands. Palms up."

Eddie Clement obliged. Todd glanced up in the rearview and caught Eddie staring just past Fred Wilkinson's head as Fred examined his hands. He was looking, Todd thought, at Nan.

"Where you from, Eddie?" Todd asked him.

"Originally? Baton Rogue."

"I meant where were you coming from when your car broke down?"

"Oh. Westover Hills."

"That in Iowa?"

"Oh, sure."

Something about him is wrong, Todd thought. *I can't put my finger on it but something is slightly out of whack.*

Kate, who must have felt the discomfort as well, turned back around and faced forward. She fished her cell phone from her purse and tried without success to locate a signal.

"It was just you and your daughter in the car, Eddie?"

"Yes."

"Why do you think she would have run off like that?"

"Sometimes she plays games. Just like I said."

"It's twenty below out there," Todd said. "A bit cold for games."

"Her name's Emily."

The rest of them were silent. For one horrible second, Todd was overcome by the feeling that this man was playing with them, toying with them. Like a cat batting around a mouse just before the final blow.

"There," said Kate, pointing.

Todd nodded. "I see it."

Kate's voice dropped to a whisper. "What the *hell?*"

It was a car, all right—stranded on the shoulder of the road, just as Eddie had promised. However, had it not been for the driver's side door sticking straight out into the roadway, Todd would have driven right past it. The whole thing was literally *blanketed* in snow, causing it to blend almost seamlessly with the packed mounds of snow running along the embankment. Except for the car's radio antenna, it looked like an igloo.

Todd guided the Cherokee to a stop then shut down the engine. He winced inwardly at the clunky mechanical whine it made before dying. He could feel Fred's breath heavy on his neck as the older man leaned forward to stare at the car-shaped hillock of snow.

"That your car, Eddie?" Todd asked, leaning over Kate's lap to grab the flashlight he'd tossed in the glove compartment.

"Oh, sure," Eddie said coolly from the backseat.

Todd climbed out of the Jeep, his boots crunching on the ice, and slowly approached the open car door. The interior light was dead, so as he crossed around the side of the car he could see nothing inside that narrow, black maw. Again, his mind summoned the image of the dead little girl strewn like a broken doll in the backseat, blood speckling the upholstery. He chased the thought away as quickly as possible, but not before it caused a cool sweat to overtake his entire body. Steeling himself for what he might find, he took a deep breath then crouched beside the open car door. He clicked on the flashlight and emptied the soft yellow beam into the front seat. He remained like that for some time before rising and turning the flashlight off.

Then he turned and called back to the Cherokee, "Send him out here."

Fred's door cracked open and the older man got out. Eddie Clement followed him, wrapped in one of the scarves Todd had also purchased back at the airport. He seemed to be walking somewhat steadier now. Perhaps his muscles had time to warm up in the Jeep.

Todd crooked a finger at Eddie. "Come here."

Without a word, Eddie shuffled over to where Todd stood before the open car door, Fred Wilkinson right on his heels. The stranger kept his head down as he closed the distance and only looked up when he'd stopped walking, just two feet from Todd. His eyes simmered like cooling embers.

"Is this really your car?" Todd said.

"I told you that it was." None of that deliberate elusiveness he'd displayed only a moment ago back in the Jeep. His voice had come out in an approximation of a growl, his head lowered just enough so that he peered straight at Todd from beneath the Neanderthal crenellation of his brow.

"This car's been here for more than an hour, Eddie. More than two hours, if I had to guess by the amount of snow it's buried under."

"It snowed hard," Eddie said, his tone unchanged.

"Not that hard." Todd clicked the flashlight back on and directed the beam to the steering column. "Where's the keys?"

Eddie blinked.

"Where's the keys, Eddie?"

"Ain't they in the ignition?"

"No."

Eddie went through the motions of patting down his pockets. Never once did he remove his eyes from Todd. When he slipped his hands back into the pockets of his flannel coat, he rolled his shoulders almost imperceptibly and said, "Guess I lost 'em."

"How come I don't see any footprints around the car? Not a single set, Eddie. Not yours, not your daughter's."

"Because of the *snow*," Eddie said. "I told you about how hard it was coming down, didn't I?"

"Yeah," Todd said, his voice nearly sticking to his throat. Back by the Jeep, Kate and Nan were standing in the glow of the remaining headlamp, huddling together to keep warm.

"What are you getting on about, anyway, buddy?" Eddie said. "I got a missing daughter out here somewhere and you're quizzing me about where I last saw my goddamn car keys."

He doesn't mean it, Todd thought then. *He's only saying that because that's what he thinks he should say. I'm looking in his eyes right now and I can tell he doesn't give a shit about any missing daughter, if there even is one to begin with.*

"I don't think this is your car," Todd said flatly. "And I don't believe your story, Eddie. Something's wrong here."

"I feel it, too," Fred piped up from over Eddie's shoulder.

"Now I don't know what game you're trying to play, but you better find someone else to play it."

Eddie blinked his eyes and took a hesitant step backward. He looked over at Fred and then at Kate and Nan before swinging his eyes back around to Todd. There was something different in them now, Todd noticed. Something muddy. Hidden.

"What's wrong with you people?" And now Eddie's voice *did* come out in a growl. "I need help out here and my *daughter* needs help, and you're going to gang up on me, accuse me of . . . of . . . well, fuck, I don't know *what* you're accusing me of . . ."

"What's the license plate number?" Fred said.

Both Eddie and Todd looked at him at the same time. Eddie managed a weak, "What?"

"The license plate," Fred said. "If it's your car, tell us the license plate number."

Atta boy, Fred, Todd thought. *That's thinking, my man.*

Eddie sucked his lower lip between his teeth and made a *mssk-mssk* sound. Again, his steel-colored eyes narrowed. Todd could almost hear the gears working in his head.

"PLO-744," Eddie said after several empty seconds. "Louisiana plates."

Fred trudged around to the front of the snow-covered vehicle, taking his time stepping up and over the jagged mounds of freezing snow, then paused at the front of the car. With his boot he swiped a trench through the snow down below the front grille, in the approximate place where the license plate should be. Todd only watched him for a moment, uncomfortable keeping his eyes off Eddie for too long. Finally, after what seemed like an eternity, he heard Fred Wilkinson sigh.

"What's the score, Fred?" Todd called to him.

"PLO-744," Fred answered. "Louisiana plates."

Eddie Clement remained expressionless. If he felt any vindication, he was smart enough to know now was not the time to show it.

"All right," Nan called to them. "Enough of this nonsense. We're wasting time out here. We should get to that town and let the police know there's a little girl lost out here somewhere."

"That radiator won't hold up too much longer, either," Fred added, climbing back over the ridge of snow on the shoulder of the road. "We should get a move on."

Eddie remained silent. His eyes were no longer boring into Todd's; he'd turned them away and was gazing down the road in the direction they had come. There was moisture in their corners.

"Get back in the Jeep," Todd told him.

Wordlessly, Eddie turned around and marched back to the Cherokee. Again, Todd saw the twin tears at the shoulders of the man's coat. When Eddie climbed into the Cherokee's open door, one of the tears parted like a mouth and Todd caught a glimpse of white flesh beneath.

CHAPTER FIVE

There's nothing here," Kate said, leaning closer to peer out the windshield. The Cherokee's remaining headlight did very little to illuminate the world around them, but what it *did* illuminate did not look promising. "There's no town here. There's *nothing*."

"Relax," Todd said, easing the Cherokee around the bend and down a ribbon of frozen blacktop. Dark pines loomed on either side of the road. Up ahead, where they had all been anticipating the soft glow of civilization was nothing but darkness. "There's bound to be someone. We took the right exit."

"Maybe it was an old sign," Fred said from the backseat. "Maybe Woodson doesn't exist anymore."

"Stop it." It was Nan, her voice cold and on edge. "All of you just stop it. You're giving me the willies."

The Cherokee shuddered and the dashboard lights flickered out. Todd felt the steering wheel grow rigid and uncooperative in his grasp.

"Did the car just die?" Kate said.

Todd cranked the wheel all the way to the right until the Cherokee bounded over a crest of snow and came to a silent demise beside a stand of towering black pines. Todd cranked the ignition but the Jeep would not start.

Slight chuckling came from the backseat. Todd shot a look in the rearview and caught Eddie Clement's dark, hollow-looking eyes staring right back at him. The man looked like a cadaver someone had propped up in the backseat. A chill raced down Todd's spine.

"Forgive me," Kate said, turning around in her seat, "but I fail to see the humor in this. Care to fill me in?"

Eddie Clement did not respond. Gradually, his laughter dissipated but he never pried his eyes away from Todd's in the rearview mirror. It was Todd who eventually looked away.

"Now what?" asked Nan.

"We get out and walk," Todd said. "There's a town somewhere up ahead and we're going to find it. Fred, I've got a duffle bag behind you filled with some clothes, some bottled water, stuff like that."

"Check," Fred said, already popping open his door. Freezing ice whistled into the Jeep. Not wanting to be left alone in the backseat with Eddie Clement, Nan quickly followed her husband out.

Todd leaned closer to Kate. "Grab the flashlight and the map. Also, my laptop's under your seat."

"Anything else?" She looked hopeful.

"You don't happen to have a portable petrol stove in your purse, do you?"

"Shoot," she said. "It's in my other purse."

They both climbed out of the Jeep. Todd went around back and helped Fred pull the duffle bag from the hatchback. Nan had already scavenged the oversized teddy bear; she clutched it now, almost childlike, to her frail chest. From where she stood against the shoulder of the road, Todd could hear her teeth clattering together.

As she tested the flashlight and folded the map into her coat pocket, Kate cast a glance back at Eddie Clement's silhouette still seated in the car. "What about him?"

"To hell with him," Todd groaned, pulling the strap of the duffle bag up over one shoulder. He unzipped it and squeezed his laptop inside.

Fred slammed the hatchback shut then gently gripped Todd's forearm. "While I'm just as anxious to part ways with our good friend," Fred whispered, "I think I'd feel more comfortable knowing where he is for the time being. Do you catch my drift?"

Todd considered. Fred was right. Walking alongside the Jeep, Todd thumped a fist on one of the windows. "Let's go, Eddie."

The man's head barely turned to acknowledge him.

Todd opened the door. For the briefest moment, a smell passed through his nose—of something moist and rotting in a hot root cellar. Inside the Jeep, Eddie's eyes seemed to glint like stones flecked with mica.

"Get out of the car, Eddie. We're going for a walk."

"I'm tired of walking."

"What about your daughter?"

For a moment it seemed that Eddie Clement would remain seated in the backseat of the Cherokee until the apocalypse showered the earth in nuclear winter. Then, expressionlessly, he shifted his considerable bulk toward the door and practically fell out onto the snow. Todd caught him with one arm. Beneath his flannel coat, the man's arm felt like the limb of an oak tree.

As they walked, it started to snow again. Lightly at first, but with each footstep it seemed to intensify. Todd's toes felt numb in his boots and, after just a good five minutes, his legs began to ache. Around them, the trees seemed to grow taller and denser and crowd in closer on all sides. If it wasn't for the road, which was covered in snow but still identifiable, they would have surely wandered off into the woods and disappeared.

"I don't like this," Kate said, saddling up beside him. Her face had gone as pale as the moon, the only exception being the tinge of red at the tip of her small nose. "Where's the goddamn town? We should be seeing streetlights, smoke coming up through chimneys."

Todd nodded then shot a look back over his shoulder. Eddie had been bringing up the rear, deliberately dragging his heavy feet like some overgrown and obstinate child. But Fred Wilkinson was apparently not comfortable with Eddie walking behind him; the older man had slowed his gait until he fell back far enough to keep Eddie firmly in his periphery.

"We should have left him back at the car," Kate said. "What was it Nan said before? He gives me the willies."

"Fred thought we should keep an eye on him."

"Why?"

"Because he doesn't trust him."

"Do you?"

"No," Todd said after a moment.

Behind them, Fred called out to Nan. Todd and Kate stopped in their tracks and spun around.

Nan had negotiated her way off the road and over into the billow mounds of snow that lay thick and heavy at the foot of the pines. Still clutching the teddy bear to her chest, she stood somewhat aloof, peering through the twirling snow and into the trees.

"Nan," Fred called again, this time hustling over to her. He gently took one elbow and followed her eyes into the shadows of the dark pines. "What is it?"

Nan blinked then shook her head. "I thought I saw someone."

"Where?" Fred asked.

"Right there. Through the trees."

Cupping his hands around his mouth, Fred shouted, "Hello!" His voice echoed and caused Nan to jump.

"There's no one there," Todd called back. "It's a trick of the snow, Nan. Makes you think you're seeing things that aren't there."

"Speaking of things that aren't there," Fred said, turning around.

Todd looked, too, and found that Eddie Clement had vanished. What might have felt like relief earlier in the night now caused a tremor of panic to ripple through him.

"God," Kate intoned. There was an octave-dropping sickness to her tone. "Where'd he go?"

"Eddie!" Fred shouted. "Eddie Clement! Where the hell are you?"

Todd rushed over to where Eddie had been standing just a moment ago. "His footprints go through here," Todd said, pointing at the ground. Eddie's big lumberjack footprints diverged from the roadway and cut straight through the trees on the shoulder of the road. The spacing between each print suggested he had taken off at a run.

"Son of a bitch," Fred muttered, coming beside Todd. "Where the hell do you think—"

But before Fred could finish, Todd had taken off through the trees in pursuit of Eddie. The duffle bag slapping against his ribs, he followed the footprints through the forest, bristling pine boughs whipping him at every turn. For some feral and inexplicable reason, he knew he had to pursue.

"Todd!" Fred called far behind him, still on the roadway. "Todd! Come back!"

At breakneck speed, Todd continued through the pines. The scent of the forest was overwhelming, infusing itself in his nose and in his skin. An image of his childhood up in Hancock flashed beneath his eyelids like subliminal advertising. Something solid and unyielding struck his right shin but he kept on running. Again, he caught wind of that awful smell—the decomposing of something dead in an old root cellar—and he reached out blindly with one hand as he ran, certain his fingers would close around Eddie's tattered flannel coat just beyond the curtain of pine needles mere inches before his face—

He stumbled out into a clearing and fell face first into the snow. His duffle bag swung around and whapped against the top of his head. Briefly, stars exploded before his eyes. When he lifted his face up out of the snow, it took a second or two for all the little pixels that comprised his vision to fall back into place. And when they did, his breath caught in his throat. It took all his strength to push himself up onto his knees.

Eddie stood maybe ten yards ahead of him in what appeared to be an open field of snow. Like Todd, Eddie was down on his knees, eye level with the little girl who stood in front of him. She was wearing a pink snow parka with the hood drawn up over her face, the hood itself rimmed in grayish-brown faux fur. Mittens hung from the parka's sleeves by colored string.

Jesus, Todd thought. *His daughter. He wasn't lying.*

Both Eddie and the little girl—Emily?—turned and looked at Todd. After a moment, Eddie stood, clumps of fresh snow falling off his knees.

The girl had no face.

Holy fuck . . .

A grin broke out across Eddie's face. "Come with us, Todd." The grin widened—impossibly wide. "It'll be warm."

As if controlled by strings, Todd felt himself rise up out of the snow. Suddenly, he wasn't as conscious of the temperature as he'd previously been. He could even feel his toes again.

"Come on, Todd." The jack-o'-lantern smile. "That's it."

The snapping of branches jerked Todd from his trance. He spun around in time to see Fred Wilkinson, followed by Kate, come stumbling out of the trees.

"Todd," Kate began, but then looked up and out across the field. "Oh my God . . ."

Todd turned back to Eddie and the little girl . . . just in time to see them bounding off into the darkness like a pair of frightened deer. The footprints left behind in the snow were spaced impossibly wide.

"Was that his daughter?" Kate said, coming down beside Todd.

"What just happened here?" It was Fred, still trying to make out Eddie and Emily even though the darkness had swallowed them up already. Nan appeared beside him, pressing the side of her face against the teddy bear's furry head for warmth.

Todd just shook his head. "I don't know."

"Come on," Kate said, slipping a hand under his armpit. "Get up."

On his feet, Todd felt the bitter cold rush back into his body. Again, he lost all feeling in his toes and he was suddenly acutely aware of every ache and pain that coursed through his musculature. When he took a single step forward, he winced as a jagged pain raced up his right shin and seemed to explode in the socket of his right hip.

Kate looked down. "You're bleeding."

"I don't want to see." But he'd already caught a glimpse of the blackened snow beneath him.

"We're here," Fred said. "Look."

They all looked up. There were no lights anywhere—no lights in windows, no traffic lights or lampposts—and it took them all a second or two to realize what they were seeing: little houses dotting the far end of the field, masked by the darkness.

"Thank God," Nan said into the bear's furry face.

"Why are they all dark?" said Kate. "There aren't any lights anywhere."

Fred rolled his shoulders. "Storm must have knocked the power out," he suggested.

"Come on," Todd said, hefting the duffle bag back over his shoulder. "Let's see if anyone's home."

Kate looked concerned. "Can you walk?"

"I'm fine."

"Let me take a look at it," Fred offered.

Todd shook his head. "No. We need to keep moving. We've been freezing our asses off out here long enough."

"Then at least let me take that bag from you."

Todd relented, letting Fred slide the duffle bag off Todd's shoulder and onto his own.

"Come on," Kate said, bringing an arm around Todd's back. She hugged him tight against her hip as they both took a step together. "Use me as a crutch."

"Did you see the little girl?" he said. His breath tasted sour and his throat burned.

"Let's not talk about them," Kate said.

"Her face," he went on anyway. "Did you see her face?"

"What was wrong with her face?"

It was just an empty socket, he wanted to say. *It was just a fleshy concavity where a face should be.*

"Never mind," he said eventually.

The snow had let up by the time they crossed the field and emptied out into a deserted street. Before them, the desolate houses along the avenue rose up like sentries. Something about them made Todd think of medieval knights, long dead and their bodies turned to powder, with their hollowed armor like conch shells propped up against dungeon walls.

"Look," Fred said, pointing down the street. "Fire."

They all looked. Indeed, where the street opened up into a quaint little town square, random fires burned. Still, there were no electric lights on; even the stars were blotted out by the heavy cloud cover.

"We should try one of these houses for help," Kate suggested. She was gazing up at the closest one, a rambling A-frame with windows like black pools of ice.

"I say we check out what started those fires," Todd said.

"I agree," seconded Fred. He, too, was looking at the houses, and there was a look of distrust most evident in his eyes. "I'm getting the vibe that no one's home around here, anyway."

"That's impossible." Kate's arm fell away from Todd's back as she crossed the street and stood on the snowy sidewalk, looking up at one of the houses.

"Kate," Todd called. "Come back, Kate."

"Are you saying an entire block is away on vacation?" She sounded adamant. "You said it yourself, Fred—the power's probably gone out in the storm. We should knock on some doors."

"That's probably true," Fred responded, "but I don't see any candles flickering in those windows, do you?"

A terrible image surfaced in Todd's mind at that moment: all the residents of this quiet little hamlet watching them from the darkness of their homes, cloaked in black, their eyes like silver dollars. *Or maybe they have no eyes at all. Maybe they have no faces.*

"Maybe the place has been evacuated," Fred added.

"For what reason?"

"I don't know."

"Get away from there, Kate," Todd called to her again, unnerved.

It was his voice that seemed to reach her. She turned around and tromped back through the snow toward them. Her eyes hung longest on Todd. They were no longer the dazzling green they'd been back at the airport bar; they now seemed drained of color and looked like steel divots.

"Let's keep moving," Fred said, slinging an arm around Nan's narrow shoulders. He administered a kiss to the top of her head and, pressed together as if one, they proceeded down the center of the street toward the fires burning in the town square.

"You're scared," Todd said, walking alongside Kate. She had not put her arm back around his waist. "It's nothing to be ashamed of."

"I'm not ashamed. And I'm not scared, either."

"Next thing you'll tell me you're not a liar."

She folded her arms across her chest but Todd could see the stirrings of a smile beneath the surface of her lips. "I can't believe this is happening. This is supposed to be Christmas. Happiest goddamn time of the year."

"Do you have a cell phone? You should probably call your fiancé, let him know what's going on."

"Yeah, thanks." She fished around in her purse for her cell phone. When she finally located it, she tried turning it on to no avail. "Shit. Battery's dead."

Todd dug his own cell phone from his coat. "Here."

"Thanks." She accepted the phone but didn't use it right away. "That guy we picked up—did that really happen?"

"Yes."

"And the little girl? I mean, what the hell was that all about?"

"I don't have a clue."

"Christ. I'm not scared," she said again, "but I *do* feel like I'm losing my mind."

Todd smiled. "And that doesn't scare you?"

"I'm a tough gal," she said, shrugging. Suddenly she looked very pretty. "It takes a lot to scare me."

Todd's smile faltered. He was thinking of the little girl with no face.

"Shit," Kate said, looking at Todd's cell phone. "Take one guess what will make this evening even better."

"No signal?"

"No signal."

"Terrific."

She handed him back the phone. "Right at this very moment, my fiancé's parents are probably catching him up to speed on all the medication they've been on for the past year, and how my soon-to-be father-in-law has been wearing the same pair of socks all week to cut down on laundry. Miserable lot."

"When's the wedding?".

"We haven't set a date yet."

"How long have you been engaged?"

Kate laughed. "See, you're hungry to do the math, right? If I say we got formally engaged over two years ago, you'll smile and say something nice and benign, but inside you'll be thinking, 'Man, this chick's crazy if she thinks this guy is ever going to seal the deal.'"

"Is that true? You've been engaged for two years now?"

"Three. We got engaged on our second date."

"Hmmmm," he said.

She cocked an eyebrow at him. "That's all you've got to say?"

"I'm still trying to think of something nice and benign."

"Forget it. If you'd seen the winners I'd gone out with in the past, you'd be all about Gerald."

"So that's his name? Gerald?"

"Yeah, so?"

"So he sounds like someone's butler."

They both laughed.

"Thank you," she said, "for taking my mind off things. I kept getting a weird feeling."

"Like what?"

She looked at the rows of houses they were passing, silent and dark and brooding. "Like there are people in there watching us."

The town square was like a Norman Rockwell painting gone horribly awry. At the center of the square was a bronze statue of a man on a horse, the horse's front legs pawing at the air. Surrounding the statue and scattered about in the snow like stuffing torn from an old mattress were strips of tattered clothing— shirts, pants, underwear, even a baseball hat. Fires burned in old oil drums that had been erected along the street, the great flames reflected in the blackened windows of the shops that circled the square. Cars had been evacuated seemingly without heed, many of them in the middle of the street with their doors ajar and their batteries dead. A bicycle lay on its side, its frame bent in the middle at a firm 90-degree angle.

"What the hell happened here?" Kate said. She surveyed the damage then looked up past the shops where the spire of a darkened church punctured the sky like a syringe.

"Looks like a battlefield," Nan commented as she slowly made her way around the bronze statue at the center of the square. "Who set these fires? Looters?"

Lowering his voice so the women wouldn't hear, Todd leaned over to Fred and whispered, "Where the fuck is everyone?"

"For their sakes, I hope they left long before whatever happened here."

"And what exactly *did*—"

Nan screamed.

CHAPTER SIX

They all hurried over to Nan, who was trembling on the other side of the bronze statue, staring with horrified eyes at something in the snow.

"What is it?" Fred said quickly, dropping Todd's duffle bag and coming up behind her. He grabbed Nan firmly by the shoulders. In her fright, the woman had dropped the teddy bear; it lay now in the snow.

"Jesus," Todd said, coming up beside them.

Here, the snow was black with what looked enough like blood to cause a tremor of fear to rise up in the back of Todd's throat. The firelight reflected in it, giving it a muddy copper hue, and there were bits of twisted, fibrous ropes trailing through the snow in every immediate direction away from the blood.

"Is that *blood?*" Kate said, suddenly right at Todd's back. "Jesus Christ, it is, isn't it?"

Fred pulled Nan against his chest. Todd heard the woman's muffled sob.

Kate pointed to the strands of ropy material strewn about the snow. "What are those things?"

"From an animal," Fred said. One of his giant hands was cradling his wife's head. "Something happened to an animal here."

"So those are *guts?*" Kate said. "Those are fucking *innards?*"

"Shhh," Todd told her, and jerked his head in Nan's direction. "Calm down, okay?"

"Todd, what the fuck happened here?"

"I don't know."

"Something bad happened here."

"We'll call the police, tell them—"

"No," Kate said. "We need to get out of here."

"We've got no car. We need to call the cops—"

"The cell phones don't work!"

"—and wait for the cops," he finished calmly. Yet his heart was strumming like a fiddle in his chest.

"We need to *leave,*" Kate insisted. She gripped him at the shoulders and stared at him hard. Todd expected to see tears welling up in her eyes, but her gaze was surprisingly sober. "Fair enough. I lied before. I'm scared now, all right?"

"We'll be okay." Todd exchanged a look with Fred, who walked back around to the other side of the statue with his wife still clinging to his chest. Todd bent down and scooped the stuffed bear up off the ground. Then he took Kate's hand and tugged her over to where Fred stood with Nan.

"There's no one here," Fred said overtop Nan's silvery hair. His eyes looked hard as steel and yellow in the firelight.

"Someone set these fires," Todd suggested.

Fred lifted one shoulder. He looked astoundingly calm. "If they're the same folks who left those entrails out on the snow, we probably don't want to go looking for them."

"Entrails," Kate repeated, as if saying it aloud would prove just how ridiculous this all was. "Fantastic."

Nan lifted her head off her husband's chest. Her eyes were glassy but she looked more composed than Todd would have suspected. "Kate's right. We can't stay here. This place feels . . . it feels—"

"Wrong," Kate finished. "The whole place feels wrong. Like there's a giant electric cable running under the earth, and we're all just vibrating up here on the surface."

Todd looked around. He didn't like the empty shop windows any more than he liked the dark houses along the outer street. The cars were worse—parked at crazy angles indiscriminately around the square, they conveyed a sense of panic and hasty evacuation. He remembered reading a book about Chernobyl a few years ago, and how thousands of people had abandoned their cars and their homes and had taken to the highway just to get the hell out of town. Yet if these people hadn't taken their cars, how had they evacuated? Surely not by foot—not in this weather.

"Okay," Todd said finally, scooping up his duffle bag and slinging it back over one shoulder, "I've got an idea. I'm going to try to find a telephone. In the meantime, you guys check these cars, see if anyone left the keys inside."

"Forget the phone," Kate said. "Let's just take a car and go."

"If none of these cars start, you'll be happy I found a phone."

Fred nodded. "All right. Just be careful, Todd."

Todd nodded. He bent down and tucked his pant legs into his boots. He was bleeding through his jeans and his leg was throbbing but they didn't have the time to spare. He'd worry about his leg later.

"I'm coming with you," Kate said, putting a hand on Todd's shoulder.

"No. Help Fred and Nan look for cars."

"They don't need my help. And none of us should be running off alone." Then she offered him a crooked smile. Suddenly she was more than just pretty—she was *beautiful*. Vaguely, Todd wondered if good old Gerald was worried about her. "Besides," she added, "I've got the flashlight, remember?"

Returning her smile, Todd nodded. "All right. Let's go."

They started by peering in the window of an old hardware store. The door was locked and Todd felt uncomfortable smashing the glass. "Let's go around until we find a shop that's unlocked."

"What if none of them are unlocked?"

"Then we break in. But I'm not too keen on making any unnecessary noise around here."

"In other words, you don't want to bring attention to us," Kate said, the underlying message being that Todd believed there were still people around someplace. Hiding.

They crunched along the icy sidewalk, stopping at each door—a bookstore, a Laundromat, a flower shop—and tugging on the door handles. Each one was locked up tight against the dark and the cold. If the townspeople evacuated in such a hurry, it seemed odd they'd take the time to lock up all the doors.

"You were going to tell me something about that little girl," Kate said behind him as he peered into the smoked glass of the flower shop. Just hearing

Kate mention the little girl caused the hairs to stand at attention along the nape of his neck. "Something about her face. What was it?"

"Forget it." He turned away from the window and walked over to a convenience store. "I was just seeing things. My mind playing tricks on me."

"You can't even convince yourself that, let alone me. Tell me."

He sighed. "It was . . ."

"What?"

But he'd caught movement inside the convenience store. "Quick, give me the flashlight."

"Anything?" Nan called from the curb.

Fred felt around the steering column of an old Buick. There were no keys in the ignition. "Nothing," he called back. Then, under his breath, uttered, "Damn it to hell." He checked the visor, under the floor mats, in the glove compartment: nothing.

He climbed out of the car and ambled over to an old Volkswagen Beetle. The driver's side door stood open but the interior lights were off. A dusting of snow had fallen across the windshield. On his way, he summoned a warm smile for Nan. Over the years, Fred Wilkinson had become quite adept at masking his fears and for the benefit of Nan. It was ingrained in him, just as it had been ingrained in Fred's old man. Those first eighteen months when they'd moved to Atlanta and the veterinary practice seemed on the brink of failure, he'd kept a smile on his face despite the hardship. Similarly, when he'd come down with cancer five years ago, Nan would have beat him to the grave with her worrying had he not been the poster child for optimism. He'd beaten the cancer and proved to Nan that positive energy could be just as effective as traditional medicine; even though he'd been scared shitless, Nan had never known. It was just how he was built, with those easy grins and strong embracing arms coming as naturally to him as breathing.

He leaned down and peered into the Volkswagen and immediately fought off a wave of nausea.

"Fred?" Nan called from the curb as he staggered a few steps back from the car, a hand over his mouth and nose. "What is it? What's the matter?"

He waved a hand at her. "Stay there, hon."

Taking a deep breath, he approached the car once again, bending down and peering inside. The driver's seat was saturated with blood, the surface of which sparkled with ice crystals. A single sneaker was wedged beneath the accelerator, and it appeared to be filled with ink. The cold kept much of the smell at bay, although it was impossible not to catch a whiff of the underlying decay that hummed like a cloud of flies inside the car.

The keys were dangling from the ignition.

"Figures," Fred muttered, leaning over the messy seat and cranking the ignition. The engine groaned but would not turn over. Which was just as well; could they have really all piled in here and driven away? All that blood . . .

Someone would have to pry that sneaker out from under the accelerator first, he thought, then immediately vomited in the driver's side foot well. Thankfully, the snow across the windshield blocked him from Nan's view.

After a few seconds catching his breath, Fred wiped his mouth with his sleeve then extricated himself from the Volkswagen. As he stood, tendons popped in his back. Nan had been on him about not doing his exercises lately. He was paying the price for his lethargy now.

"No good?" Nan said.

He shook his head. "Wouldn't start. I think it might—"

A man was standing directly behind Nan, no more than five feet away. His clothes hung off him in tattered ribbons and were splattered with blood. The man's eyes were dead in their sockets, his face as expressionless as an Egyptian mummy.

"Hon," Fred said quickly, holding both arms out toward his wife. "Come here. Quick."

"Fred, what in the—"

"Come here," he repeated. "Now."

Todd pressed the flashlight against the window of the convenience store to eliminate the glare. Inside, the flashlight illuminated overturned aisles, bags of potato chips and popcorn on the floor. Soda had congealed to the tiled floor and busted soda cans were scattered about like spent shotgun shells.

"What do you see?" Kate said in a low voice by his ear.

"Place is a mess."

"Is there someone in there?"

"I thought I saw movement . . ."

"But now you're not so sure?"

"I'm not—"

The flashlight's beam fell on what at first appeared to be a strange tropical plant caught in the process of blossoming. It took several seconds for Todd's brain to register what he was actually seeing, and he jerked backward away from the glass. The flashlight clattered to the snow, causing the beam to cut out.

"What?" Kate said. "What'd you see?"

"Someone's dead in there," he managed. "Head was split open . . ."

"Oh my God . . ."

Again, movement from within the store caught Todd's attention. He jerked his head up and squinted through the darkness just as a whitish shape flitted across the aisles. Whoever—or whatever—was inside was heading for the door.

"Get back," Todd shouted at Kate. Together, they both stumbled backward off the snow-packed curb.

The convenience store's door flung open, Christmas bells on a strip of rawhide rebounding off the smoked glass, and a shape sprung out into the night. There was the sound of a long-barreled gun being charged and Todd felt his body brace for impact.

Nan took a hesitant step toward Fred, an odd, almost coy smile playing across her features.

"Fred, what is it?"

But Fred was through pampering. He reached out and grabbed Nan's wrist, yanking her down off the curb and into his arms. He was still staring at the man in the tattered and bloodied clothes, who was staring right back at him with inkblot eyes. Holding Nan in a strong embrace, Fred began to back away from the curb.

Nan pushed off him, looked up at him. "What the hell has gotten into you?" But she must have noticed that he was looking at something over her shoulder, because she turned and followed his gaze. When she saw the man in the bloody clothes on the sidewalk, mere feet from where she'd just been, Fred felt her entire body go rigid.

"Are you hurt?" Fred said, addressing the stranger. He continued walking backward, unwilling to take his eyes off the stranger. "Hello? Are you okay?"

"Fred . . ."

He rubbed Nan's head with one hand. It didn't appear that the stranger had a weapon; if he were to rush at them, Fred was pretty confident he could fend him off. Still . . .

"Todd!" he shouted. "Kate!"

The stranger hunkered down, like an animal preparing to pounce. A silvery rope of spit oozed from the man's bottom lip.

Fred froze in mid-step. He felt his bowels clench. In Nan's ear, he muttered, "Run."

"Who are you?" said the stranger who'd just come bursting out of the convenience store. It was a woman—that much Todd could tell from her voice—and she was pointing a rather angry-looking rifle at them.

"We're lost," Todd said, somehow finding his voice. "Our car broke down just outside of town."

"What happened here?" Kate said from behind him.

The woman appeared to scrutinize them from behind her rifle. After a few drawn out seconds, she said, "Turn around."

"Please," Todd muttered.

"I said turn around."

"Don't shoot us," he said, turning around as the woman requested. He consciously stepped in front of Kate, although he wasn't sure if his body would be enough to arrest any bullets that came shooting out of that gun.

"You, too," the woman said to Kate. "Turn around. I want to see your backs."

Kate did as she was told, her hands up in the air.

The woman with the rifle came up behind them, grabbed fistfuls of their coats, and patted them down like a police officer searching for weapons. "Okay," she said, and Todd and Kate turned back around to face her. With the gun lowered, it was easier to make out her features. She was young, perhaps in her early twenties, and for the first time Todd saw how she held the rifle somewhat awkwardly, as if doing so was new to her.

"I'm Todd Curry," he said, hoping an introduction would break the ice. "This is Kate Jansen. We were driving and our car—"

"There was a man," Kate blurted.

Todd nodded. "Yeah. He—"

From across the square, Fred's voice carried in a wavering echo: "Todd! Kate!"

The woman jerked the rifle in the direction of Fred's voice. She looked nervous and too thin, and she was practically swimming in her clothes. Todd noticed a fresh slick of blood running down the left leg of her pants.

"That's our friend," Todd said. Then, shouting: "Fred! Over here!"

The rifle swung back around to face Todd. His hands shot up immediately. "Calm down. Those are our friends. We're lost. We're not here to hurt you."

"They're running," Kate said.

Todd turned and looked out across the square. Nan was careening across the ice, amazingly balanced, her thin arms and legs pumping like machinery. Fred followed close behind, though he was not facing forward: something, it seemed, was following them.

"Shit," said the woman with the rifle. "Get in the store."

Todd shook his head. "Those are our friends."

"Get in the fucking store!"

In her panic, Nan practically slammed into a parked car. Todd reached out and grabbed her before she lost her balance and spilled to the ground. There was a look of pure terror on her face.

Fred came next, shouting something indecipherable as he ran. Also . . . there was someone else closing the distance behind him . . .

"What the hell is going on around here?" Kate muttered.

Fred barreled up over the curb and collided with Todd and Nan, his breathing whistling audibly. Fred's pursuer slammed on the brakes, skidding to a clumsy stop on the ice before his legs pulled out from under him. Had the circumstances been different, the fall would have been comical. But as it was, tensions were high, and the man did not stay down on the ground for more than a split second. Back on his feet, he appeared to waver in the air, his weight moving from foot to foot, like a swimmer about to dive into the deep end of a pool.

The sound of the rifle fire was almost deafening.

In the street, the man's head evaporated into a red mist. The body sagged forward then dropped straight to the ground, its legs folded neatly beneath it.

Nan screamed and Fred cursed. Kate clawed at the back of Todd's neck, gripping a fistful of hair.

Then something else happened. The headless body in the street bucked once, twice, three times. Hot blood spurted from the abbreviated neck and coursed like an oil slick across the ice. There was the impression of levitation, although the dead man's never actually left the ground; rather, something from *within* the man's body was rising up, up. For one insane moment, Todd actually believed he was witnessing the dead man's soul vacating the body.

But this was no one's soul. What rose up was a hurricane swirl of snow, funneled and compacted so that it was nearly tangible. It held the vague form of a human being, though as it continued to withdraw itself from the man's body, Todd could see its arms—or whatever served as arms—were nearly twice the length of a normal person's. It had no definable characteristics beyond the vague suggestion of humanity. And as it peeled away from the corpse—from *out* of the corpse—it hovered briefly above the body, nearly solid and comprehensible, before it dispersed into a scattering of snowflakes and was gone.

The silence that followed was thundering.

CHAPTER SEVEN

W hat the hell was that thing?" Todd asked.

They were locked inside the convenience store now, trapped in the dark with a young, rifle-toting stranger who looked barely old enough to drink legally. Fred and Nan sat against one wall, a dazed look on poor Nan's face. Fred absently rubbed the back of her head while occasionally peering back out the store's windows at the corpse in the street. Whatever the thing was that had exited the dead man's body, it hadn't come back.

The woman with the rifle said nothing. She went around peering through all the windows then headed to the back of the store where she proceeded to load another round into the rifle.

Todd stood shivering in one darkened corner, his eyes volleying from the corpse out in the street to Fred and Nan and, finally, to Kate. Kate was sitting on the floor between two overturned racks of canned food and potato chip bags, her legs drawn up against her chest, her whole body vibrating from the cold. She was staring at the body that lay sprawled over a fallen crate of soda—the body Todd had glimpsed while shining the flashlight into the store moments ago. Two dead bodies: one out in the street, one in here with them.

Todd frowned. "You gonna answer me or just hold us hostage?"

The woman looked up at him. "You wanna go out there again, be my guest."

"What about the power? The electricity?"

"Dead."

"And the telephones?"

The woman leveled her gaze at him, clearly showing her displeasure in answering such mundane questions. "Dead. One of those things must have cut the lines."

Todd caught a look from Kate. Her skin looked nearly translucent in the moonlight issuing through the store windows.

"Who's this guy?" he said, acknowledging the body bent over the crate of soda.

"Jared."

"Can we cover him up with something?"

"There's some trash bags on one of the shelves," said the woman.

Rubbing his hands together for warmth, Todd walked down the aisles until he found a box of trash bags. He tore into the box and pulled out a number of bags then carried them over to where the body lay in one corner. Its head was split open like a ripe melon, the innards frozen and nearly sparkling. Todd draped the body in the plastic garbage bags, trying to not look at it too closely.

"Thank you," Todd said after he'd finished.

The woman shrugged. "Not my trash bags."

"I meant about what happened out in the street. I guess you saved our asses."

The woman set the rifle down on the counter . . . then, looking over the rest of them, must have thought better of it and picked it back up again. She went around to the rear of the counter and produced a case of bottled water. She heaved it up onto the countertop. "This water's fresh. If you're thirsty."

"Christ, yes," Kate said, getting up. She looked to Fred and Nan, both of whom nodded, and she approached the counter. It was obvious she was keeping her distance from the woman with the gun.

"Eat whatever you want, too," said the woman.

Kate screamed and staggered backward, her hands over her mouth. She was looking down at something on the floor. Todd couldn't see it; the rows of junkfood blocked his view.

"What is it?" Fred asked, his voice hard.

"Another one," Kate practically groaned. "There's . . . there's blood all over the floor."

Todd stepped into the aisle to see a second corpse—this one much more mangled than poor Jared, whom he'd just covered up with trash bags—strewn like roadside garbage against one wall. It was nearly impossible to discern any sense of humanity from the black, glistening heap. A dark smear of blood trailed behind it like the tail of a comet.

"Jesus," Todd breathed.

"That's Mr. Farmer," said the woman with the rifle. "He used to own this place."

Kate looked up at her. "Did you kill him, too?"

"He wasn't Mr. Farmer when I killed him."

"What's your name?" Todd asked, pulling fresh plastic bags from the box. He moved closer to the glistening heap on the tile floor. Glancing down, he could see where the blood was beginning to congeal and where ice crystals had started forming along the sections of exposed white flesh.

"Shawna Dupree."

"You from around here, Shawna?"

"Spent my whole life in Woodson." Then, as if it were a humorous observation, she added, "Might die here in Woodson, too, you know."

"What's going on?" Fred asked from across the room as Kate, all too anxious to get away from Shawna and the mangled corpse on the floor, brought him and Nan bottles of water.

"It started earlier this week," Shawna said. "They came in with the snow." She seemed to consider this, then added, "They *are* the snow."

"Who came in with the snow?" Todd asked, draping plastic bags over the thing that had once been the proprietor of this little convenience store. "What was wrong with that guy out there in the street? He looked about ready to kill us."

"He was," said Shawna.

"Why?"

"Because he wasn't himself," she said. "He was one of those things."

"What things?" said Kate.

"Whatever came out of him when I shot him," Shawna said. "Didn't you see it?"

"What *was* it?" Todd pressed.

Shawna Dupree took them all in, as if deciding what to do with them. Finally, she propped the rifle over one shoulder and headed around the counter. "I have to pee. I suggest you all keep that door locked."

When she was gone, Nan sighed and looked down at her hands. She said something to her husband about their daughter Rebecca.

"Here." Kate handed Todd a bottle of water once he'd finished covering up the second body.

"I guess we're lucky it's so cold in here," he said. "Otherwise these two would be stinking to high heaven." Kate grimaced.

"Sorry," he said, popping open the bottle of water.

"Your leg's still bleeding. Let me see."

"It's fine."

"Let me see."

"Fuck." He hunkered down, his back against a freezer door. He tried to roll up his pant leg but it would only go so high before it caused him too much pain. "I can't."

"Take your pants off."

"Miss Jansen, you're engaged."

"Ha. Very funny. I'm being serious."

"Just let it be. It's not that big a deal."

Fred appeared over Kate's shoulder. "Let me have a look."

Todd managed a pained smile. "You gonna put me out of my misery?"

"You should be so lucky," Fred said, bending to his knees with some difficulty. Todd noted that maybe the old guy wasn't in as good a shape as he'd initially thought. "I can cut the pant leg or you can take them off. It's up to you."

"Christ. You two should buy me dinner first." He unbuttoned his pants and managed to worm his way out of them, until they were bunched up at his ankles. He didn't bother looking down at the wound.

"Not so bad," Fred said, leaning over him. "How'd you do it?"

"Chasing that son of a bitch Eddie through the woods. I think a tree limb came out and took a bite out of me."

Fred told Kate to seek out some implements from the shelves—adhesive bandages, rubbing alcohol, gauze pads, whatever else she could find. When she returned, she was juggling a bunch of boxes and had a bag of pretzels under one arm.

Fred unscrewed a bottle of peroxide and emptied it over the wound. It fizzed and burned slightly. Todd glanced down and saw a lightning bolt tear along his right shin, perhaps three inches long. Blood ran in muddy tributaries down his leg.

"Pretzel," Fred said, as if requesting a scalpel from a nurse, and Kate popped a pretzel into his open mouth. As he crunched, he blotted the wound with a sanitary napkin then proceeded to dress it in a gauze wrap.

"Some bedside manner," Todd commented, and Fred chuckled.

A shadow moved out from the darkness. It was Shawna, looking younger and smaller than ever without her rifle slung over one shoulder. "Hey," she said to no one in particular. "You think you could help me, too?"

They all looked over and saw that the left leg of her pants was saturated with blood. She had been walking with a considerable limp, too, although Todd hadn't put two and two together until now.

As Todd pulled his pants back on, Fred turned to Shawna. He reached out and lifted the hem of her pant leg. Her entire sock and sneaker were black with blood. A firm look passed briefly over Fred Wilkinson's face.

Without a word, Shawna carefully stepped out of her pants. Her naked skin looked nearly blue. Striations of dried black blood coated her left leg, and there was a deep gash along her left thigh that made Todd's injury look like a pinprick.

"Good Lord," Fred mused, leaning closer to examine the wound. "How long ago did this happen?"

"Yesterday evening."

"Did you put anything on it?"

"I cleaned it out with some peroxide. Oh, and some bourbon."

"You wouldn't happen to have any of that bourbon still lying around, would you?" Kate said, probably only half joking, Todd thought.

Fred turned to Todd. "Can you help her up onto the checkout counter?"

"Sure." Todd looped one arm under Shawna while Kate came around and lent her support on the other side. This close, the girl smelled of days old sweat and unwashed flesh. "How long have you been holed up in this store?" he asked her as they carried her over to the counter and hoisted her up.

"Since this afternoon." Shawna winced as Fred came over and straightened her injured leg. "Before that, I locked myself in my house on Fairmont Street. That's two blocks over, by the church."

"Do you still have that flashlight?" Fred asked Kate.

"Hold on," Kate said, and went over to dig around in her purse.

"No flashlights," Shawna said. "I don't think they know we're here."

"I have to see what I'm doing," Fred said. "I promise we'll keep it to a minimum."

"Cover it with a towel," she suggested, and reached down beneath the counter to produce a shoddy-looking dishtowel.

Kate returned with the flashlight and Nan at her side. For some reason, the arrival of the older woman caused Shawna to blush, and she self-consciously tugged down her shirt to cover her panties. Until that point, Todd had hardly realized the poor girl was practically naked and on display to a roomful of strangers. He reached over the counter and found another dishtowel, which he draped over Shawna's hips. She looked up at him and offered wordless thanks.

"This is going to sting," Fred said, and poured some of the peroxide into the wound while he held it open just slightly with a finger and thumb.

"*Oh*," Shawna cried, and bucked her hips. One hand shot out and grasped Todd about the wrist. "Oh, *shit!*"

"Easy-easy-easy-easy," Fred crooned. It was probably how he muttered to the dogs and cats he worked on in a typical day at the office. "Atta girl . . ." Glancing over at Kate, Fred said, "Give me some light, will you?"

Nan held up the dishtowel to shield the soft beam of the flashlight from anything that might be just beyond the convenience store's windows. Todd snuck a glance over Fred's shoulder. The gash was deep, the tissue dark red and fibrous inside. Something wet rolled over in his stomach.

"How did this happen?" Todd asked.

"One of those things took a swipe at me."

"What things? You mean like that guy out there dead in the street?"

"No," she said, gritting her teeth as Fred addressed the wound once again. "I mean like what was *inside* that guy dead out in the street. What came out of him what I shot him." She grunted and added, "That was Bill Showalter, by the way. Owned the hardware store since I was a kid."

Todd and Kate exchanged a glance from overtop Fred's head.

"Shit, that hurts!"

"Hold still, darling," Fred said, his nose nearly pressed to the wound. "Kate, would you give Nan the flashlight? I need you to find me one of those portable sewing kits."

"No fucking way," Shawna said, and attempted to draw her injured leg up to her chest. Fred's hand was surprisingly firm and held her down on the counter. "You're not seriously gonna sew me up, are you?"

"You need stitches. It's the best I can do."

Kate handed the flashlight to Nan then slipped down the nearest aisle in search of the sewing kit.

Shawna's grip on Todd's wrist tightened. She looked up at him with dark, bleary eyes. Her face looked muddy and out of focus. "That bourbon I mentioned," she said. "It's down behind the counter."

Todd nodded then liberated his wrist from her grip. He dipped down behind the counter and was uncharacteristically heartbroken by the tiny dog bed, blankets, paperback novels, and random snacks stacked back here: Shawna's makeshift hideaway. He located a bottle of Wild Turkey and unscrewed the cap.

"One for you, one for me," he said, taking a swig, wincing, and handing the bottle over to Shawna.

"Down the hatch," she said, and embarrassed Todd with the amount of alcohol she downed in one swallow.

Kate returned with a little plastic case full of various threads, some sewing needles, and spare buttons.

"Perfect," Fred said. "I've got a lighter in my right coat pocket. Heat the needle to sterilize it."

"Fuck," groaned Shawna. She took another swig.

Kate fished the lighter out of Fred's coat pocket and proceeded to heat the needle while Nan balanced the flashlight beneath the tented dishtowel.

"They're almost not even there," Shawna said. She was looking blankly across the store, her eyes unfocused. "They're like smoke. They showed up with the snowstorm earlier this week. They look just like little . . . little tornados of snow, just twirling in the air, until they let themselves be seen. Then they only look like ghosts . . . like the suggestion of a person, an unfinished drawing. Not all there."

Once again, Todd thought of the little girl with no face. Emily. Who the hell was Emily? Who the hell was Eddie Clement? Or *what* the hell was he?

Kate handed over the sterilized needle to Fred, who managed to thread the eyelet on the first shot.

"They can pass right through you and you wouldn't even know it," Shawna went on. She was in a different place now, her eyes so completely unfocused she could have been staring at the surface of a different plane of existence. "Except for their arms. They can concentrate and make their arms solid, just long enough to get inside you. See, that's how they do it—with their arms. But they're not like regular arms. They're more like those big curved sickle blades. Like the kind of blade you see Death carrying in the movies."

"A scythe," Todd said.

"They can make those bladed arms solid just long enough to drive them inside you. They go in through the shoulder blades and they walk people, like puppets. Ouch!"

"Sorry," Fred murmured. He was stitching up her leg now.

Shawna took another hit from the bottle. Todd had to steady her hand to prevent the gingery liquor from spilling all down her chest.

"That's how I got cut," she went on. "One of those bladed arms came swinging out of the blizzard and split me right open. But, see, they can't be solid long enough on their own. That's why they climb inside people. In people, they can move around and do whatever they want." Her muddy brown eyes swung back to Todd. "They can feed."

This can't be real. This can't be happening. I'm probably on the airplane right now, snoring loudly in my seat and disrupting half the passengers, on my way to Des Moines. Because this isn't real. It can't be.

"Ugh," Shawna groaned, and her head slumped backward on her neck. Todd was quick to slide his hands against her shoulders to prevent her from cracking her skull on the countertop, but he wasn't quick enough to catch the bottle of Wild Turkey before it rolled off the counter and broke on the floor.

"Ease her down," Fred said serenely. "She's okay. She just passed out."

"Was she delirious?" Kate wanted to know. "All that talk of . . . of whatever the hell that was?"

No one answered.

CHAPTER EIGHT

And there was Justin, tiny baby Justin, just a pink and puckered smear in Brianna's arms, the smell of him—of the baby—infused throughout the nursery: that smell of powder and warmth and new skin. Eyes squinted into piggy little slits, knuckled fists pumping blindly at the air, the baby cried a soundless cry. Brianna fed the child, looking tired and worn out but looking somehow refreshed and vivacious and full of some indescribable light, too, all at the same time. It was a wonder to behold, all of it. And Todd thought, *I'm going to be a better man for you, little baby. I'm going to do things better than I've ever done them before, harder than I've ever done them before. I'm going to do all that for you, little baby. I'm going to try to make the world just one iota better for our little family and for you, for you, for you.*

He grunted awake, a moan caught somewhere in his throat. Kate was lying beside him on the floor where they'd spread out pads of foam from egg crates they'd found in the storage room. One of Kate's arms was draped over his side.

He sat up stiffly and looked around. Fred was awake, the rifle in his lap while he kept guard by the darkened windows. On the floor beside him, Nan was sleeping soundless on her own foam bedding, Fred's coat draped over her. Snoring loudly by the checkout counter, Shawna slept beneath a bundle of dirty dishtowels and aprons.

"I can't believe I actually fell asleep," Todd whispered. He eased Kate's arm off him and she rolled over, murmuring in her sleep. "How long have I been out?"

"Only about an hour."

"Seen any action?"

Still peering out the windows into the pitch black night, Fred said, "I thought I saw movement between the barbershop and the bank across the square, maybe fifteen minutes ago. But I can't be sure. And there's been nothing since."

Todd looked across the store to where Shawna slept fitfully beneath heaped towels and aprons. "Will she be okay?"

"Unless infection sets in, she should be fine."

"What do you make of what she told us?"

"I think she was talking real fast and real loopy because I was driving a sewing needle into a hole in her leg."

"That doesn't really answer my question. Do you believe her?"

Fred spat a gob of brown saliva into a Pepsi bottle. He must have found a packet of dip somewhere. "I believe she's scared pretty bad and has been trapped in this town for the better part of the week, fending off people who appear to have . . ."

"To have what?"

"You saw that man, Todd. I don't know what to call it, do you?"

"It reminded me of those fucked up zombie movies I used to love when I was a kid."

"Yeah," Fred said, chuckling. He spat another gob into the Pepsi bottle. In his lap, the steel of the rifle gleamed a ghostly blue. "Maybe something got in the town's water supply, made 'em all a little bonkers. Some chemical spill or something."

"What sort of chemical would do that?"

"I haven't the slightest idea."

Todd sighed and rubbed his face. "So what do we do now?" he said after a few moments listening to the women breathe.

"We need to get out of here." Fred jerked his chin out the window. "I've been thinking. All the cars we tried in the street have either died or the keys are nowhere to be found. But those houses we passed along the street to get here? They had garages. There're probably cars in there, full of gas, and keys hanging from a peg on the wall or something. That's our way out."

Todd felt himself nodding in agreement . . . although the thought of entering one of those dark, soulless houses did not appeal to him.

Fred went on, "I think that if—"

"What?"

Fred was staring out the window. One hand gripped the rifle stock tighter.

Todd turned and looked out the window, too. There was movement halfway across the town square, a shadow hustling among the fires that still burned in the oil barrels. More shadows. A woman emerged from behind the pedestal of the bronze statue, completely naked except for a pair of rubber boots, her hair hanging like a frozen wet mop over her face, the points of her pelvic bones jutting like bullhorns. She staggered through the snow, seeming to sniff at the air, and finally dropped down on all fours when she reached the bloodied slick on entrails that had been sprayed across the snow on the far side of the statue. As Todd and Fred watched, the woman began stuffing bits of flesh into her mouth.

"We're not seeing this," Todd whispered. "Tell me we're not seeing this."

"Look at her back. What is that?"

Todd looked. He could make out twin slashes in the woman's flesh, cut diagonally at each shoulder blade. It was as if she was an angel whose wings had been shorn off. Instantly, Todd thought of the slits in Eddie Clement's flannel jacket.

Fred murmured, "Now what do you suppose that is?"

"Shawna said something about . . . about those things cutting into people's shoulders, wearing them like puppets." His face was so close to the window now he was fogging up the glass. "Remember?"

Across the square, a second figure emerged. This one was male, dressed in a bathrobe that hung open. He walked with the lumbering gait of a crippled deer. When he bent down to join the woman eating entrails from the snow, Todd could make out similar cuts along the back of the man's bathrobe, just like those that had been on the back of Eddie Clement's jacket.

"We can't go out there," Todd said.

"They're just people."

"No, they're not. Look at them. How can you say that?"

"What I meant is they can *die* just like people. That kid sleeping back there took that guy's head off and he dropped to the street like a wet sack of laundry."

"But then that thing came out of him," Todd said. "Who knows what that thing can do?"

As if the two people out in the street could read their thoughts, they perked up and sniffed at the air again. Moving much swifter this time, they scrambled to their feet and darted directly toward the convenience store at a steady run.

"Oh, shit," Fred groaned, sliding down against the wall while fumbling with the rifle in his lap. "Get down."

But Todd was already down, just barely peering over the window's ledge to watch the two figures charge at them from across the street.

But they were not heading for the convenience store. They stopped when they approached the headless corpse in the street. The woman dropped again to her knees and began to feed. The man in the bathrobe remained standing, swaying now in the frigid night air, the strong wind bullying his hair. He began to shudder, the man's head lolling back on his neck. Pasty white foam began frothing from the man's lips.

"What the hell's going on, Fred?" Todd whispered, just as Kate sat up wide-eyed beside him. He grabbed her and pulled her down out of sight, pressing her face very close to his.

"Oh my God," he heard her mutter.

The man in the bathrobe began vibrating like a tuning fork. At his feet, the nude woman continued to devour the headless corpse, hardly aware of what was happening to her companion.

Kate squealed and Todd quickly clapped a hand over her mouth. Their commingling exhalations were fogging up the glass to the point where it was becoming harder to see out.

Then, instantly, the man in the bathrobe simply *caved inward,* as if he was a piece of paper someone had folded down the middle. A gout of blood arched up out of his mouth just as his body, like a used husk, sagged to the snow. What remained where he stood was a partially translucent visage that, for a split second, appeared almost human. Todd could make out the suggestion of a head and limbs branching from a central torso, and there was something hideous and depraved in that resemblance. Then its arms raised and Todd suddenly knew Shawna Dupree had been exactly right in her estimation: the things arms were twin scythes, like curved blades that ended in needle-sharp points of glittering light. The bladed arms reared up in a bizarre mockery of the bronze horse at the center of the square. Then the creature vanished into a whirlwind of giant snowflakes. The whirlwind twisted and floated, practically *breathed,* then dispersed into the night until no semblance of it was left behind.

Kate was spilling silent tears over Todd's hand, which he still held tight to her mouth.

The nude female stood, moon-shimmering gore spilling down her body, and took off into the shadows. She just barely left footprints behind in the snow.

It took several drawn out seconds for the world to come crashing back down around them. In that time, no one spoke, no one moved. When Todd finally pried his hand away from Kate's mouth, the imprint of her teeth was impressed upon his palm.

"I'm going to throw up," she croaked, and quickly got up and rushed to the bathroom. The noise caused Nan to jar awake. She groaned and swatted feebly at the air until Fred slid over and soothed her.

Todd couldn't pull his eyes away from the square. It seemed no matter where he looked he could see the velvet twist of shapes moving through the shadows. How many of those things were out there? Every floating ember of snow caused his stomach to clench. Was it really snow or was it something else?

"Did you see?" It was Shawna, her voice like that of a ghost speaking through the darkness. Todd turned to find her sitting upright, the towels and aprons draped about her like a homeless person. Her hair was askew and her eyes were as wide as hubcaps. "What did I tell you? Did you see them?"

"How many are there?" Todd asked.

Shawna just shook her head.

"The rest of the town," Fred said. He was squeezing Nan to his side while she peered worriedly out the windows at the darkness. She was lucky to have just missed the display. "Is everyone else dead?"

"I don't know. Someone was ringing the church bells earlier today but I haven't heard them since. And I haven't seen anyone else on the street . . . except for those . . . things."

"There could be more people," Todd said. He was aware how ridiculously hopeful he sounded. "They could be hiding out just like us."

"I still think our best bet is to get a car and get the hell out of here," said Fred.

Todd chewed on his lower lip. Peering through the window, he again surveyed the square. "It's a long walk back to those houses."

"I know." Fred pointed to the wall at Todd's back. "But it's a quicker walk right next door."

"What's next door?" Todd asked.

"A gun shop." It was Shawna who answered.

CHAPTER NINE

In the tiny, foul-smelling bathroom, Kate clicked on the flashlight and nearly screamed at the cadaverous appearance of her reflection in the mirror. Sunken, hollow eyes, drawn features, skin the color of soured milk. She set the flashlight down and turned on the hot water. It felt good to run her hands under it—she could feel its warmth cascade all the way down to her toes.

The sparkle of her engagement ring caught her eye. She stared at it for a very long time. Trapped in a lousy Pack-N-Go, she wondered what Gerald would do. *Gerald*. There would never be a wedding. She'd known for quite some time now. They'd gotten engaged on a whim, two free spirits who felt empowered when they acted strictly on impulse. But in the intervening years, their impulses had mellowed. Before either of them knew what had happened, she was strutting around like some fool with a giant glittering chandelier on her ring finger. How unfair was it they both had to come to their senses so quickly? And now they were stagnant, trapped in some quasi-committed relationship that had become derailed somewhere along the line.

She loved him but she didn't *know* him. They lived in different cities and had their own lives. Had he slept with other women? Probably. Very likely, in fact. Had she slept with other men since the engagement? In fact, there'd been two. There had been the college professor whom she'd actually dated for several months, amused at how her abruptness had enchanted him. He was clumsy in bed but sadly grateful, which had been his downfall in the end. And then there had been the funky frat boy from the university with whom she'd spent a glorious yet tumultuous week. He'd been virile and overzealous, and their lovemaking session had left her feeling like she'd been riding a horse over the Rocky Mountains.

Six month ago, during a camping trip to the Great Smoky Mountains and following a brief and unsatisfying stint of lovemaking in some seedy, out-of-the-way roadside motel, she'd rolled over in bed and stared for a long, long time at Gerald's profile while he pretended to sleep.

—Is this ever gonna happen? she'd asked him, her voice cracking the silence of the motel room like the crack of a whip.

—What's that? he'd said.

—This whole wedding thing.

He went silent, though his breathing was like a large jungle cat's. After a long while, he said, We've been over this, Kate. We're just not in the right place.

—If you don't want to marry me, she'd told him, just say so. I won't be mad. I just need to know.

Gerald had rolled over, the pitiable little mattress groaning beneath his weight.

—I love you, she'd said . . . and it had been true enough at the time and on that night. But what had been even more truthful was her request of him: to *just say so*. If it was never going to happen, she needed to know. She couldn't spend the rest of her life in pantomime, in this lovers' limbo. Her only twinge of personal regret was that she hadn't been strong enough to leave him that night.

Glancing back at her reflection, she laughed at herself nervously. What kind of whacko was she? Thinking about all the times she'd been unfaithful to

Gerald while trapped in a convenience store in the middle of goddamn rural nowhere . . .

"You're fucked in the head, lady," she told herself before leaving.

"Do you think it's safe to go out there, even if it's just to go next door?" Todd asked. He was still peering out the windows, certain he was seeing the shadows across the square shifting around.

"We'd have to be quick," said Fred. He was standing by the counter now, looking disappointedly at the one remaining box of ammo. "The door's probably locked, too, so we'll have to break in."

"That'll make noise," Nan said. She was sitting on a stack of Coke cases, clutching her bottle of water in two hands. "Won't those people come back?"

Against Todd's suggestion, Fred had filled his wife in on what had happened while she slept. He'd left out the gory details but the story was still enough to cause a permanent crease to form in the fleshy pocket between Nan's eyes.

Hands on his hips, Todd turned away from the window and surveyed the store. "What if we waited till daylight?"

Fred shrugged. "What would daylight do except make us more visible?" He looked to Shawna. "Are they less active in daylight?"

"Ask Jared," she said. "The guy you covered up in trash bags. I shot him three times in broad daylight. The sun didn't seem to slow him any. They're not fucking vampires." Shawna glanced in Nan's direction and, embarrassed at her language, muttered, "Sorry."

"Fuck it," said Nan.

"Fuck what?" Kate said, coming out of the bathroom.

"You feeling okay?" Todd said. She looked hung over and worn out, like someone who'd just come down from a bender.

"I'm fine."

Fred shuffled over to Shawna. "How about you? How's that leg?"

Shawna was propped up on the checkout counter, her left leg wrapped in bandages that had turned a bright red at the center. "Won't be running any marathons for awhile, but I guess I'll live." She laughed nervously. "Or not."

"You know . . ." Todd began, taking a step back and examining the row of freezer doors against the wall.

"What is it?" Kate asked.

He began stacking cases of soda in front of the freezer doors. "I'm just wondering . . ." There was a ventilation grate above the freezers, large enough for a man to squeeze through. He stood on the soda cases and peered through the slats of the grate. Of course, all he saw was darkness.

"I know what you're thinking," Fred said. "You think it goes straight through to the other side?"

"I put myself through law school in two ways," Todd said. "The honest way was working construction during the summers. Old buildings like these, right up against each other—they share all the ductwork for the heating and air conditioning. They'll have their own controls and vent shafts but the main ductwork should be the same."

"So the plan is to crawl through the wall into the gun shop?" said Shawna.

"There's a gun shop next door?" Kate said. "Did I miss something?"

"I think it'll work." Todd was beaming; he could feel the stupid grin on his face as he looked at all of them. "It's worth a try, anyway."

"You're right," Fred agreed. "I'll go with you."

Todd shook his head. "No. I can do it. Stay here with the girls."

"Shit," Kate said. "That sounds absolutely high class, Todd."

"I don't care. We're not gonna squabble about women's lib right now, Kate, okay?" He was already shucking off his coat and cuffing his sleeves. "I'm gonna need a screwdriver to get this grate off."

"Check," Nan said, hopping off the Coke cases and dodging down one of the aisles.

"I'll go with you," Kate said, pulling off her own coat now.

"Not a chance. I can *do* this."

"What, do you think you're suddenly on *Survivor* or something?" Kate said, pulling back her hair. "Didn't we already have the 'nobody goes off alone' talk, buddy? Or do you need a refresher?"

"Here you go," Nan said, handing Todd a screwdriver.

Todd climbed back up on the stack of soda cases and began unscrewing the ventilation grate.

"I can bitch and moan with the best of them," Kate said, her arms now folded obstinately across her chest.

With the vent cover off, the ventilation shaft looked smaller than Todd originally thought. Standing on the cases of soda and peering into the opening, he could see that it cut sharply to the right. It would be a narrow squeeze. Although he wasn't claustrophobic by nature, the idea of getting stuck in there suddenly terrified him.

He thought of Justin fast asleep in his racecar bed, the flannel blankets tucked securely under his chin. Glancing down at his watch, he saw that it was only ten minutes past midnight. With some uncertain emotions, he wondered if Brianna was still up waiting for him.

Kate and Nan returned with armfuls of supplies: plastic bags, rope, broom handles, two more flashlights, and a couple of long, serrated kitchen knives.

Shawna hobbled over and handed Kate a pair of makeshift sheaths for the knives, made out of Bubble Wrap and electrical tape. "Stick 'em to your belt," Shawna explained, "and those knives will slide in and out."

"We're like a couple of accidental warriors," Kate replied, trying hard to sound upbeat.

"Use this so you won't break your neck, Todd," Fred said, carrying over a four-foot stepladder. "Those cases of Coke are starting to buckle."

Todd nodded and clapped a hand on Fred's shoulder. A brief father and son moment passed between the two men. Then they both became embarrassed and the moment was gone. *Men are often their own worst enemies,* Todd thought, setting up the stepladder beneath the ventilation opening.

"You sure you guys don't want to take the rifle?" Fred asked.

"No. You hold onto it. We're breaking into a gun store; we'll have all we need right at our fingertips."

"Just be careful, Todd."

Again, Todd nodded.

"Look." It was Nan, standing in the center of the store, looking out the plate glass windows. Fresh snow was falling outside.

"I used to think that was so beautiful," Shawna said. The saccharine tone of her voice sounded very unlike her. "But now I find myself distrusting it all." She shot a worried look over at Todd. "That could be them. They're the snow."

Kate took a deep breath and moved one step closer to Todd. Instinct kicking in, Todd nearly reached out and took her hand, just barely catching himself at the last possible moment. Instead, he offered her a wan smile which she returned with equal enthusiasm.

"Merry Christmas," he said. "It's after midnight."

"It seems like we've been here a week already."

"You ready to do this?"

"Yes."

"All right. Let's move."

CHAPTER TEN

A serrated steak knife affixed to his belt in its Bubble Wrap scabbard, Todd climbed the stepladder and hoisted himself up into the ventilation shaft. His legs kicked out behind him and it required much more strength than he had originally thought to drag himself forward those first few feet. The shaft itself was about as wide as a coffin—and the comparison did very little to settle Todd's nerves. His breath reverberated off the aluminum, echoing back into his ears.

He crawled a few feet farther then paused while he listened to Kate follow him inside. She was a tough chick, Kate Jansen, although he knew there was a softer, more emotional side beneath the surface of her tough, self-reliant exterior. He had caught brief glimpses of it this evening, particularly out by the bronze statue when they'd first come across what looked like the guts of some large animal—or possibly a human being—strewn about in the snow. She was similar to Brianna that way. But of course, just look how all that turned out.

The divorce wasn't Brianna's fault, he thought now, breathing warmth into his cupped hands, his shoulders pressing against the ceiling of the shaft. *Brianna wasn't the one with the problem. I can spend the rest of my life blaming her and hating her, but that won't change the truth. And it won't fix the future.*

"Okay," Kate whispered behind him, her voice echoing up through the aluminum chamber. "I'm good."

Todd began to crawl along on his elbows, feeling the flimsy metal beneath him buckle slightly beneath his weight. It was foolish to have two people in here; their combined weight risked collapsing the structure. Then where would they be?

They continued crawling. Todd hoped to see moonlit slits spilling into the shaft from the ventilation grate on the gun shop's side, but he could see nothing. Temporarily arrested by panic, he paused and wondered what the hell they'd do if the ductwork *wasn't* connected. His heartbeat vibrated against the aluminum.

"You okay?" Kate said, very close behind him. He felt one of her hands graze his ankle. "Is it your leg?"

"Yeah," he lied. "Just give me a sec."

Coward, he thought, then pushed on.

He didn't realize he'd had his eyes pressed shut until he finally opened them and saw those moon-colored slats of light issuing through the gun shop's ventilation grate. Relief burned through him like a fever. "Up ahead," he muttered.

"Now we're cooking," Kate returned, some humor in her voice.

He reached the grate and pressed his palms against it. It was identical to the one in the Pack-N-Go. The screws would only be accessible from the other side; he'd have to bang this one out of the frame to get it off, and only hoped that it wouldn't make too much racket.

Before he did so, he pressed his nose to the slats and peered down into the gun shop.

The place looked as quiet and undisturbed as an ancient tomb. Moonlight spilled through the front windows through the twirling snow, casting a bluish-silver haze over the whole place. At that moment, he could have been convinced that he was the only living person on the planet.

"What do you see?" Kate whispered.

"Place is empty."

"Are you . . . sure?"

"As sure as I can be, sitting up here in the crow's nest." He turned and tried to make out her features in the darkness. "You ready?"

"Let's go."

He fisted his hands and proceeded to bang them against the grate. It made less noise than he had anticipated, which was good, but it also felt sturdier than he'd thought, which was *not* good. It took a good minute to bang the grate out of shape enough for Todd to slip the blade of the knife between the grate and the drywall, and saw away chunks of the sheetrock. The shaft quickly filled up with floating particles of drywall.

"Try not to breathe this shit in," he told Kate.

"Just hurry up." Her voice was muffled, as if she were speaking through the fabric of her shirt pulled over her mouth.

Finally, another two strikes against the grate, and the panel popped off the wall and clattered down to the floor below. Neither Todd nor Kate moved right away, listening to see if the noise had alerted anyone—or anything—else. But all remained silent. Todd pushed himself forward and was soon hanging upside down from the opening in the wall. Kate gripped hold of his ankles and helped ease him forward, but her strength wasn't enough to combat his weight; she lost her grip and he went crashing to the floor.

"Shit." Kate's head poked out of the shaft. "Are you okay?"

"Yeah." He sat up, rubbing the side of his face and jaw. He'd managed to catch himself mid-fall, and landed mostly on his left shoulder.

Standing, he held up his hands to assist Kate. She took his hands and he pulled her out with little difficulty, the blade of her knife scraping along the aluminum as she went. He caught her awkwardly in his arms, almost like a groom about to carry his bride across the threshold, and their eyes lingered on one another for perhaps a second longer than necessary. Then he swung her legs down to the floor as she began slapping the drywall dust from her clothes.

"Do you know anything about guns?" he asked.

"You pull the trigger and it kills someone," she replied. The shop was cold enough so that they could see their breath.

"That's about the bulk of it. I say we stick to simple handguns—nothing too complex. I wouldn't know what to do with anything too fancy."

Kate was already digging around behind a glass counter. Setting boxes of ammo into stacks, she worked quickly and diligently.

Todd went to the display wall, which was decorated with countless rifles and semiautomatic pistols. He'd fired guns before and had even kept one in the apartment for awhile, particularly after the Atlantic City incident when he thought every creak and groan of the apartment was one of Andre Kantos's men coming to cut his throat. But anything beyond a typical six-shot revolver was a bit out of his league.

The little he knew about guns he'd learned on his own. His father hadn't been the type of man to take him hunting, fishing, canoeing. Todd's old man had spent much of his time carousing and getting drunk, until one spring afternoon Todd's mother, a typically meager and browbeaten woman with a charitable heart, was struck by an uncharacteristic streak of boldness and spoke the one word which would regain her misplaced sense of self-worth and grant his father the freedom he so obviously desired: *divorce*. Often, Todd wondered if his old man had been a different person, if *he* would have turned out to be a different person, too—if things would have been different with Brianna and if he would have been able to see Justin growing up.

You're an adult now, came a voice in the back of his head—a voice very much like Bree's. *You can't hand your blame over to other people anymore.*

"So, back in the convenience store," Kate said from behind the counter, "you said you put yourself through law school in two ways. You said the honest way was working construction. What was the dishonest way?"

"Gambling," he said, selected various guns from the display wall. He examined each one in the moonlight coming through the front windows.

"You made a lot of money gambling?"

"In the beginning, yeah."

"But not in the end?"

He looked over at her but she was busy examining rounds of ammunition. "No one does in the end," he said.

"That was a racing form in your wallet, wasn't it? The slip of paper with blood all over it? I recognized it because my dad used to take me to the track when I was a little girl."

He hefted a nine-millimeter in one hand, surprised by how light it was. "That's right."

"You said it was a reminder. A reminder of what?"

"Do we really need to talk about this?"

"No. Not at all. Forget it."

He tucked the handgun into his waistband and began searching for more like it. After a few moments of silence, he said, "It's a reminder of how I fucked up. Brianna—she's my ex—she left me because I had a problem, got in over my head. There was a time when I owed a lot of people a lot of money. It wasn't fair to her and it wasn't fair to our son. After she left, I just kept digging myself a deeper hole. I got involved with some not so nice guys in Atlantic City, a fella named Andre Kantos and some of his goons, and they showed me the brutal reality of what it meant to owe someone like Kantos a lot of money. That's my blood on the racing form. They took it out on me pretty good that day, and I spent a lot of time recovering. I was supposed to spend time with my son soon after, but I couldn't have him see me like that. And I haven't seen him since."

The memories burned. Looking down, he saw that his hands were trembling.

Kate came around from behind the counter, her arms burdened with boxes of ammunition. She set them down on a tabletop display then, much to Todd's surprise, she hugged him around the shoulders. He smelled the top of her head, a scent that reminded him of waking up in bed with Brianna, and he felt his heart flutter.

"You'll see your son again soon, Todd," she told him, finally letting him go. "Real soon."

He smiled at her, half her face shadowed in darkness, the other half a brilliant white from the moonlight coming in at his back. They were close enough that he could have kissed her without awkwardness, but he let the moment slip by and hated himself an instant later.

"What do you have?" Kate asked, examining the guns Todd had selected. "I want to make sure we've got the right bullets."

"Here." He handed her one of the handguns. "Do you know how to use this?"

She popped out the magazine then snapped it back into place. Gripping the slide, she went through the motions of charging the weapon, then pulled the spring-loaded trigger. It clicked dully. "Piece of cake, right?"

"Piece of cake," he said.

"Todd . . ."

He was going through the motions with his own weapon now. "Yeah?"

"Todd . . ." There was slightly more urgency to her voice now.

Todd looked up and saw the frozen expression on Kate's face as she stared past him and out the front windows. He whipped around, taking an instinctive step backward at the same time. His left shoulder thumped against Kate's chest.

At first he couldn't see what Kate saw—just a pitch-black night choked with a heavy snowfall. But then a moment later his mind grasped the *wrongness* of it. Like a puzzle piece sliding out of position, a section of the snow seemed to *unhinge* itself from the rest, a compact little vacuum of twirling white filaments sliding *into* the wind. It passed in front of the windows and paused just at the door where it seemed to take on a gradual density. The snow began to congeal, the flakes adhering to one another to form physical shape.

"Oh, Jesus," Todd breathed. Kate clinging to his back, they proceeded to back farther away from the windows.

A silvery tendril of light briefly ignited at the center of the whirling snow, shimmering like Christmas tinsel. For one horrible moment, Todd was certain he could make out the insinuation of a head taking shape. The thing approached solidity then wavered back into nothingness over and over again, as if pulsing with some living current.

"It's got arms," Kate said. Her lips brushed against his ear. He could feel her entire body trembling against his. "Does it see us?"

"I don't think so."

Suddenly, one of the creature's limbs became a solid, hooked blade, which it raised above its partially formed head. Kate screamed. Its arms was pale like a corpse's, its forearm tapering not to a wrist and hand but to a crescent-shaped claw that made Todd think of scythes used to hack down fields of wheat. The arm held solid form long enough for the creature to drive it down into the plate glass. The sound was like an explosion. The entire wall of windows shook. At the point of impact, a bullet-hole opening appeared, a thousand spidery cracks networking like tributaries in every direction.

"Todd!"

A second swipe of that massive, bladed arm turned the window into a shower of ice.

"Run!" Todd screamed, lunging forward to grab the bag of ammunition. Freezing wind filled the shop and blew his hair back from his forehead. He grabbed the bag and yanked it down to the floor. When he looked up, he saw that Kate hadn't moved; she was standing mesmerized at the whirlwind of snow that floated through the busted window. "Kate! Get out of the way!"

But she didn't move.

The cloud of snow appeared to rear itself up and, only briefly, looked like a wave about to crash to shore. Todd caught a glimpse of that silvery filament twining in the center of the blustery cloud again. Then he rushed forward and tackled Kate's legs, dragging her to the carpet. A second later, one of those scythe-like arms crashed through the glass display counter, showering them with crystals of broken glass.

"Come on!" he screamed at her, crawling along the carpet toward the shattered front windows.

There came a sound like the screeching of car tires as the thing behind them shrieked into the night. Blood pumping, Todd jumped to his feet and dove through the opening in the shattered window. Outside, he struck the icy pavement with enough force to fill his mouth with powder from pummeled tooth. He scrambled quickly to his feet just in time to have Kate slam against his chest, knocking them both backward into the street. Todd's head rebounded against hard ice and for one terrible moment he feared he was going to pass out.

But Kate was yanking him up on his feet. He stumbled but rose and she jerked him forward. Like a cartoon character, his boots couldn't get traction on the ice-slicked ground at first . . . but when they finally did, he shot forward and hurried after Kate.

Close behind them, that screeching cry shook the world.

They hurried across the square just as two figures emerged from darkened alleyways. They were two of the possessed, human beings with feral faces and eyes that gleamed like jewels. Kate screamed and cut to her right, Todd sticking close to her heels. A third figure sprung out of the darkness and Kate swung the bag of ammo at its head, knocking the shape backward into the shadows.

"There!" Kate shouted, pointing to a narrow avenue that wended through more deserted-looking house. At the end of the street, the dark fingerlike structure of the church rose up against the black sky.

"Go!" Todd shouted, not daring to catch a glance over his shoulder. "Run!"

Kate took off toward the church, the bag of ammunition swinging like a pendulum. Todd stumbled but got back on his feet quickly, chasing after her. He felt the gun in his waistband beginning to come loose, so he grabbed it and held it in one hand as he ran.

The church was at the crest of a snow-covered hill and surrounded by burly lodgepole pines. Through the curtain of snow, the building seemed to tremble in the night. Kate rushed up the steps to the massive doors. She tugged on the wrought iron handles but the doors wouldn't open.

Todd hurried up the steps beside her. It was only then did he pause to look down at the road. "Shit." A few of the townspeople were running after them up the street.

"It's locked," Kate said, nearly in disbelief. "It's a church and it's fucking locked . . ." She began banging on the doors and shouting.

"Better give me some of that ammo," Todd barked. He'd already popped the magazine out of the pistol.

Kate dropped to her knees and sifted through the bag. Down below, the townspeople were closing in. Worse still, it appeared that sections of the sky were shifting, coming together to form partially solid masses that oozed across the treetops.

"Oh, fuck," he groaned.

"Here! Here!" Kate shoved a box of nine-millimeter rounds at him. Then she spun around and screamed, her back against the locked doors of the church.

Todd fumbled with the box of ammo. His hands numb from the cold, he dropped it, sending the rounds in every possible direction. "Shit!" Dropping to his knees, he began to scoop them up and load them one at a time into the clip.

"Hurry, Todd!"

"I'm trying!"

A man in ripped jeans and a blood-soaked sweatshirt was already scrambling up the stone steps of the church.

"Todd!"

Todd slammed the magazine home and charged the pistol. He needn't aim; their attacker was a mere three feet from them when Todd pulled the trigger and took the man's face apart. Again, Kate screamed. She had both hands clamped to her ears. Todd's hand trembled as he kept the gun aimed in. The man's body folded backward down the steps like a Slinky, his limbs rubbery and lifeless. Then, just as they'd seen happen when Shawna had killed that man in the street outside the Pack-N-Go, the newly dead man's body began to tremble and buck. Something vaguely vaporous began to withdraw itself from the corpse. Except for a milky opaqueness, it was practically invisible . . . although looking through it was like looking through heat waves rising off a desert highway. Behind it, the world was distorted.

Kate shrieked and pointed toward the road. Two more townspeople were running toward them, their strides impracticably long. They galloped like horses.

Todd fired two shots but both missed.

"Shoot better!" Kate screamed. "Shoot better!"

"I'm trying!"

The thing that had extricated itself from the dead man's body now hovered before them like a phantom. It was comprised of snow, though the snow itself shimmered like crystal, and again Todd could make out that slender filament of silver at its core. *That's its soul. I don't know how I know this, but I do. It's alive and it has a soul.*

Todd fired the pistol at it but the bullet passed right through it. In his head, he heard Shawna saying, *They're like smoke.*

That silvery filament grew brighter just as the semblance of an arm began to form. Once again, Todd could make out the curling blade of its arm . . . and he could see it grow into solidity right before his eyes.

This is where we die, he thought. *We die now.*

Then suddenly Kate was gone. He turned in time to see her legs being pulled inside the open door of the church.

Rolling onto his side, Todd thrust himself forward and through the doorway of the church. He struck the marble floor with enough force to knock the wind out of his lungs. Directly behind him he heard the massive door slam shut. And a moment after that, there came the sound of the creature's bladed arm striking the wood. The sound was like a gunshot.

Todd Curry passed out.

CHAPTER ELEVEN

C an you see them? Where'd they go?" This was Shawna, leaning against a magazine rack for support. Both Fred and Nan were peering out the windows, trying to locate exactly where Todd and Kate had gone.

"They went up that road," Nan said, pointing. "Where does it go?"

"To St. John's," said Shawna.

"I don't see them anymore," said Nan. "It's too dark." She turned away from the window, a weakened expression on her face. "There were people chasing them."

"Those weren't people," Shawna said.

Clutching the rifle, Fred turned away from the window and strode across the store toward the checkout counter. "They had guns," he said, digging around in the ammo box again. "I could see them. They'll be okay."

"Will they?" Nan protested. "Will they really? You don't know that."

"They're both quick and they're both smart. With guns, they've got a good shot."

Nan seemed to tremble. Shawna braced herself against the magazine rack and worried that the woman might actually explode.

"Stop it!" Nan shouted at Fred. "Stop lying to me! Stop telling me things will be all right when they're not!" Tears burst from her eyes and spilled down her pale face. Her whole body trembled. "Just stop it!"

The outburst caught her husband off guard. "Nan . . ."

"I'm tired of it! I can't pretend to believe you anymore!"

Without saying a word, Fred rushed to her and gathered her up in his big arms. Nan struck him once with a small fist, but there was no power behind it. He held her tighter and the sight of their embrace caused something vital to weaken inside Shawna. Then she looked up at the opening in the wall above the freezers that led to the ventilation shaft. Cold dread overcame her.

"Fred . . . Nan . . ."

They both turned to look at her.

"Look," Shawna said, and pointed.

Like sparkling confetti, a light snow fell from the ventilation shaft and drifted down in front of the freezer doors. The snowflakes did not collect on the floor, however; they seemed to remain buoyant, as if by some invisible force, and they hovered in midair.

Fred slowly released Nan. He took a few silent steps backward toward the checkout counter where he'd set down the rifle.

The cloud of snow coiled and twisted. Almost imperceptibly at first, a billow of snow bulged from the mass like a bud blossoming on a vine. Then, as quick as a lightning strike, the tendril of snow shot out and struck the rifle, knocking it down behind the counter.

Nan shrieked and staggered backward behind an aisle of canned goods. Fred froze, uncertain what to do next. The mass of snow began to clot, to become solid, while simultaneously encircling Fred as if in an embrace.

"Don't let it touch you," Shawna warned. She, too, had backed up behind an aisle of goods . . . only she already had her eye on a can of bug spray at the edge of the shelf. She reached for it, never taking her eyes from the swirling cloud of snow.

Fred seemed to be in a trance. He stared up at the swirling mass before him, eyes wide like those of a child. Almost hesitantly, he brought one hand up and actually grazed the snow; his fingers passed through the trembling snowcloud leaving grooves in their wake. A look of absolute awe fell across Fred's face.

"Don't be fooled by it, Fred," Shawna said. She had made her way closer to Fred, the canister of bug spray down at her side and hidden.

The distinct shape of a head peeled from the snowcloud and swung around to face Shawna. It was the face of a ghost, with dark, sightless pits for eyes. The longer she stared at it the less tangible it became.

Fred slowly withdrew his hand from it, bringing it back down at his side . . . which was when the snowcloud became dense and sprouted overlong arms tipped in curling blades. A sound like a train squealing to a stop emanated from the creature. Nan screamed and knocked over an aisle of canned goods. The creature flickered briefly into nonexistence then appeared again, this time facing Nan Wilkinson, its bladed arms raised like swords to strike.

"Fuck you!" Shawna screamed, and aimed the bug spray at the thing. As she depressed the trigger on the can, she brought up a Bic lighter and thumbed a flame into existence. The result was a makeshift blowtorch. A dazzling yellow pyre closed the distance between herself and the creature. The thing screamed in pain—a sound like a million windows shattering at once—as the heat from the flame forced the creature into solid form. In the firelight, Shawna could make out its humped, pale-skinned back and the vague nubs of its spinal column pressing the flesh taut. The flame ignited half its face, too, and it glared at her like a skull on fire. Its single eye burned like a fiery ember.

The creature swung one of its massive arms, knocking the can of bug spray from Shawna's hand. Its back and the side of its face still on fire, it whirled around and shrieked at Shawna, bearing down on her like a looming thunderhead. The smell of the thing was like burning rubber, like human waste set ablaze.

Shawna rolled into the next aisle just as soda cans exploded from the heat. She felt something sharp and unforgiving strike her right hip then ricochet off into the darkness. Jumping to her feet, she ran to the other end of the store and didn't look back until she'd struck the far wall.

The creature was directly above Fred, who was staggering down one of the aisles toward his wife. Those bladed arms materialized again and were poised like the arms of a praying mantis. Before Shawna could react, she saw the thing plunge the twin knives of its arms into Fred's shoulder blades. Speared, Fred jerked and floundered, his feet swinging loosely beneath him. Blood frothed at his lips and his eyes bugged out like headlights.

The fire had burned itself out along the creature's back, leaving behind the merest hint of a charred and rubbery-looking carapace. It raised itself up on Fred's shoulders, working its twin blades deeper and deeper into the man's flesh. Blood soaked the back of Fred's shirt. Petrified, Nan could only watch while cowering in a corner.

Shawna dove behind the checkout counter and fumbled around in the darkness for the rifle. Something leaked into her eyes—blood?—and for a moment she couldn't see anything. Then one hand closed around the butt of the gun and she yanked it up off the floor. Gun at the ready, Shawna popped up from behind the checkout counter.

The creature was halfway inside Fred Wilkinson. It dematerialized into a shadow, an apparition, and melded with Fred's body like a soul reclaiming its corpse. Fred's eyes blinked and some bastardization of life resurfaced in his face. Like a marionette, his head swung wooden toward Nan. The grin on his face was that of a Halloween pumpkin.

Nan cried out and tried to make herself smaller in the corner of the store.

Shawna leveled the gun at Fred and fired a single round. The bullet missed, striking one of the plate glass windows instead, where it webbed the glass with fissures.

The Fred-thing pivoted in Shawna's direction. For a millisecond, Shawna could see the creature riding Fred's back, working him like a puppet, engineering the man's movements and expressions.

"Don't shoot him!" Nan screamed from the other end of the store. "Please!"

Shawna focused her concentration and fired a second shot. This one struck Fred in the lower abdomen, sending a fountain of blackish goop spouting out from his back. The grin never faltered from Fred's face. He took a step toward her, the leg a bit unsteady, the body wobbly.

It's a new body, Shawna had time to think. *It's still getting used to working it.*

She attempted to fire a third shot but the rifle just offered a hollow click.

Empty.

Motherfucker!

She drove one fist into the carton of ammunition and hastily loaded one round into the rifle. Fred was closing the distance more steadily now. Black strips of foam slavered from his mouth and each footstep left behind bloody prints on the linoleum.

Shawna charged the weapon, swung it against one shoulder, and pulled the trigger one last time.

Fred Wilkinson's head was replaced by a cloud of red mist.

Shawna wasted no time—she grabbed another fistful of rounds then hopped over the checkout counter, the rifle slung over one shoulder. As Fred's body began to buck and tremble on the floor, Shawna slammed against Nan and shoved her toward the front door.

"Fred! Fred!" Nan wouldn't stop screaming.

Shawna shoved her aside and flipped the deadbolt on the door. As she kicked the door open, freezing air washed into the Pack-N-Go like a tidal wave. It whipped her hair into her face, temporarily blinding her. She groped for Nan, caught a fistful of the woman's coat, and yanked her through the doorway.

The town square was deserted. Still dragging Nan behind her, Shawna hurried across the square toward the opposite end of the street. She knew all the shops were locked up and, in some cases, barricaded. They would get no reprieve there. Instead, she dragged Nan toward the nearest vehicle— a Volkswagen Beetle with its driver's side door standing open.

Nan collapsed to the snow, sobbing. Shawna staggered, considered leaving the old woman right there on the ground . . . then thought better of it.

"Come on!" she shouted at Nan. "We have to go!"

"Oh, Fred," Nan sobbed. "Oh . . ."

Shawna dropped down beside her. "Please, Nan. We have to go. Please, okay? I don't want to die out here. Please."

Nan nodded. She swiped at her eyes with the heels of her hands then stood up without any assistance.

Across the square, the windows of the Pack-N-Go exploded.

"Get in!" Shawna screamed, shoving Nan forward into the open door of the Volkswagen. The older woman lost her balance and went sprawling over the seat, her frail legs kicking. Shawna didn't wait for Nan to climb into the passenger seat; she jumped in on top of her and slammed the driver's side door shut.

CHAPTER TWELVE

Slowly, Todd's eyes unstuck. And his first thought was, *I'm blind.* He couldn't see a damn thing. He was lying down on something hard and uncomfortable, and although he was without sight, he got the sense that the darkness was expansive. Like waking up in a giant cave.

He groaned and rolled over on his side. He heard movement in the darkness close by, which sent him into self-preservation mode. He recalled having a gun at one point; he patted himself down but could not locate the weapon. Also, his head throbbed and he thought he tasted blood at the back of his throat.

"Who's there?" he asked the darkness.

"Shhhh," came a voice. Female. "You'll be all right."

"Where am I?"

"St. John's. A church. You're safe here."

He swallowed what felt like a chunk of obsidian. "Who are you?"

"My name's Meg."

He felt the girl slide closer to him in the darkness. A moment later, he felt the fabric of her clothing brush against his bare hand. She sat beside him and he could smell the staleness of her flesh. Panic raced through him. He imagined the faceless little girl sitting beside him in the blinding dark, taking to him with a mouth she did not have.

A scrape of a match, the stink of sulfur, and a candle was lit. Above the flame, the girl's face was a quilt of candlelight and shadows. She looked like a teenager, possibly younger.

"Are you okay?" she asked him.

"I think so." He looked around and realized he was sitting up on one of the church pews. Deep in the shadows, the altar loomed atop the pulpit like a Stonehenge pillar. "Where's Kate?"

"That lady you were with?"

"Yes. Where is she?"

"She's getting cleaned up in the back. You can get cleaned up, too, if you like."

"Who are you?" he asked again.

"I told you. I'm Meg."

"I meant, where did you come from? How did you get here?"

"Our folks brought us here when it started. They said it would be safe."

"So you're from town? From here in Woodson?"

"Yes." She looked him up and down. Her clothes were grimy and in tatters. Her dark hair hung in unkempt coils at either side of her face. "But you're not," she said.

"No," he said. "My friends and I were driving through. Our car broke down back on the highway. We came here for help."

The girl giggled, covering her mouth with one hand. Then she quickly apologized. "Sorry. I didn't mean to laugh. It just sounds funny, saying you came *here* for help. Of all places."

"Yeah, right," he said, running his hands through his hair. He sniffed and smelled blood in the air. "How many of you are hiding in this church?"

"It's just me and my brother. His name's Chris."

"What happened to your parents?"

The girl looked away. Her profile made her appear more adult than Todd guessed she was.

"I'm sorry," he said, not waiting for any answer. Anyway, he didn't think one would come. "Do you have access to a car?"

"I can't drive."

"But is there a car here at the church? Something we can drive away in?"

"I don't know. I don't think so. We didn't come in a car. We ran here." She blew the candle out, dousing them both in darkness once again. "Chris says not to leave the candles burning for too long."

"Where is Chris now?"

"In the tower. He can see the whole town from up there."

"What happened to my gun?"

The girl didn't answer.

"I had a gun," he said. "What happened to it?"

"Chris took it."

"Why?"

"For protection. He said we needed weapons and God provided one for us."

"God?"

"God sent you to us for protection. That's what Chris says."

"Terrific. How old is Chris?"

"Twenty."

"And how old are you?"

"Fourteen."

Todd was startled to feel the girl's hand slide into one of his. He was too shocked to pull away. "I think I should see my friend now," he said.

"What's her name? Kate?"

"Yes. Can you take me to her?"

"I can do it in the dark," the girl said. "I don't even need to light the candle to take you."

"I won't be able to see where I'm going," he said . . . although he was beginning to make out the lighter shades of darkness as moonlight stuck a series of stained glass windows. Directly above the chancel, he thought he could make out panels of glass in the ceiling, though the cloud cover on this night was too great to permit the moon's light full penetration.

"Just hold onto my hand," she said, and stood up.

Head back against the headrest and her eyes closed, Shawna took in great whooping breaths. Beside her in the passenger seat, Nan wept almost soundlessly into her hands. As her heartbeat regained its normal rhythm, Shawna opened her eyes to find herself staring at a windshield that was completely covered in snow. She slid the rifle between the two seats then gripped the steering wheel, if for no other reason than to anchor herself to some tangible form of reality. She could have been in a convertible cruising down a desert highway, the sun glinting off the chrome and the wind in her hair. It was all she could do to fight off the reality of her surroundings . . . and she surrendered to it before too long.

Also, the fucking car *stank*. She shifted in the seat and heard ice crystals crunching beneath her weight. Leaning forward, she could make out what appeared to be frozen blood on the dashboard and along the console. She reached up and adjusted the rearview mirror until she could get a view of the backseat.

There was something dead back there. A person. She could make out a white, blood-streaked hand.

Oh Jesus oh Christ oh fuck oh Jesus . . .

"Calm down," she told Nan. She reached down and cracked the window the slightest bit. The wind that whistled in was ice cold but it helped clear out the smell. "Nan, please calm down."

Nan swiped at her eyes. Once she got her crying under control, she stared down at her hands. Her breath came out in little clouds of vapor and fogged up the windshield. "He's dead. He's really dead. You shot him."

"He was dead before I shot him," Shawna promised. "Believe me."

"I know."

Shawna reached out and felt the steering column. A sudden spark of hope ignited within her as her hand closed on a set of car keys in the ignition. She turned them but the car made no sound. "Goddamn it."

"Fred already tried this car," Nan said, her voice so small it was practically nonexistent. "He tried every one on this side of the street. That's when that . . . that man came out of the shadows and started chasing us. The man you shot." Nan turned to look at her but Shawna could not face her. "What are we going to do?"

We're going to sit here and freeze to death in this car, Shawna thought. Amazingly, the thought nearly sent her into a fit of laughter. Surely that would have calmed Nan. Sitting in a car with a crazy person . . .

"What if we just walked back out to the main road?" Nan suggested. "We could wait for another car to drive by and flag them down."

"We'd never make it."

"Well we certainly can't sit here all night, can we? We'll freeze."

"I know. I'm thinking."

"It . . . it became real for a minute in there, didn't it? That *thing.* When you set it on fire, you made it whole."

"I know. I noticed." She ran a hand through her tangled nest of hair. "Those oil drums outside, the ones with the fires burning in them? That was Jared's idea. He noticed those things tend to stay away from anything too warm. Heat makes them tangible, and when they're tangible they can be hurt, probably even killed. I think that's why they get inside people to feed—the warmth of the human body makes them whole enough so that they can eat."

Nan said, "Who's Jared?"

"My boyfriend. The dead guy back at the Pack-N-Go." Lowering her voice, Shawna said, "They got to him two days ago. I had to shoot him. This is his rifle. He used it to hunt deer."

Suddenly, she laughed. And her laughter turned into tears. Nan draped an arm around her neck and drew her closer. Together, they cried.

Through absolute darkness, Todd followed the girl deep into the bowels of the church, her slender hand cold in his. When they reached a narrow corridor, Meg relit the candle, casting tallow light down along the wood paneled walls.

"Come on," Meg urged him, continuing down the hallway.

Todd followed. Lithographs of Jesus Christ and the Virgin Mary glared accusingly down at him from the walls. At the end of the hall, Todd could make out a single closed door beneath which radiated a soft orange glow. Meg stopped outside this door, resting her hand on the doorknob.

"Don't be mad," she said.

"What do you mean?"

"Just promise. Don't be mad."

Stupidly, he nodded. "Okay. I promise."

Meg opened the door and led him into the room.

Kate was tied to a chair in the otherwise empty room, a series of candles burning in ceramic plates on the floor. Kate lifted her head, her hair a stringy mess before her eyes, her shoulders and arms bound by rope. Her sweater had been removed—it sat balled up in one corner of the room, dangerously close to one of the burning candles—leaving her in nothing but a flimsy satin bra.

"Jesus, Todd," Kate groaned.

Todd rushed to her, dropped to his knees in front of her. "What the hell happened?" He glared at Meg. "What'd you do?"

"You promised not to get mad."

"There's another one," Kate said quickly. "A boy. He tied me up . . . took my cluh-clothes off . . ." She was shivering from the cold, her skin bristling with gooseflesh.

"Hang on," Todd said, moving around back to untie her.

"You shouldn't do that," Meg said. "Chris tied her up for a reason."

"Oh, yeah?" Todd returned. "What reason was that?"

Angry, Meg did not answer. She blew out her candle, which was pointless since the room was littered with them.

The ropes untied, they dropped to the floor and onto Kate's lap. Kate squirmed her way out of them and up out of the chair, hugging her bare chest. Her breasts were small and prickled with goose bumps, the nipples straining against the fabric of her bra in the cold. Embarrassed, Todd looked away. He gathered up her sweater from the floor and tossed it to her.

"Did your brother take the bag of ammunition, too?" he asked Meg.

But Meg was insolent. She would not answer.

"I think so," Kate told him, tugging her sweater down over her head. "I . . . I don't really remember what happened."

"Are you hurt?"

"No."

"All right." Todd turned to Meg, who was watching him with a bored expression. "I want you to take me to your brother Chris. I want to meet him."

"He saved your life," Meg said.

"But Chris said God sent me here to protect you, didn't he? So let me do my job, kid."

Conflict flickered behind Meg's small black eyes. After a moment of quiet deliberation, she turned and marched out of the room. Crossing over the threshold, she once again relit her candle. Casting a look over her shoulder, she said, "Well come on, then."

Todd and Kate followed.

CHAPTER THIRTEEN

W hat is it? What do you see?" Nan asked, leaning closer to Shawna to peer out of the driver's side window. Shawna could hear the older woman's teeth rattling in her head. Sure enough, if they stayed here much longer, they'd both turn into popsicles before morning.

Shawna pressed one finger against the glass. "I keep seeing something out beyond those buildings. A bright light. Flashing."

"I don't—" Nan began, but was cut off as the light flashed once again. It was like a camera's flashbulb going off in a dark alley across the square. "Yes! What *is* that?"

"I don't know."

"What's back there?"

"That's Fairmont Street. My house is back there."

"What could be flashing like that?"

"I don't know."

"Do you think it could be help?" Nan's voice was sadly optimistic.

"I think," Shawna said, "it could be absolutely anything." She pulled the rifle up into her lap and proceeded to load it to capacity. "I should probably check it out."

"Alone?"

Shawna surveyed the woman. She was in fantastic shape but was she mentally prepared for another trek across town? She'd witnessed her husband turn into a monster then have his head blown off less than an hour ago . . .

"I don't want to sit in this car by myself, Shawna. I'll go crazy."

Try locking yourself in a convenience store with your boyfriend's headless corpse, she felt like saying, but didn't.

Shawna nodded. "All right. But we have to be quick and careful."

"If there's—*oh!*" Nan had turned and caught sight of the mess in the backseat. She stared at it, her jaw unhinged. "Dear Jesus."

"Don't look at it."

"Oh. Oh. Oh."

"Are you with me, Nan?"

Nan took a deep breath then turned away from the backseat. She sat, facing forward, her hands planted firmly in her lap. After a few seconds, she said, "I'm with you."

Meg led them both up a flight of narrow, attic-like stairs that creaked beneath their collective weight. The flame of her candle caused their shadows to jump and bob along the walls. Despite the drop in temperature and the fact that he'd left his coat back at the Pack-N-Go in order to fit in the ventilation shaft, he was sweating profusely. Something was roiling around in his guts—a warning. Something was very wrong here.

There was a hatch directly above their heads at the top of the stairs. Meg knocked on it twice then pushed it up and opened. Hinges squealed. Before crawling up, the girl castigated them with a disquieting stare that made her seem much older than her fourteen years. Then she climbed up and out of the hatch.

Todd followed, bracing himself for anything.

Topside, he found himself in a square room with windows on every wall—thick, hand-blown glass panes reinforced with iron piping. The whole town was visible from this vantage. Directly above his head, an ancient copper bell hung from recessed rafters. He caught a whiff of something in the air, something that was not necessarily dangerous but still did not belong nonetheless. It took him a moment to place the smell: corn chips.

Meg crept off into the shadows where the silhouette of another person—her brother Chris?—sat slouched in a folding chair. As Todd helped Kate up out of the hatch, Meg thumped the figure on one shoulder. The silhouette jerked and sat upright, bags of potato chips crunching beneath his shifting feet while he smacked his lips together.

"What?" the boy growled . . . then saw Todd and Kate standing before him. He sprung up out of the chair and sauntered into the panel of moonlight coming in through the nearest window. He was tall and broad-shouldered but possessed a child's face, with doughy cheeks, a dimpled chin, and an infant's squinty eyes. Like a vagabond, he wore several layers of clothing from beneath which his sizable gut protruded almost comically, and there was a strip of purple satin tied around his forehead like a bandana. Todd was quick to notice his pistol stuffed into the boy's waistband.

"Are you Chris?" Todd asked.

The boy looked him up and down. Then his piggy little eyes sought out Kate and scrutinized her as well. Turning to Meg, he said, "Who told you to untie her?"

"I didn't," Meg said. She pointed at Todd. "He did."

Chris's hand shot out and slapped her across the face.

"Hey!" Kate shouted. "What the hell's the matter with you?"

"Who are you both?" Chris demanded. "Where'd you come from? You're not from town."

Todd held up both hands in an effort to show his intentions were not of the hostile variety. "Just take it easy. You're right, we're not from around here. Our car broke down tonight and we came into town looking for help.

We have absolutely nothing to do with anything that's been going on around here."

"The girl's got cuts on her back," Chris said.

"What?" Todd stammered. For a second he thought Chris was talking about Meg. But then he remembered the lacerations he'd seen on Kate's bare back as he untied her from the chair and at least some of this madness began to make sense. "No," Todd said, "you're wrong."

"I saw the cuts myself." The boy was adamant.

"She's not one of them," Todd said.

"Me?" Kate said, incredulous.

"Turn around," Chris demanded of Kate. "Lift up your shirt. I want to see."

"Fuck off, you perverted little twerp," Kate barked.

Chris yanked the pistol from his waistband. Todd sidestepped in front of Kate, his hands still up. "Take it easy. She'll show you. Kate, turn around and lift up your shirt. He thinks you're one of them."

"This is insane."

"So is getting shot by Lord of the Flies over there," Todd countered. "Just do it."

Slowly, Kate turned around and pulled her shirt up over her shoulders. The smooth canvas of her back was marred by flecks of broken skin and jagged lacerations—probably from when the gun shop's window imploded, sending spears of glass every which way.

"See?" Todd said, tracing a hand along Kate's back. She shivered at his touch. "They're just cuts. We've been running from those things and got hit with some broken glass. Okay? She's normal. We both are."

Chris was chewing on the inside of one cheek. His distrustful, oil-spot eyes darted from Kate to Todd to Kate again. Finally he returned the pistol to his waistband with an unfavorable grunt. "Okay," he said, though he sounded miserable at having been wrong.

Kate lowered her sweater then hugged herself with her arm. She was shivering fiercely. Todd rubbed a hand along one of her arms and asked Chris if they had any extra clothes.

Chris dropped back down in his folding chair. He glared at his sister. "Take her down to the trunk. She can pick out whatever she wants."

Wordlessly, Meg approached Kate, took her by the hand, and led her back down the hatch. Kate cast one last glance at Todd before disappearing down the darkened stairwell in the floor.

Todd moved to the nearest window. He could see the town square clearly from up here. Beyond that, a community fire hall, a building that may have been a school, and a sheriff's office—all dark. Cars lay overturned in ditches and near the outskirts of town Todd could make out an ambulance that had died along the shoulder of the road, its rear doors flung open, the whole thing powdered with snow. Then a sinking feeling overtook him when he noticed that the windows of the Pack-N-Go had been blown out. "Oh, shit . . ."

"I saw you run across the square," Chris said from his folding chair. He had a voice like a squeaky trumpet. The stink of corn chips was cloying, reminding Todd of awful foot odor; it was all he could do not to gag. "There's more of you down there."

"There were," Todd said. "I hope they're okay."

"Two ladies made it out of the store," Chris said. "I saw them, too."

Todd turned to him. "You saw them? Where'd they go?"

Disinterested, the boy shrugged. "Don't know." Then, adopting an exasperated tone, he said, "I can't see *everything*, you know." The sound of his voice suggested Todd was an imbecile for maybe thinking otherwise.

Beyond the square Todd could make out intermittent white lights flashing. They looked like gunshots reflected off the buildings. "What's that?" he asked the boy.

"Those lights? Downed power lines."

"So that's why the power's out."

"*They* did it," Chris said. "Those *things*."

"Do you know if there's anybody left in town?"

"What's the matter with you? Don't you know?" Chris said, nearly snorting. "The whole *town* is still here. It's just that most of 'em are . . . well, they're different now."

"That's an understatement."

Chris sat upright in his chair. "What'd you say?" he nearly shouted at Todd.

"Never mind."

"Don't tell me to never mind. I asked you a question." Those bags of chips crunched beneath his feet again.

"I said, 'that's an understatement.' It was sarcasm."

"Don't make fun of me. I was left in charge. I'm running things around here now."

"Left in charge by whom?"

"My dad. So go fuck yourself." He licked his lips and sounded instantly nervous. Todd assumed "fuck" was not typically part of the boy's vocabulary. "You're a stranger here, anyway."

"I'm not trying to do anything. I'm not trying to take over, either. You want to be in change, Chris, that's just fine with me. I just want to get out of here."

"You can't. You can't get out of here."

"Why's that?"

"Those things won't let you. There's no way out." He leaned forward in his chair and tapped the stained-glass windowpane with the handgun. Todd hadn't even seen him take it from his pants this time. "They're in the snow, haven't you noticed? They *are* the snow."

"Still," Todd said, "there's gotta be a way. If we can get to a car that will start, we can drive out of here—"

"The cars out in the square are dead. My parents tried to start one. That's when they got taken."

"Taken?"

"Taken away," Chris said, irritated. "By the snow."

This chubby bastard is off his rocker, Todd thought.

"My dad came back but we stopped that. I don't know what happened to my mom."

"What do you mean?"

Chris frowned and faded back into the gloom.

My dad came back but we stopped that . . .

"Are you religious?" Chris asked suddenly. "What religion are you?"

"I was born Catholic," Todd confessed, "but this is the first time I've been in a church in maybe a decade. Why?"

Chris made a snorting sound but didn't answer.

Todd turned and looked back out the window. "Holy shit. That's Nan and Shawna." He went to pry open the window and call to them but the window was stuck.

"Stop that!" Chris shouted, jumping out of his chair.

"Those are my friends down there!"

"They're as good as dead. Hey, stop trying to open that window!"

"I'm just try—"

A dull crack to the back of his head sent Todd sailing off into darkness.

Surprisingly, they crossed the town square without difficulty. In fact, it unnerved Shawna just how easy it was. With Nan close behind her, she crept down an alley between two storefronts and climbed through a wedge of pine trees on the other side. Several times she glanced over her shoulder to make sure Nan was keeping up. Each time, the older woman offered Shawna a tired smile but showed no signs of fatigue. *She's a tough old broad,* Shawna thought.

"Be quiet," Shawna said as they reached the cusp of the pine trees. Together they crouched down in the snow and peered across the street. The houses along Fairmont were just as dark and silent as the rest of the town. Shawna could make out her own home, nearly a stone's throw away, with the dilapidated porch swing and the Christmas decorations drooping from the eaves. Was this really Christmas morning? It seemed impossible.

The street itself was utterly quiet. From what she could tell from sitting in the Volkswagen, this was where those flashes of light had been coming from . . . but now she could see nothing but the infestation of deepening shadows. Snow still fell lazily—a sight that caused Shawna growing discomfort. *I'm never going to look at snow the same way again,* she thought . . . then on the heels of that: *If I live through tonight.*

"There," Nan said just as a white spark of light exploded on the front lawn of the Barristers' house. "A downed power line."

"Damn," Shawna muttered. "I was hoping it would be the National Guard."

"Which house is yours?" Nan asked.

Shawna pointed.

"Can we go there?"

"No. We can't go in any of those houses."

"Why not?"

"Because they're not empty."

"What do you mean?"

"There's roughly twelve hundred people in this town. Those who aren't dead are something else now. There are puppets in those houses. They look like people but they're not people. Not anymore."

"Like those people that chased Todd and Kate up to that church? And like what happened . . . happened to Fred?"

"No. They were something different. Those people were like socks—they serve a quick and hasty purpose. These other people . . . I think it's what happens if the creatures take up permanent residence. Not just to feed, but to live among us. They act like people but they're not really people. Real *Invasion of the Body Snatchers* bullshit."

"Lord," Nan said. "I've seen one. We picked him up out on the highway. He said his name was Eddie Clement and he was out looking for his daughter. And there *was* a daughter, and they ran off together."

"It's like if those creatures stay inside you too long they get stuck there. They become some strange hybrid of monster."

"And they're . . . in those houses?"

"Yes. Some of them, anyway. No way to tell which ones."

"But if they're still half people, we can talk to them. They might listen to us. They could—"

"No. They only look like people. They're different now."

Across the street the power line sparked and popped, lighting up the front of the Barristers' house.

"We need to find a warm place to hide," Shawna began. "I think we can make it over to—"

"Look." Nan pointed farther down the street. "A little boy."

But it wasn't a little boy. Shawna knew better. The child—maybe six or seven years of age, judging by his size—stood in the center of Fairmont Street in nothing but his pajamas and bare feet. If it wasn't for the considerable distance between them and the wedge of pines that were shielding them from the roadway, Shawna would have sworn the damn thing was staring straight at them.

"What if he's normal?" Nan said. "What if he needs help?"

"He's not human," Shawna assured her. "Not anymore."

Nan was looking hard through the darkness at the boy's frail and seemingly trustworthy frame. After a moment, she said, "Is there . . . there something wrong with his *face?*"

Shawna was busy patting down her pockets for extra rifle rounds. "Just stay back, Nan. Don't leave the trees."

"I think—"

Nan's voice cut out. Shawna whipped around to see a blurry-faced figure emerge through the pines, one hand covering Nan's mouth. The poor woman's eyes blazed above the soot-covered knuckles. Nan's legs kicked out as the figure dragged her backward through the trees.

Shawna lunged forward and grabbed Nan's ankle. With her free hand, she swung the rifle around and jammed the butt against her shoulder. Aimed high. Pulled the trigger.

The pine trees shuddered. A low howl emanated from within the copse of trees. Nan's legs were still kicking furiously, her body buried in the pines from her waist up. Shawna yanked Nan toward her but only succeeded in tearing Nan's pants. Shawna fell back on her buttocks, the rifle thumping to the snow.

A strangled cry broke through the trees as Nan's legs were swallowed up into the pines.

Grabbing the rifle, Shawna charged forward, pine branches whipping at her face. She cried out for Nan but the woman did not answer. She got the sense that the figure was dragging Nan through the trees just mere *feet* in front of her, but she could not catch up. Risking it, she raised the rifle up high and fired another shot. This one vanished into distant space. Shawna's ears rang.

Finally she burst through the trees and spilled back out into the alleyway. Directly ahead of her, the figure was running at breakneck speed, dragging Nan behind him by her hair. Again, Shawna leveled the gun and fired two shots in a row. Both struck the figure in the back but did not slow him down.

"*Shawwwwnaaaa!*" Nan screamed as the figure dragged her out into the town square.

Shawna pursued, her lungs burning, her feet numb. Just as she reached the street, she saw the upper portion of the man's body blur and lose consistency.

It became a wavering shimmer of bright light and twirling snow. The figure launched up off the ground as it simultaneously became a cloud of rattling snow, carrying Nan Wilkinson with it.

Shawna raised the rifle . . . but there was no longer anything to shoot at . . .

Nan let out one final scream as she was carried off into the night sky.

"Jesus . . ." Her throat rasped.

The barefoot child in the pajamas appeared at the opposite end of the square. At this closer distance, Shawna could make out the smooth, unmarred convexity of flesh that made up the child's face. There were no eyes, no mouth, no nose—just a fleshy bubble that appeared to drip down from the boy's hairline.

Two more white moon-faces rose up from behind a parked car. Farther down the avenue, a mound of snow rose up off the ground like a missile rising up out of an underground silo.

Shawna turned and ran.

CHAPTER FOURTEEN

This was Father Finnick's stuff," Meg said, lifting open the priest's trunk. They were in a small room deep in the rectory, which was attached to the rear of the church. A tiny bed clung to one wall above which hung an iron crucifix. In the closet, dark slacks and buttoned shirts hung neatly from wire hangers. There was a small circular table on which sat a potted plant in desperate need of water.

"Thank you," Kate said, kneeling down before the open trunk. It was filled with hand-stitched garments, embroidered stoles with gold trimming, and lavish robes made of a material that looked like silk but felt much heavier. "These are priest's clothes."

"I told you that already."

"What happened to Father Finnick?"

"He changed."

Kate sifted through the trunk. "Is there anything else? A coat or something?"

"Chris said to take you to the trunk. This is the trunk."

Kate looked up. Her gaze lingered on Meg. In the glow of the candle she held, the girl looked almost savage. What had Shawna said about checking the shoulders? Could this girl actually be one of those things?

"Could you turn around for me?" Kate asked, trying to sound as innocuous as possible.

Meg's expression—one of stupid incomprehension—did not falter. She did not turn around, either.

"Remember how Chris tore my shirt off?" Kate pursued. "Remember how he looked at those scratches down my back?"

"You want to see if I have scratches, too," Meg said. It was not a question. The candle's flame danced just inches below her chin.

Kate struggled to come up with something soothing and placating with which to respond, but in the end her mind came up blank. She said simply, "Yes."

"Dad had them."

"Your father?"

"Straight down his back," said Meg. "Two long cuts. Like someone . . . like someone chopped him with an axe . . ."

"That's horrible." One of Kate's hands advanced the slightest bit, moving to touch the girl and offer some semblance of comfort . . . but she stopped herself at the last minute.

"He came back to the church," Meg went on. Her voice was monotone. "He banged on the door for hours. I wanted to let him in but Chris said it wasn't our dad anymore."

"What happened?"

"He went around to the side of the church to try to break the windows," Meg said. "That's when Chris went up into the bell tower and dropped a fountain on him."

"A fountain?"

"One of those marble water fountains at the front of the church," Meg said. "I forget what they're called. Chris knows."

"Chris killed your dad?"

"It wasn't our dad. Chris said so."

"But he killed him?"

"He dropped the fountain on him and one of those things came out. The things that turn into snow."

Despite the chill, a tacky film of perspiration now coated Kate's face and neck. Resigned, she turned back to the trunk and stared noncommittally at the garments inside. "Isn't there anything else? Anything at all?"

"This is the trunk," was all Meg said. She'd taken a single step back; the repositioning of the candlelight caused the shadows to shift.

Kate looked up. A corduroy blazer hung in the closet. She got up and took the blazer down from the hanger. It would be a bit long on her but she much preferred it over some religious robes.

"No," Meg said. There was a strictness in her voice that caused an icy finger to prod the base of Kate's spine. "Chris said to take you to the *trunk.*"

"And you did. But I don't want to wear any of that stuff." She pulled on the blazer.

"No!" Meg threw the candle down and the light blew out, dousing the room in blackness. The girl stomped out of the room. Standing in absolute darkness, Kate listened to her footfalls recede down the hallway.

I need to get Todd and we both need to get the hell out of here, she thought. Suddenly, she found she'd much rather be back at the Pack-N-Go with the others than here in this church with these two strange kids.

Kate hurried back out into the narrow hallway. Ahead of her in the darkness, Meg's footfalls struck hollowly as she took off. There was another sound, too—a consistent thumping coming from somewhere above her head, like someone rhythmically dropping a fist over and over against the rafters.

"Meg," she called after the girl, her voice swallowed up by the darkness.

Dragging one hand along the wall, Kate headed back in the direction of the main body of the church, moving strictly by intuition. Without lights, it was like passing through an enclosed maze. Once, she even thumped against one wall.

Eventually she felt the space around her expand and she could make out the dimly lighted stained glass radiating with the moon's glow, and she knew she was in the heart of the church. As her eyes grew accustomed to the dark, the bracketed shape of the altar, like white bone, was visible on the chancel. To her immediate right, rows of pews stretched out like the exposed ribs of some giant fallen carcass.

Someone else was in the church with her; Kate could make out the indefinite shuffling of nervous feet across the dusty floor.

"Is that you, Meg?"

"You're going to make Chris angry," Meg called back. The vastness of the church made it sound like she was speaking from every direction at once. "He'll hit me again."

"No," Kate assured her. "No, he won't."

"You don't *know!*"

"Where is Chris now?"

Almost as if on cue, the thumping sound increased. It was coming from directly behind Kate, as if straight through the wall at her back.

Kate spun around, her hands pawing at the heavy shadows. The movement stirred up cobwebs; they wafted down from the nearby rafters and got tangled in her hair.

A door opened somewhere close. Kate could hear heavy, labored breathing. That same instant, a candle flickered to life, frighteningly close to her. It was

Meg, having snuck up beside her in the dark, the candle causing the shadows to swim across her narrow little features. Kate peered at the open doorway to see Chris's broad shoulders come backward through the opening. He was bent over, dragging something . . . and Kate felt a sickness knot up in her belly.

It was Todd, unconscious or dead. The thumping sound she'd heard had been Todd's boots thumping down the bell tower stairs.

"What'd you do to him, you son of a bitch?" Kate shouted. Beside her, Meg recoiled.

"He was going to open the windows," Chris rasped, out of breath. He let go of Todd's arms and Todd's body slumped motionless to the floor. "He was trying to let those things inside."

"That's bullshit. He wouldn't do that."

Chris whirled around on her. In the light of the candle, his piggy eyes gleamed like seabed stones. "Were you *there?* Do you *know?*"

Through clenched teeth, Kate said, "Is he dead? Did you kill him?"

"I'm in charge," said the boy. He still had Todd's pistol tucked into his belt. The dead priest's flowing clothes were tight around the boy's shoulders but too long so that the hems bunched at his feet and dragged on the floor. "You both have to do what *I* say."

"I told you he'd be mad," Meg muttered at Kate's elbow.

On the floor, Todd groaned but did not wake up. Relief washed over Kate. She hadn't realized just how bad her hands were shaking until that moment.

Chris climbed the chancel steps and approached the altar. In the flickering yellow light, Kate could make out a number of implements lined up there—what appeared to be a golden chalice among them. Also recognizable was the plastic bag full of ammunition for the handgun as well as the flashlight Kate had brought with them. Chris sorted through the implements until he located what he was looking for, then trudged back down the steps and bent down over Todd's body.

Kate stepped toward him. "You leave him al—"

With surprising speed, Chris turned and had the pistol pointed at her. Kate's heart froze, as did her advance on the boy. "Don't come closer. I'll shoot you. Won't I, Meg?"

Meg nodded furiously. "He will. He'll kill you."

"If it's meant to be," Chris said, "then it's meant to be. It's all part of God's plan. Are you religious?"

"I don't know."

Chris seemed puzzled by the answer. His chubby baby-face creased. "What does that mean?"

"Please don't hurt him." Kate was trying to see what Chris had in his other hand, the item he'd taken off the altar.

"What would God think about your insolence?" Chris said.

"Do you even know what that word means?" Kate countered, though she knew it was a mistake the moment the words came from her mouth.

Chris bolted to his feet, enraged. "Don't make fun of me!" he shouted, his voice echoing through the chamber. The gun wavered in his hand. "If it wasn't for me, you and your friend would have died out there! I saw what was happening! I could have left you to die!"

"I didn't mean to make fun of you."

"You *did!* You . . . you *fucking* did!"

Again, Meg recoiled. Kate could almost hear the girl's heart thudding against the wall of her chest.

"Kneel down," Chris demanded of Kate. He thrust the gun at her. "Do it!"

Shaking, Kate dropped to her knees. The floor was hard and unforgiving and her whole body suddenly ached.

"Don't shoot her, Chris," Meg said, although there was very little compassion in her tone.

The barrel of the gun looked enormous. The longer she stared at it, the more Kate believed she could just reach out and shove her whole fist into the chamber. The thing was suddenly the size of a cannon.

"They persecuted Jesus Christ for all the good He did for people," Chris said, the gun vibrating in his meaty hand. His face was speckled with sweat. "He tried to save them and they nailed Him to the cross!"

In her horror, Kate caught a whiff of freshly-spilled urine, and wondered if the almighty Chris had just wet himself in his excitement.

"He gave his *life* for the wretched and worthless animals who took His!" Then he pointed the gun at Meg. "Blow out that candle!"

Meg puffed and doused them all in darkness.

Kate pressed her eyes shut and braced herself for the shot. Chris's heavy respiration seemed to be coming from every angle, every direction, all around her. His Clydesdale footfalls paced all about.

Think of something happy, think of something beautiful, a favorite memory, a happier time, something wonderful that I want to have as my last and final thought before this little son of a bitch drives a bullet through my brain . . .

Several seconds went by before Kate realized she was still alive. She could hear Chris moving about in front of her where Todd's body lay supine on the floor. There came a muted ruffling noise, like someone rifling through laundry, followed by a solid thump. Kate's heart was strumming in her throat.

Then she heard Chris stand. A second later, she could smell his breath—a poisonous concoction of Fritos, beef jerky, and onions—directly in her face. She thought she could smell the oil of the gun, too.

"Please . . ." Her voice was almost nonexistent.

His lips brushing the side of her face, Chris whispered, "Judge not and ye shall not be judged; condemn not and ye shall not be condemned."

A dull strike echoed down the nave. Kate felt Chris tense and stand up. Kate opened her eyes and squinted down the dark throat of the church. On either side of the narthex, the bluish stained glass windows seemed to float like apparitions. At first, Kate could not tell what had made the noise. But then as her eyes acclimated themselves to the gloom, she thought she saw a single palm, all five fingers splayed, pressed against one of the windows.

"They're out there," Kate whispered.

Chris must have spotted the hand, too; his respiration increased its tempo again. Under his breath, he muttered, "I told you not to light those candles."

Meg said nothing. For all Kate knew, the girl had vanished into smoke.

"They know we're in here," Kate said.

"Of course they do." There was unmasked disgust in Chris's voice. "I should have never opened those doors for you."

She heard Chris hurry across the narthex. A moment later, the silhouette of his overlarge head appeared before one of the windows as he peered out. "Oh," he said, his voice almost comically small. "Oh."

"What is it?" Kate said.

"Outside. There's a lot of them."

Somewhere behind Kate, Meg began to whimper.

Quickly, Kate stood. Her whole body groaned in protest. Blindly, she reached out in the dark until her hand fell on one of Meg's shoulders. The girl did not move beneath her grasp. Kate's fingers slid down into the collar of the girl's shirt and worked their way over the twin hubs of Meg's shoulder blades. There were no lacerations that Kate could feel. Bending down very close to Meg's ear so that Chris wouldn't hear, she whispered, "What about your brother?"

"He's not one of them, either."

So he's just your typical sociopath, Kate thought . . . and was astounded to find that the thought nearly sent her into hysterical laughter. It was all she could do to keep from braying like a donkey.

"There's . . . maybe twelve . . . thirteen . . . thirteen people just standing out there in the snow," Chris said, still looking out the window. He sounded completely dazed by the situation. "Maybe they've been sent here to help."

"No," Kate said. "Everyone in this town is fucked."

Meg trembled at the word. Kate quickly withdrew her hand from the girl's shoulder. Careful of her footing, she negotiated around Meg and climbed toward the altar, working mostly by feel and from memory. When she reached it, she ran her hands gingerly over the top of the altar, her fingers trailing over the various implements until she located the flashlight.

She slipped the flashlight into the rear waistband of her pants. Then her fingers closed around the plastic bag full of ammo. She winced at the sound the plastic made crinkling between her fingers, certain Chris would spin around and start firing shots at her. But he was too occupied with their new visitors out in the snow to pay her any further mind. Kate slid the bag off the altar and set it down beneath it—someplace she knew she could get to in a hurry, if need be.

Down on the floor, Todd moaned. Much louder this time.

"They're going to hear him," Meg cautioned.

Chris hustled back across the narthex, his multiple robes rustling. "I should shut him up for good."

"It doesn't matter," Kate said, sliding back into place beside Meg. "They already know we're here. What we need to do is wake him up so we can all figure out what to do next."

"What do you mean?" Chris demanded. "What do you mean, 'what to do next'? I don't need him to tell me what to do."

"That isn't what I meant. I just think that with the four of us trying to figure this out, we might stand a better—"

"I don't *need* him for *anything*."

"All right." She knew better than to keep up the argument.

"They won't get in here. This is sacred ground."

"I don't think that matters to them."

"You don't think *God* matters?" Chris boomed. Behind him, more hands appeared on the stained glass windows. "You don't think the Almighty is powerful enough to keep evil at bay? Because that's what they are—they're pure evil! Sent to punish us all for our sins! Sent straight from hell to do the devil's bidding!"

If I rush him in the dark, surprise him and get him off-balance, I could probably wrestle that gun away from him, she thought. *He's a chunky son of a bitch but as long as I kept his weight off me, I think I'd actually be able to do it.*

She started sweating all over again.

"Kate?" It was Todd's groggy voice filtering through the shadows. "You there, Kate?"

"I'm right here," she called to him.

"Stop it," Chris said. But there was little strength left in his voice now.

"What's . . . what's going on?" Todd continued.

"We're at Judgment Day," Chris said. "This is the End of Times."

"I can't move," Todd said. His voice sounded more lucid now. "I'm tied up to something. Kate?"

Like starfish clinging to the underside of a boat, countless hands now papered the windows.

"They're going to get in, Chris," Kate said, her voice level. She desperately wanted to sound logical and calm at the moment. She also deliberately spoke Chris's name in hopes that whatever memory had been temporarily knocked from Todd would return to him the moment he heard the boy's name. "We need to untie Todd so he can help us keep them away."

"I told you," Chris retorted. "They won't be able to get in here."

"I'm scared," Meg said—startling Kate, who had forgotten that the girl has been standing right next to her.

"Don't listen to these people," Chris told Meg. "They're on the side of evil. That's clear to me now. They want to coax us into battle when there is no need. God will protect us, Meg. Just like Mom and Dad have always taught us—God will see us through this."

Sensing her opportunity, Kate sprung down off the pulpit and landed on Chris's chest in a clumsy but effective tackle. They both dropped to the floor, Kate on top of the boy, and she heard the distinct sound of the gun clatter to the tiles. *Shit!* Nonetheless, she straddled him and sought out his neck with her hands. He sent his big fists swinging, connecting over and over again with the sides of her head. Sparks flew beneath her eyelids. One punch rushed up to meet her nose and tears exploded from her eyes. Beneath her, Chris bucked like a hog being tied. He shouted to his sister in throaty lamentations.

"Stop it!" Meg screamed from the pulpit. "Stop it! You're hurting him!"

Kate's fingers closed around the boy's throat. Chris's spittle flecked her face as his thick-fingered hands attempted to loosen her grasp on him.

Distantly, Kate was aware of a looming presence . . . and she was reminded in that instant of being a young girl out on the softball field, and how cool it had been when airliners would pass overhead, their shadows like the shadows of a giant bird bulleting across the outfield . . .

Kate let go of Chris's throat and rolled off him just in time to glimpse a dark, wavering shape floating just beyond the panels of stained glass in the ceiling high above the altar. Then, a second later, something came crashing through the windows, sending a shower of jagged spearheads raining down on them all. Kate blocked her eyes with one arm but still managed to see a figure, undeniably human, fall through the shattered windows and plummet like a sack of potatoes to the altar. The figure struck the altar with a bone-crunching din and nearly buckled in half at the force of the landing. A cone of moonlight poured in through the ceiling, spotlighting the altar and the twisted, mangled corpse that lay folded overtop of it.

Meg screamed.

Kate quickly scrambled to her hands and knees and ditched forward, pawing for the handgun. Its blue steel practically glowed in the moonlight. Gripping the gun by the hilt, Kate then swung around and hurried over to

Todd, who sat half-cocked against a pew staring up at the wound in the ceiling with stark disbelief.

"Where are you tied?" she said, nearly knocking her forehead against his ear as she slid into him.

"My hands." But he wasn't looking at her; he was staring numbly at the ceiling. His face was a network of small cuts and bleeding lacerations from the shower of glass.

Kate reached behind him and found that Chris had tied Todd's hands around the front leg of the pew. Quickly she felt out the knot and managed to dig her fingernails between the sections of rope, prying them apart.

"Oh, fuck," Todd said, his voice sounding like it was sticking to his throat. "That's *Nan*."

Kate paused in her work just long enough to look back up at the altar. Had Todd not said anything she would have never recognized poor Nan Wilkinson due to the stage of her mutilation, but once she locked eyes on Nan's face—the frozen grimace of fear and pain, the bulging, milked-over eyes, the skin pulled taut like the flesh of a balloon—she couldn't *not see* her.

"Oh, Christ," Kate whispered breathlessly into Todd's ear. "Oh . . . Christ, Todd . . ."

"Untie me."

She quickly went back to work with the rope. Peripherally, she saw Chris scoot away from her in the darkness, possibly looking for sanctuary behind one of the pews. Up on the pulpit, a pinpoint of light sparked through the darkness: Meg's lighter. The flame shook and wavered until the girl was able once again to light the candle. This time, her brother did not yell at her to blow it out.

Meg approached the altar and the mangled corpse that lay across it. One bloodied arm jutted out at an unnatural angle. Meg moved with the lethargy of a somnambulist while the candle's flame jittered in her hand. Above the girl's head, it began to snow through the opening in the roof.

Kate finally got the rope untied. Todd pulled his hands into his lap and rubbed his wrists before climbing to his feet. He was staring up at the snow coming through the roof. "We need to get out of here. Fast."

Kate rushed up to the altar and snatched the bag of ammo from beneath it. As she stood, she locked eyes again with Nan Wilkinson's corpse. Ice clung to the woman's silvery hair and her skin looked cold and brittle, like porcelain.

"Come with me," Kate said, grabbing Meg by the wrist. The motion caused Meg to drop the candle.

"My brother," Meg said.

"We all need to get out of here."

The hands against the windows began banging on the glass—all of them in unison, like some orchestrated percussive beat. Kate pulled Meg down off the altar just as the snow above their heads began to solidify and come together. At the center of the blustery mass was a tendril of silver light, like light spilling out of a keyhole.

"Here!" Kate shouted, tossing Todd the handgun. Dragging Meg by the wrist, she ran toward the farthest wall. Meg was as lifeless as a rag doll in her grasp.

Chris began whimpering from behind one of the pews.

Todd press-checked the nine-millimeter then took several steps backward. The mass of snow rotating above the altar seemed to darken and take on form, like a shadow. Watching it, Kate found herself hoping that Chris had been right—that perhaps this was sanctified land and no evil would dare cross its threshold. But as the swirling mass of snow and light above the altar became thicker and more prominent, she knew that was not the case.

They were going to die.

The carpet beneath the altar suddenly went up in a blaze of white flame: Meg's dropped candle. A second later and Nan's outstretched arm went up, too, filling the nave with a dark black smoke and the acrid, gunpowdery reek of burning flesh. As the black smoke rose up out of the hole in the roof, it commingled with the twirling mass of living snow hovering just above the altar. Briefly, like a sheet draped over a mannequin, the smoke brought the creature into frightening relief—the human-shaped head with the distended jowls and the hollow pits for eyes; the thin stalk of its neck; the heart-shaped scurf of its upper chest . . .

Todd fired two, three shots at it. The rounds passed right through the cloud of smoke, carving funnels in their wake. Meg clamped hands to her ears while her brother shouted something unintelligible, the fear in his voice undeniable now.

The creature swooped down and glided just above the pulpit, its near-formless arms trailing behind it like the tentacles of a giant squid. Its belly licked the flames, causing the massive thing to shriek in agony and pull up toward the ceiling. Kate felt the wind of its movement against her face.

"Burn it!" Meg screamed beside her, clutching onto Kate's forearm with both her hands. "Burn it!"

Indeed, the creature's scaly flank glowed as red as embers in a bonfire as it pulled rotations above their heads. Charred bits of scurf fluttered to the altar like confetti.

Just as one of the windows shattered behind her, Kate lunged forward and pulled one of the wall sconces from its seating. Charging up to the altar, she plunged the sconce into the flames, the heat from the growing inferno stinging her eyes and causing sweat to pop out of her pores.

"Kate!" Todd yelled at her. "Get down, Kate!"

Meg wailed and curled up in one corner. Directly above Meg's head, one of the townspeople was attempting to climb in through the shattered window.

Proffering the flaming torch above her head, Kate stepped down off the altar and joined Todd, who was holding the pistol in both hands now, a look of utter perplexity on his face. Blood streaked his white skin—cheeks, forehead, neck and chin.

Kate waved the torch and the creature pixilated into dust. Snow rained down from the rafters while more poured in through the opening in the roof.

Farther down the narthex, more windows imploded as fists were driven through the glass. Ghoulish shapes shimmied up over the sill and dropped down into the church.

"There's a side door!" Todd shouted, pointing clear across the pulpit.

"Okay!" Kate shouted. It felt like the building was getting ready to shake apart. She turned to Meg and called for the girl but Meg wouldn't move; she'd drawn her legs up into a fetal position and simply sat, rocking back and for in the corner.

"Come on," Todd said, grabbing Kate's arm.

Kate pulled her arm loose. "Wait!" She ran to Meg and pulled her to her feet. Meg stumbled but followed. Kate shouted for Chris, too . . . and the boy popped up behind one of the pews, his flesh prickled with sweat and his priestly garbs hanging off him like quilts. He hurried toward them just as something—something *big*—moved behind him in the shadows. The darkness seemed to separate from itself just as a white curl of powder engulfed Chris, bringing him screaming to the floor.

"Chris!" Meg shouted, and it took all of Kate's strength to hang onto the girl.

Chris attempted to stand . . . but just as he got his feet under himself, something partially transparent and shaped like the blade of a hunting knife (only much, much bigger) speared out of the mist and plunged straight into Chris's right shoulder.

Chris's eyes bulged. His mouth dropped open and, a moment later, a black string of blood oozed out. He staggered and would have fallen had he not been speared to the thing behind him.

A second curled talon appeared, this one the size of a school bus fender and about as solid as a strip of film projected onto a cloud of smoke. It sprung forward, reminding Kate of nature specials she'd seen as a kid where scorpions jabbed their poison-tipped tails into the backs of spiders. The talon pierced Chris's left shoulder, making the boy's head roll loosely on his neck. Blood continued to spill from his agape mouth, staining the holy vestments he wore.

Meg buried her face in Kate's chest.

Later on, Kate would recall Shawna Dupree's words when thinking back on this event—about these things wearing people like puppets—because that's exactly what it appeared was happening. The darkened shape behind Chris seemed to loom up over him as it slid its bladed arms further into Chris's back. As it did so, Chris's body jerked and squirmed, like a sock being fitted with an oversized foot. The cloud-shape then seemed to fade *into* Chris's back, as if sucked through a black hole, and as the last vestige of the creature withdrew into him, Chris's eyes flipped open and his neck cocked at an angle on his neck in a mockery of life.

Everything went deathly silent. In the shadows behind Chris, Kate could make out the crenellated silhouettes of the townspeople inside the church while others paused halfway through the broken windows. They were surrounded.

"Hey," said the Chris-thing. "Hey, Meg. Come on. Come here."

Meg would not look at it. Kate hugged her tighter.

"Come on, Meg. Sis. Come on, little sister." The Chris-thing shuffled forward, its steps as awkward as a toddler's. He had the same empty look in his eyes as Eddie Clement had when they picked him up on the side of the road. "Hey, now . . ."

"Fuck this," Todd said, and kicked through the doors at the other end of the church. Freezing air filled the church. For a second, it seemed the torch in Kate's hand would be extinguished, but the flame was strong and held on. Todd marshaled through the door and Kate followed, Meg still clinging to her.

Behind them, the Chris-thing screamed—a sound like a passing locomotive.

Todd staggered in the snow. His shoulders appeared to slouch. From over his shoulder, Kate saw what had deterred him: scattered around the grounds of the church were twenty or so townspeople, each one staring them down with dark, soulless eyes. Todd raised the gun, pointed it at one of them.

Directly above them, the sky looked like a volcanic eruption. Lightning flashed horizontally from cloud to cloud. There was no moon.

Todd grabbed Kate's hand. "Use the fire if they get too close." He pulled her through the snow while Kate, in turn, pulled Meg. The townspeople began closing in on them. Todd let a few rounds rip from the handgun but that didn't seem to deter any of them, except for the one or two that went down from the force of the bullet. When clutching hands got too close, Kate singed them with the torch. One of the townspeople howled . . . and suddenly dropped to the snow like someone shucking off an old housedress. Something semitransparent and hulking flitted off into the night.

The church grounds sloped downward to Pascal Street. There were a number of dead vehicles staggered at intervals down the street and two tipped over on their sides in a nearby ravine. Todd led the charge, panting and out of breath by the time they reached the street. Kate nearly slammed into his back and managed to hold onto the torch before it tipped out of her hands and clattered down into the frozen culvert.

Kate chanced a look behind her.

The church was a black smear at the top of the hill. Thick smoke billowed up through the rent in the roof and melded with the low-clinging clouds. The lower windows were alive with firelight as the interior of the church burned. The townspeople still stood on the snowy slope, staring down at them. Strangely, none had pursued.

Something's wrong here, Kate had time to think. *Something is very, very wrong . . .*

Though he was still breathing hard, Todd straightened up and began moving farther down the road. "Come on. We can't stop now."

Kate lifted the torch above her head and gripped Meg's hand. It felt limp and lifeless; the girl was no doubt shocked into immobility by what she'd just witnessed happen to her brother. Kate tugged her through the icy streets, close on Todd's heels.

"Where are we going?" Kate called to him. Before Todd could answer, she looked over at Meg. "Where do you think we should go? Where would be safe?"

The girl only stared at her without expression. She was still in shock.

"When I was up in the bell tower," Todd said, "I saw a fire hall and a police station up this road. I don't know the condition they're in but we need to—"

A mound of snow burst up from the ground along the shoulder, showering the night in white crystals. A lion's roar shook Kate to the marrow of her bones and she nearly dropped the torch. The snow rose up and towered over them, three stories high, undulating like the segmented body of a worm. A blade of ice protruded from it and reared up—

Kate charged forward and drove the torch into the wall of snow. She had expected the flame to immediately extinguish upon impact, but instead the snow solidified and turned the color of a catfish. Kate could make out the vague suggestion of a ribcage and, beneath the translucent scurf, the throb of a white light at the center of the being. The flame ignited its flesh and the creature emitted a bone-numbing shriek that shook the tops of the nearby pines. Then it folded in on itself and scattered in a cloud of sparkling mist across the snowy ground.

Todd could only stare at the space where the creature had been just a moment ago. It looked like he was holding his breath.

Kate put a hand on his shoulder. "It's okay," she said, though she thought her voice sounded too nervous and uncertain. "We're okay."

"Right," he said, nodding without really hearing her. "Right . . ."

She pushed him forward. "I'm right behind you," she told him.

CHAPTER FIFTEEN

Crouching behind a veil of holly bushes, Shawna peered at the back of the Rita Tubalow's house. Shaking from a mixture of cold and fear, Shawna counted to fifty until she could feel her heartbeat regain its normal rhythm again. The rifle clinging to her side, she surveyed Rita Tubalow's backyard, now blanketed in an undulating carpet of snow. The moonlight made the snow radiate with nacreous light.

A doghouse sat at an angle beneath the deck, and a concrete sundial, the top of which held about eight inches of compacted white powder, rose up out of the center of the yard like a lighthouse on rocky shores. The house itself looked deserted, all the windows black like a mountainside pocked with caverns.

What she had told Nan Wilkinson had been the truth—that while many of these houses *appeared* empty, that was far from the truth. She'd seen the worst of what had come to Woodson over the past week, and it was all too horrible to attempt to relay to any outsider who hadn't witnessed it all first-hand. As Shawna had.

It had started quietly in the night, without anyone's knowledge. Like a sneak attack from an advancing army, they had entered the town under everyone's radar. And maybe that analogy wasn't too far off—after all, what were those things and where had they come from? It was anyone's guess. It *was* a sneak attack from an advancing army; the only difference was that their attackers hadn't been human.

The snow had been falling steadily since the middle of November, so it was impossible to pinpoint exactly when things changed. If they had come in on some special storm, or if they were actually the storm *itself,* Shawna had no clue. For all she knew, they could have been here since November, among the town unobserved and biding their time until the right moment. But what Shawna *did* know was that the horror hadn't begun until earlier that week. And it had started with Jared.

She'd known Jared from high school, although they hadn't dated until after they'd graduated and took fulltime jobs together—merely by chance—at the local Ben Franklin. He was a bird-chested, narrow-faced lover of classic rock who couldn't grow a full beard if someone said they'd pay him a million dollars, and in truth, Shawna hadn't even liked him at first. She knew of him from school—it was a small town, needless to say—but they hadn't been what you'd call friends. While she'd hung out primarily with girls from the soccer team, Jared Calabrese had smoked dope behind St. John's with the motorheads from Mr. Barnholdt's shop class. So when Jared had asked her out after two weeks working in adjacent checkout lanes at the Ben Franklin, she was taken aback. She'd merely smiled and told him she had a boyfriend—an utterly ridiculous and easily refutable lie, since everyone knew everyone else's business in Woodson. Yet Jared hadn't called her out on it; he'd only grinned his goofy grin and gave her what approximated a two-fingered salute that had coaxed a surprised laugh from her before he returned to work.

Eventually, though, he'd cornered her in the stockroom where they shared a cigarette and where she finally succumbed to his persistence. (Shawna had taken up smoking after her father, a health-conscious marathon runner, had died from lung cancer, which was when Shawna figured fuck it, there were no guarantees in life, bottoms up and smoke 'em if ya got 'em all that.) She hadn't even been attracted to him but, in the face of total honesty, there really weren't a whole lot of prospects around Woodson. So they'd gone on a number of dates, Jared keeping his hands astoundingly to himself in a display of self-control worthy of some award, and before she knew it she found herself falling for the son of a bitch.

They'd spent the next few months rutting like feral cats. Twice she feared pregnancy and sweated her period, wondering what her mother would say, until it eventually arrived and she was able to breathe normally again. Jared was clumsy in bed but Shawna found the trait surprisingly endearing, and it soon erased all doubt about whether the stories she'd heard about him back in high school—about his sexual deviance—were true. He'd gotten her flowers and candy for her birthday—rather uninspired, but appreciated nonetheless—and this Christmas would have marked their one-year anniversary. She had been looking forward to it. (Back in her bedroom on Fairmont Street, in the top drawer of her dresser wrapped in a tube sock, was a Timex watch with a silver band and their initials engraved on the back—a Christmas gift that had cost her four months' salary, meticulously saved.)

But then earlier this week, all that had changed.

It started at the high school. During a fresh snowfall, a group of kids sledding down the steep hill behind the school never returned home. Frantic parents donned hats and gloves and poured out into the streets. At this time, Jared had come to pick Shawna up after her shift at the Ben Franklin—it was his day off, something they were unable to coordinate due to a lack of employees at the store—and he'd filled her in on the mystery of the disappearing children with the excitement of someone who'd just come from seeing a kick-ass rock concert.

"Where'd they all go?" she'd asked.

"Don't know," he'd said simply, jerking his shoulders up to his ears. "But that's not the weird part. Just as I was leaving, I heard from Mr. Dormer across the street who was outside talking with some of the neighbors. They were talking about the sheriff being called out to the school, too, and that some of the parents had come running back into town saying stuff about the snow rising up off the ground and covering people." His grin had looked fiendish in the glow of the Subaru's dashboard lights. "Like, the snow fucking came up in a wave and swallowed them whole."

"Are they okay?"

"You don't get it, 'Na. They're fucking *gone.*"

She scowled, searching through her purse for her lipstick. "What do you mean they're gone?"

"Gone. Vanished. Disappeared. Snow swallowed 'em up. They can't find them."

"That's bullshit. That's Dormer fucking with your head."

"You wouldn't say that if you were there. Mr. Dormer looked scared enough to shit bricks. I could hear the cop cars racing through the snow from the house."

"They're probably just out looking for the kids."

"They won't find them, either."

"Why's that?"

"Snow got 'em," he'd said, as if this were the most logical thing in the world. "Swallowed 'em up like popcorn."

Arriving back at her house, her mother was quick to usher her inside. As she watched Jared drive off through the snowy streets, Shawna felt an awful premonitory pang resonate in the center of her chest. Her mother, a frail woman encumbered with a perpetual scowl, rushed her to the kitchen before Shawna could even take her coat off, her sneakers squeaking wetly on the linoleum.

In the kitchen, all the lights were off. Shawna went to flip them on but her mother slapped her hand away. "Ouch! Mother, what's going on?"

"Be quiet!" her mother chastised. She grabbed Shawna's wrist in a pincer-like grip and dragged her over to the bank of windows that overlooked the backyard. The rear porch lights were off, too, but orange-pink sodium light from the nearby streetlamps filtered through the bare branches of the surrounding trees.

Shawna leaned closer to the window. There was someone out in the yard. Just standing there in the snow, staring at the house.

"Is that Mr. Kopeck?" Shawna asked her mother.

"He's been there for over an hour now. I shut the lights and locked the doors but he hasn't moved."

"But what's he *doing?*"

"Waiting," said her mother.

"Waiting for what?"

"I don't know. But it can't be good." Her mother pointed past their yard to their neighbors', the Samjakes. "Look."

Someone was standing in the Samjakes' backyard, too. The distance was too great to know for certain, but Shawna thought it looked like plump old Delia Overmeyer from over on Port Avenue. Just like Tim Kopeck, Delia Overmeyer was standing up to her shins in the snow, staring at the back of the Samjakes' house.

"What's going on out there?" Shawna murmured, her breath blossoming on the glass.

"I got a phone call from Lizzie MacDonald about twenty minutes ago," said her mother. "She said George Lee Wilson is in her yard, too. Just standing there, staring up at her house, just the same way, Shawna. She said her dog Brutus was out there barking his head off. She called to the dog but he wouldn't come. He ran out into the yard and disappeared into the shadows. Then she said she didn't hear him no more."

A twinge of icy terror rippled through Shawna's body. "Jared said some kids disappeared down at the school tonight. Said their parents went looking for them but some of them disappeared, too."

No, that's a lie, she thought immediately afterward. *That's not exactly what Jared had said. He'd said they were eaten up by the snow. Eaten up like popcorn.*

But she couldn't tell this to her mother. The poor woman already looked on the verge of a nervous breakdown.

Shawna leaned over the counter and pulled the telephone to her ear.

"There's no answer at Joe's," said her mother. Joe Farnsworth was the sheriff.

Shawna dialed the number anyway. It was printed on the phone's handset in her mother's spidery handwriting.

Her mother finally let go of Shawna's wrist. The woman gripped the sill of the window with both hands, her face very close to the windowpane. Her breath was fogging it up but she was still able to keep an eye on Tim Kopeck out in the yard. Tim Kopeck, who had undoubtedly lost his frigging mind . . . along with Delia Overmeyer . . . along with George Lee Wilson . . .

No. That's impossible.

The telephone at the other end of the line kept ringing, ringing, ringing. Shawna caught her mother's worried stare. "No one's going to answer,

Shawnie. Poor Joe's probably got his hands full tonight." There was moisture glittering in the corners of her mother's eyes. "Don't tie up the line. Lizzie's been calling every few minutes."

Shawna hung up the telephone while chewing on her lower lip. "I don't understand," she said after a time. "What does this mean?"

"It means—" began her mother, but then the words dried up in her mouth. The older woman's eyes were locked back on the window. "He's gone," she said in a low utterance.

Shawna practically pressed her face up against the windowpane. Her mother was right: Tim Kopeck was no longer standing in their backyard.

Shawna cast her eyes over to the Samjakes' yard and saw that Delia Over-meyer—or whoever that had been—was also gone.

"Where'd he go?" said her mother. Her voice was paper-thin.

"There's no footprints," Shawna said. "Look in the yard."

"What are you talking about? That's impossible." But her mother looked and could say no more. It was obvious—there were no footprints in the snow, save for the two divots where, only a moment ago, Tim Kopeck had been standing. It was as if the man had simply vanished into thin air.

Above their heads, rafters creaked. Both women jerked their heads toward the ceiling. It was an old A-frame house built in the early '70s, and both women had lived in the place long enough to become familiar with all its typical creaks, groans, and rumblings. This sound was not one of them.

"Is something upstairs?" said her mother, still staring heavenward.

"Sounds like someone's on the roof."

In the summers, squirrels would tromp about the shingles and drop acorns down on the roof where they'd roll like tiny boulders down into the gutters. Even those pedestrian sounds had resonated with amplification, and Shawna would imagine squirrels up there the size of small dogs and acorns as big as apples. Right now, whatever was up there sounded like a pickup truck slowly ascending the pitched roof.

"Stay here," Shawna said.

"Where are you going?" her mother called after her, but by that time, Shawna was already halfway down the hall on her way to the stairs. "Shawnie!"

Upstairs, the house was dark, the moonlight sliding in shafts through the windows. Pausing on the landing, Shawna held her breath and listened for the sound again. But all was silent.

Shawna had loved her father very much and, since his death, thought of him often, but this was the first time since perhaps the funeral she actually tried to *will* him back into existence. If he were here, this wouldn't be happening. If he were here, she wouldn't have to be checking the upstairs hallway, the bed-rooms, making sure the windows were locked. That had been her father's job.

She went quickly from bedroom to bedroom, making sure all the windows were locked. They were. Tight. Outside, the snow continued to fall. From her bedroom window she peered down into the yard. Mr. Kopeck was still M.I.A., but those two footprint-shaped divots stared up at her like eyes.

Downstairs, her mother screamed.

Shawna raced back down the hall and took the stairs two at a time. She grabbed an umbrella from the umbrella rack at the foot of the stairs—the only weapon she thought of at the moment—and rushed toward the kitchen amidst the sounds of pots and pans clattering loudly to the kitchen floor.

"Mom!"

She arrived in the kitchen just in time to see a fleeting shape yanked backward through the doorway at the opposite end of the kitchen. One of her mother's slippers skidded across the floor.

Shawna charged forward, wielding the umbrella like a sword, and crossed the threshold into the living room. What she saw there would be etched into her memory until her dying day.

It was her mother, her housedress torn down one side, her ample bosom clad in a padded bra fully exposed, a look of incomprehensive terror on her face. She was on her back ... but not necessarily on the *floor*, because something was sliding wetly beneath her, something big, keeping her up off the floor. The sight caused Shawna to freeze, her eyes blazing like the headlamps of a tractor.

"*Shawwwwnieeee!*"

The thing beneath her mother bucked and the woman slid to the floor. Then, impossibly, what looked like a narrow funnel of snow corkscrewed up from the floor. Wind blew Shawna's hair off her forehead and sent loose papers and napkins fluttering about the room. There was a smell, too—something thickly rotten and unearthly.

Something separated from the funnel of snow—something long and tapered, pointed at the tip. In her stupefaction, Shawna thought of a shark's dorsal fin. Then reality rushed back to her and she lunged forward, swinging the umbrella at the twirling mass of snow like a baseball bat.

The umbrella passed right through it, unencumbered.

"*Shawww-NIEEEE!*"

It was the last thing she would ever hear her mother say. The dorsal fin blade pitched downward, lightning quick, and buried itself into her mother's chest. A gout of black blood erupted in a geyser from her mother's mouth. Around Shawna, the house shook. That hideous, dead animal stink intensified until Shawna's eyes burned.

She blinked her eyes, her vision sliding away from her.

And when she opened them again, she caught the final vestige of the snow-funnel withdrawing up through the chimney. Her mother was gone now, too, but her other slipper lay in the hearth of the fireplace, powdered in soot . . .

The days following that event had been pure madness. By the time she reunited with Jared, half the town had vanished and those who remained had either turned into drooling savages or had simply become *different.* Some of the neighborhood children had simply vanished . . . but the ones that lingered became ghosts of their former selves, faceless little nymphs hiding out in the surrounding woods. It was as if the creatures could not properly meld with children, that they corrupted them visually and ruined them.

Jared's plan was to get out of town ASAP, but unfortunately he was having trouble starting his Subaru. Gunning the accelerator while the vehicle strad-dled a snow bank achieved nothing except for igniting a small fire beneath the undercarriage. Jared cursed and panicked but, as it turned out, the fire kept the snow-things away. Fire, Jared told her, could hurt them, maybe even kill them. It was Jared's idea to hurry over to the Pack-N-Go for containers of lighter fluid so they could make torches . . . but when they got there, the proprietor, George Farmer, had changed. And something had gotten inside Jared, too.

She'd had to shoot him, bring him down. She could still see his head com-ing apart in her mind's eye . . .

These thoughts, along with a thousand others from the past week, clut-tered Shawna's mind as she crouched down in the holly bushes staring at the back of Rita Tubalow's house. Her whole body felt numb and her breath was becoming shallower and shallower. As much as she hated to consider this alternative, she knew she had to get out of the cold as soon as possible, not to mention away from those things that were pursuing her . . . which meant ditching into the nearest shelter.

What if those things are in that house? Those things like Tim Kopeck and Delia Overmeyer?

It was a risk she'd have to take.

When she finally felt more in control of herself, she stood. She was aware of a ripping sensation followed by a surge of pain that raced up her left leg— Fred Wilkinson's stitches coming undone.

In pain, she hustled across the snow-covered yard toward Rita's house. Glancing over her shoulder, she was horrified to find spatters of blood left behind in the snow.

She hid briefly in the shadow of the raised deck, catching her breath. Sud-denly, the rifle hanging from her shoulder weighed about a thousand pounds. Her breath wheezing through her tightening throat, she leaned forward and looked in either direction, examining the neighboring yards for signs of life. Or signs of . . . something *other* . . .

There were no broken windows that Shawna could find at the back of the house. That was how they got in. Through the chimneys, too, of course. Or open doors. Any way in at all.

Slinking along the concrete wall, Shawna made her way to the basement door. Curling her numb fingers around the doorknob, she said a silent prayer to a god she did not believe in before trying to turn it.

It turned. Blessedly.

She eased it open and waited to see if anything would rush out at her. The rifle at the ready, she counted to ten. Nothing came for her. She leaned into the doorway and examined a basement as black as the solar system. Sniffing the air, she braced herself for that decaying, dead animal stink they carried with them, but the place just smelled musty and unused. Not dangerous.

Maybe.

Shawna slipped quickly inside, toeing the basement door shut behind her.

The darkness was absolute. Hulking behemoth shapes rose up out of the ether like beasties from some fabled world—a billiard table, sofas, tables and chairs, boxes of old clothes and appliances. She smelled sawdust and paint thinner and, beneath all that, rodent feces.

She wended her way to one dark corner where she proceeded to stack boxes around her as a sort of improvised shelter. Then she eased herself down onto the cold stone floor, using the butt of the rifle as a crutch. The pain in her leg was a raging conflagration now; it was all she could do not to shout out as she attempted to unbend her knee.

Something thumped on the floor above her head.

Please no please no please no, she prayed. *Just give me some time to rest. Please. Just a few minutes.*

She waited but the noise did not repeat. Setting the rifle down, she unbuttoned her pants and, over the course of the next fifteen minutes, managed to slide out of them despite the agony it caused. Her fingers grazed the wound. The pain was one thing but actually *feeling* it caused her gorge to rise; she leaned over on her side and vomited a stringy acidic paste into one of the cardboard boxes.

The easy thing would be to stick that rifle in my mouth and pull the trigger. After all, it's not like I'm going to get out of here. It's futile. And if these things live in the snow, if they are *the snow . . . well, around these parts, snow's liable to stick around until early March. My luck's bound to run out before then.*

It was very unlike her to think like that. Wiping her mouth with her sleeve, she righted herself against the wall and began patting herself down for the flashlight she'd slipped into one of her coat pockets. But the flashlight was not there; she must have dropped it in all the commotion. And this thought caused her mind to summon the image of Nan Wilkinson being swooped up into the night sky where she disappeared.

That's it . . . a single pull of the trigger and this nightmare is over, Shawnie. It frightened her to think that was her mother's voice.

Scrounging around in the pockets of her pants, which were now bunched up at her ankles, she managed to locate her cigarette lighter. She considered the implications of flicking it on—was it possible the flame could be seen from outside?—but in the end decided she had little choice. If she didn't attend to her wound, she'd die right here, frozen and bleeding to death.

Shawna clicked on the lighter and brought the flame down to her left leg.

Again, she felt her gorge rise . . . but this time, did an admirable job keeping her ground. The injury was bad, made to look worse by the way half the stitches had come undone and giving the wound a half-pursed, mouth-like appearance. Her entire thigh down past the knee was brown and matted in sticky, dried blood.

She let the flame flicker out. Leaning her head back against the wall, she silently counted to one hundred. When she'd finished, she began systematically sifting through the surrounding boxes for loose articles of clothing. She found a number of old shirts, which she collected in a nice pile beside her. She'd use some to dress with and keep warm, others to use as blankets and pillows. Lastly, she'd use the fabric from others to bandage up her leg.

Taking one of the shirts—a long-sleeved button-down—she set it in her lap and proceeded to tear one of the sleeves off. She wrapped the sleeve just above the wound to prevent any future blood loss. With the second sleeve she tied it over the wound—gritting her teeth as she did so—and pulled it snug. The pain was unbearable and didn't let up until she finally loosened the bandage. Lastly, she located a pair of sweatpants and decided to pull these on instead of trying to wriggle back into her cold, wet, and blood-soaked slacks. The sweatpants were several sizes too large but they felt heavenly.

Her eyes were already beginning to droop by the time she'd piled extra clothes beneath her head and body and laid down on the floor. She pulled a tattered old shawl that smelled of camphor over her shoulders then dragged the rifle closer to her in the darkness.

Soundlessly, she slept.

PART TWO

SURVIVAL

CHAPTER SIXTEEN

As the milky pink of predawn bruised the sky, Todd jerked awake. Both hands were still clutching the handgun. The three of them were hidden in the back of the ambulance Todd had seen from the church's bell tower, the doors pulled shut and locked against anything that might be out there waiting for them. Through the sliding panel of window that separated the rear of the ambulance from the cab, Todd could see daylight bleeding up from behind the distant trees. He could also see the sky, and the bizarre cloud cover that seemed to hermetically seal the town, like the lid on a boiling pot. The clouds looked dense, solid, tangible . . . and the color of pond moss . . .

Kate stirred behind him. She had curled up behind Meg and slept straight through the early morning hours despite her initial protest that she'd never in a million years be able to find sleep. She looked at him now and offered him a crooked yet somewhat seductive smile while she ran her fingers through her matted hair.

"Sleep well?" he said.

"The best. We're on vacation, right? In the Bahamas?"

"Of course. Would you like a mimosa with your breakfast?"

"Ooh," she chided, playfully grimacing. "Don't say breakfast. I could eat a whole cow right now."

"Yeah," he said, looking back through the sliding panel and out the windshield beyond. "I'm starving, too."

Kate crept up next to him and looked out the window. She smelled of sleep and dried perspiration, the combination of which caused something to stir within Todd. Upon their first meeting back at the bar at O'Hare, he'd found her attractive . . . but something overwhelming was working on him now and he realized, with bittersweet embarrassment, that he was trying to fight off an erection.

"My God, the sky's funny," she said. "I've never seen clouds like that in my life."

"Maybe they're not actually clouds," he suggested. "Just like those things out there aren't actually snow."

The thought caused Kate's face to draw into a frown. He suddenly wanted to hug her, to cradle her.

"There's smoke, too," she said.

"It's the church." He'd seen the column of thick black smoke spiraling up into the atmosphere, where it flattened out and spread like oil against the low clouds.

"It burned all through the night?"

"Seems that way."

"Do you think it's completely gone?"

"I don't know." His stomach growled and he blushed when Kate turned and smiled at him.

Then her smile faded. She was looking at Meg.

Todd looked at the sleeping teenager, who had her back turned to them as she lay curled on a gurney. She wore a threadbare blouse of thin material smudged with dirt, the collar of which had been torn away at some point during their escape from the church. What was exposed was a narrow serration in the soft flesh of her shoulder, nearly mouth-like, that ran midway down her back and disappeared beneath the fabric of her blouse. The lips of the gash appeared to respire.

"She wasn't like that before," Kate said, backing up against the opposite wall of the ambulance. "I checked her back at the church. It must have happened while we were escaping. One of those things must have . . . must have gotten inside her somehow . . ."

Todd pointed the gun at the back of Meg's head.

"Oh." Kate began to cry. "Oh fuck, Todd . . ."

His hand shook. He watched the girl's chest rise and fall as she slept. *No,* he tried to convince himself, *she's not a little girl. She's different now.* But that did little to assuage his guilt.

He lowered the gun. He felt Kate's eyes hanging on him, burning through him. Instead of looking at her he just nodded toward the ambulance's rear doors and mouthed the words, *Get out.* Comprehending, Kate peeled herself off the wall and practically glided past the sleeping teenage girl. Kate picked up her sconce and somehow managed to unlatch the ambulance doors without making a sound. Todd crept out after her, the freezing temperatures a sudden shock to his system the second he dropped down to the slushy road.

He stood for a long time staring into the open doors of the ambulance. If this were a movie, he'd be cursing the hero, telling him to go back in there and pull the trigger, pull the trigger, pull the fucking trigger. But this was real life, and sometimes people are just as foolish as the fake people on screen.

Let's be honest, he thought then, his hand holding the gun trembling. *I'm not even sure shooting this girl would kill the thing inside it. The one Shawna shot outside the Pack-N-Go just seemed to flit away. Maybe they're injured and weakened when they come rushing out of people like that, but I don't think shooting them kills them.*

Fire, on the other hand . . .

The thought caused him to turn and watch the conical of black smoke rising up from the trees. The church. It was a goddamn funeral pyre, all right, smoldering straight through the night. He wondered what was left of the building and, moreover, what remained of the creatures inside.

Kate was staring at him by the side of the road. She looked cold and wet and uncomfortable. "Are we going?" she said, her voice just barely audible.

He nodded, and they began walking down in the culvert, out of sight from the road.

In the light of day, the massacre that had come to Woodson was horrifically apparent. Blood stained the snowy hillsides and froze in red rivulets in the ravines and gutters along the roadways. Shredded bits of clothing were strung up into trees like discarded party favors. Worse still, human bones were strewn about at random as if they'd fallen off the back of a passing truck; many of the bones still had chunks of meat on them that glittered with frost. A human head caught in mid-scream was propped in the Y of a yew tree, the eyes frozen into black marbles, the skin a nightmarish blue-green. At one point Kate asked if she should light the torch, just in case one of those things burst out of the snow again, but Todd said it was probably best to keep a low profile. "Besides," he said, "it seems like they're hiding now that it's daylight."

"Shawna said daylight didn't matter, that they're not vampires."

Todd shrugged. "Maybe they are. Maybe these things are what we've come to know as vampires."

"The sky looks funny. I've got a bad feeling. And that swirling electrical cloud over the hill up there?" She pointed over toward the rotating black eyelet beneath the dome of clouds. "It's unnatural."

Todd laughed—he couldn't help it. "This whole fucking *thing* is unnatural, love," he said, sending her laughing, too. He was starving—surely they both were—and laughing only aggravated his empty stomach . . . but it also felt good, too. Suddenly, Todd couldn't remember the last time he'd laughed.

"Where do we go now?" Kate asked after they'd walked for another few minutes, the laughter having subsided.

"I say we stick to the original plan. Hit one of those houses, steal a car, get the fuck outta Dodge."

"What about the others?" There was genuine hopefulness in her voice that suggested she actually believe they were still alive. "I mean, once we find a car, do we . . . we just leave them here? Leave them behind?"

"Nan's dead," Todd reminded her. "That doesn't bode well for Fred and Shawna, either."

"But you don't know that."

"When I was up in the bell tower with Chris, I could see that the windows of the Pack-N-Go had been blown out. Chris said he saw two women come running out of there."

"What about Fred?"

"He said nothing about Fred."

"That doesn't mean he's dead. And what about Shawna? We don't know that she's dead, either. Not for sure. She's lasted the whole week out here on her own holed up in that convenience store, it's possible she's still around, hiding and waiting things out."

"Listen," he said, "I don't like the idea of leaving them behind any more than you do. I feel like shit about Nan. But it's not like we can tool around the neighborhoods honking our horn and shouting their names, Kate. What do you suggest we do?"

She paused. He thought she was angry with him but when he looked at her, there was a strange expression on her face.

"What?" he said. "What is it?"

"I have to pee."

He snorted, smiling. "So pee. I'll wait here."

"No. I'm not traipsing off by myself. Just turn around. I'll do it right here."

He took the torch from her then turned around. He stared at the treetops while she unzipped her pants and, a few seconds later, he tried not to get embarrassed by the sound of her urinating in the snow. To make light of the scenario, he said, "Man, I hope you're pissing on one of those fuckers right now."

She barked laughter then scolded him: "Don't make me laugh! I'm squirting all over the place back here."

When she'd finished, she balled up some snow in her hands to clean them then took the torch back from Todd. Together they continued walking along the muddy culvert until they could see the houses looming up on the other side of the street. Someone had driven a Ford Taurus into a fire hydrant, the car's occupant gone. A stop sign was bent at a perfect right angle, the large white STOP printed vertically.

They crossed up over the embankment and out into the street with considerable trepidation. Every footfall seemed to echo down the street. It was like walking onto a movie set. Nothing seemed real and everything was eerily quiet.

"Where do you think they all are?" Kate said. She was holding the unlit torch like a baseball bat now.

"I have no clue. But let's not take it for granted."

"Deal. Which house?"

"The closest one."

They moved up the snow-packed sidewalk, their feet sinking straight down to their ankles in the freezing muck. Beyond a copse of pines, Todd thought he recognized the backs of some of the buildings. "I think we're on the other side of the town square," he said, trying to peek through the trees.

"God." Kate froze.

"What is it?"

"I feel like someone's following us."

"Someone?"

"Or one of those things."

Todd surveyed the empty road, the strip of houses, the surrounding wedges of trees. "I don't see anything."

"I think that's the idea." She shivered, hugging herself. "Let's keep going. I feel like a moving target out here."

They hurried up the sloping lawn to the first house, a quaint little Victorian with Christmas decorations in the darkened windows. Off to their left, something sizzled. Todd spun around, the gun aimed in. Kate said, "What was that?"

Across the street, a thick black cable snaked through the snow, occasionally spitting sparks from its truncated end.

"Downed power line," Todd said. "I saw that from the bell tower, too."

"You're a regular Quasimodo."

Kate advanced up the lawn but Todd grabbed her sleeve. "Wait. I think we should go around back."

"Okay."

The backyard was protected by a wooden fence roughly six feet high. Todd could just barely see over the top but there was no hope for Kate. However, an ivy trellis clung to the side of the house, flimsy but workable. Todd slipped the handgun into his waistband then propped a foot into one of the diamond-shaped grooves. Hoisting himself up, he felt just how weak the trellis was. He managed to secure another foothold before leaning over the fence. A quick survey of the yard showed nothing out of the ordinary—a drooping hammock dipped in ice and a bird feeder that was, like everything else in this town, deserted. In fact, it occurred to him at that moment that he hadn't seen a single animal—not a bird or a squirrel—since arriving in Woodson. It troubled him to think of what might have happened to all the little woodland creatures . . .

He clambered over the fence and dropped down on the other side, his boots plowing through several inches of snow. Kate's head appeared over the fence next, looking nervous and unsteady.

"What's wrong?" he said.

"I'm afraid of heights."

"You're eighteen inches off the ground. Come on."

She managed to swing one leg over the fence then panicked when she didn't know how to get the other leg over. Todd lifted her up beneath her thigh and buttocks and hoisted her over and into the yard. It wasn't until she thanked him and turned back toward the rear of the house did he register his disappointment—he had hoped she'd kiss him.

Brilliant, asshole, he thought. *Great time to start thinking with your libido.*

It wasn't his fault—the last woman he'd slept with had been some floozy he'd picked up in a bar in the Village; both of them drunk, they'd stumbled back to her place and he'd gored her like a bull in heat right on her loveseat. Then she'd gotten up and vomited in the bathroom where, presumably, she'd spent the rest of the evening.

What a life I lead, he thought. *Makes me wonder why I'm trying so desperately to stay alive.*

But he knew the answer to that.

His son.

They went to the back door, which was a sliding glass door behind which hung heavy drapes. If it had been his hope to peek in through the glass, he was shit out of luck. He produced the gun from his waistband and held it by the barrel, intending to use the butt of the weapon to shatter the glass.

"Wait," Kate said. "Try the door."

He tried the door and it shushed open, unlocked.

"I grew up in a small town," she said, beaming. "No one locks their doors."

Todd pulled aside the curtain to reveal a house that looked relatively unharmed. They stepped into the kitchen, a cozy little room with bright ceramic tiles on the wall and plastic fruit in a basket on the table. Photos of children cluttered the refrigerator.

Out of habit, Todd's hand went immediately for the light switch . . . but of course, nothing happened. Kate went directly to the telephone on the wall, picked it up and listened, then shrugged and hung it up. "Was worth a try," she told him with a wry grin. "You think we could hit that fridge?"

"Let's do it quickly."

They devoured sliced lunch meat, half a loaf of bread, two pieces of strawberry shortcake, and washed it all down with half a carton of milk.

"I think that was the best meal I've ever had in my life," Kate said through a mouthful of cake.

"Those five-star dives in Manhattan have got it all wrong," he agreed.

When they were done eating, they walked through the rooms of the lower level, but the place was deserted. The sunlight that spilled through the windows looked dirty, like a sepia-toned reel of film. It had something to do with the sky, Todd was certain, and that bizarre cloud cover. In fact, it even occurred to him that the *air* tasted funny, as if the whole *atmosphere* was slowly deteriorating. He tried to think how long the air had tasted like that and remembered some sense of disorientation when he'd followed Eddie

Clement through the trees only to arrive in the field that overlooked Woodson. It had started back then . . . but he'd been too preoccupied with other matters at the moment to notice something so subliminal. Now, however, everything was suspect.

"Go check the drawers in the kitchen for car keys," he told Kate. "I'm going to take a look in the garage."

It was a single car garage, housing a dust-covered Ford station wagon. He frowned, wondering how far they'd get on the icy roads in this piece of shit. Well, at least the tires looked to be in good shape.

Kate appeared behind him, dangling a set of keys. She peered at the station wagon from over Todd's shoulder and grimaced. "That looks like my grandmother's car."

Todd took the keys and headed around to the driver's side of the car. He reached out for the door handle then looked up at Kate. "I'm going to start the car. Once it kicks over, pull open the garage door."

"Isn't it automatic?" She sounded like she wanted to get in the car with him.

"Power's out. It won't work." Then he tossed her the keys. "Okay, you kick it over and I'll open the door. Then I'll hop in the passenger seat." He forced a wink and it earned him a smile. "Just don't leave without me."

"Not on your life," she said, hurrying around to the driver's door. "You've got the gun."

Todd went to the garage door, unlatched it, and prepared to shove it open once the station wagon kicked over. Kate climbed into the driver's seat and sat there for a long time.

"Go ahead," he said to her eventually.

"I *am*," she told him, leaning out the door and gaping at him. "It won't start."

"Are you sure?"

"I know how to start a car."

"Let me try."

"I'm not an idiot."

He leaned against the driver's side door, frowning down at her. "Let's not do this, okay? I just want to get out of here."

"So do I." Then with a huff, she climbed out of the car and Todd got in.

Slid the keys into the ignition. Gave it a good crank.

Nothing.

Todd and Kate exchanged a look. "I told you so," she said.

He popped the hood and climbed out. Examining the engine, he couldn't find anything obviously wrong with the car.

"Do you even know what you're looking for?" she asked him, peering into the engine block, too.

"Just the usual stuff," he said, "but I'm not an auto mechanic."

"Wonderful. Now what?"

He chewed his lower lip. "I hate to keep pressing our luck, but I think we hit the house next door and try it all over again."

The house next door was in worse shape. For starters, the doors were locked and they had to break a window and shimmy through it. Inside, the furniture had been toppled over and there were broken dishes on the kitchen floor. The television set in the living room was busted and the whole house smelled like it had been fried in the electric chair. In the laundry room, something that had once been a small dog or cat had been turned inside out and resembled something one might find in a dumpster behind a slaughterhouse.

"I don't like this place," Kate said for the record.

"Duly noted."

There were a set of keys hanging from a pegboard beside the pantry. BLESS THIS HAPPY HOME was painted on the pegboard in bright blue letters. They went quickly to the garage and found a Toyota Corolla, freshly detailed.

"Let's try this again," he said, tossing Kate the keys and going to the garage door. He undid the latch on the door as Kate slid into the car. This time, Todd could hear her twisting the keys. But the car would not roll over.

After several more tries, Kate got out of the car and stood there in the half-light like she was about to scream. Todd went to her and hugged her. It was a warm and lengthy hug. She smelled like Brianna's pillows did in the morning after she'd gotten up out of bed. It made his head dizzy and his heart hurt.

"I'm starting to think . . ." he said after a moment.

"No," she said. "Please don't say it. Something is preventing us from starting these cars. Just like it cut the power and killed the phones."

"I think so."

"Todd," she said, and moved in as if to hug him again. He brought her closer . . . then felt a rush as her lips touched his. She tasted like sea salt and felt very warm despite the cold all around them. If he could, he would have stretched this moment in time out to infinity.

A mechanical tone sounded from his pants pocket just as Kate pressed her thigh against his. She flinched at the sound, startled. "What was that?" she breathed directly in his face.

"Looks like you've activated my cell." He fished his cell phone out of his pocket and ran his fingers along the keypad to activate it.

"Please tell me that's an incoming call," Kate said. Her hands slid slowly down the lengths of Todd's arms until they were no longer touching.

"No such luck. You just leaned against the keypad. Still no signal."

Then a notion seemed to strike them both simultaneously. In the dark cave of some stranger's garage, they glanced briefly at each other, their faces illuminated by the cold glow of Todd's cell phone.

"Other cell phones," Kate said.

"Might get different reception," Todd added.

"Might have closer towers," Kate finished. It was like an epiphany.

"There must be some around the house," Todd said as they stormed back into the kitchen. "Laying around on tables, on phone chargers, maybe upstairs in one of the bedrooms—"

Kate rushed over to the kitchen counter where a small flip phone sat in plain view. She flipped it open and beamed. "Battery works!"

Todd rushed to her side just as her face fell. "What is it?" he asked.

Kate held out the phone so that he could examine the display screen. "Look at the numerals. Look at the time."

"I . . ." But then he saw it. When he looked back up at her, she had the face of a frightened child.

"How's that possible?" she said.

According to the cell phone, the time was currently F9:KA.

He took the phone from her and scrolled through the electronic phone-book. "Jesus Christ, will you look at this . . ."

The first entry was nothing but gibberish:

SH%AMSA <, TWSWSV

1028734601283746109739117

"It's like the goddamn thing got scrambled," he said, flipping through more names. Each one was in some similar form of hieroglyphics. "Let me see your phone."

"I don't have it. It's still in my coat, back at the Pack-N-Go."

Todd looked around. He began going systematically through the kitchen drawers until he located a ruby red cell phone with unicorn stickers on the casing. He powered it on and the screen blinked with the following cryptic missive: DWELLDWELLDWELLDWELLDWELLDWELL. Todd scrolled through the rest of the phone, each of the alphanumeric entries comprised of similar nonsense. Frustrated, he tossed the cell phone back in the drawer.

"Our situation just got worse, didn't it?" Kate said. "None of the cars in this town will start, will they? All the electrical shit is out and all the battery powered things have gone to shit. Everything's either dead or scrambled."

"Kate," Todd said, suddenly backing up behind the kitchen counter with his gun drawn. "There's someone behind you."

CHAPTER SEVENTEEN

U pon waking, the first thing Shawna was aware of was the pain in her leg. The bandages had come loose in the night and the wound had reopened, soaking the left leg of her sweatpants in fresh blood. She sat up with much difficulty, utilizing the wall behind her for support, and managed to grab hold of the pant leg in one fist and slide her leg out straight in front of her.

The pain was like a thousand holocausts.

Gritting her teeth, she adjusted her leg and slid one hand inside the waistband of the sweatpants, then farther down her thigh until she felt the swollen, tender tissue just below the knee. Her entire calf had swollen to twice its normal size.

That's because it's infected, she thought, instantly miserable. *One of those fucking snowmen took a chunk out of me and now I'm infected with whatever malignant diseases those fucking things carry.*

Miserable.

She reached down into the nearest cardboard box in hopes of finding a fresh pair of pants and another bandage to tie her leg. Instead, she wound up planting her hand firmly in the still-warm vomit from last night.

"This is certainly not one of my better days," she muttered . . . and the ruined, parched sound of her own voice nearly frightened her as much as her injury. It was as if she was becoming less and less herself . . . changing as everyone else in town had changed . . .

I won't let that happen, she thought, her eyes shifting to the rifle that had remained by her side all throughout the night. *I've still got Old Blue here.*

The next thing she realized was just how hungry she was. Her stomach caterwauled. Holed up in the Pack-N-Go, it was easy to take food and drink for granted—she'd had all she could want at her disposal. Now, out here in No Man's Land, she was on her own. Was it possible old Rita Tubalow had some food stowed away down here?

Sure, she thought, her misery increasing. *Everyone keeps food in the basement!*

It briefly occurred to her that she was losing her mind.

Anyway, there was sure to be food upstairs. In the kitchen. If anyone was up there, she'd let Old Blue do the talking. If, of course, she was actually *capable* of climbing the stairs . . .

Using the rifle like a crutch, she hoisted herself up amidst a fog of pain. It was all she could do not to scream when she straightened out her leg and actually set her foot down on the floor. She'd kicked off her shoes in her sleep and now the cold concrete of the basement floor radiated up through her sock and into the depths of her bones. Her sock was dark with dried blood . . .

Come on come on come on come on comeoncomeoncomeon—

She stood, and let out a meager cry. Tears streamed down her cheeks. Climbing the stairs would be tantamount to climbing Everest. Hell, just *making* to the stairs would be an incredible feat. Nonetheless, she proceeded, crutching along with the rifle, limping and in excruciating pain. Each time she put weight on her injured leg, she swore she could feel the wound separating and tearing further up her calf, straight up to her kneecap. Was it possible for kneecaps to come undone, to fall out and clatter like dinnerware to the floor? A hideous mental image of plastic Tupperware rolling out of a gash in her thigh suddenly filled her mind and it was all she could do to keep herself from breaking down into uncontrollable laughter. Tupperware containers full of frozen meatballs and lasagna, of fruit salad and leftover green beans . . .

Think of Jared. That'll sober you up, you imbecile. Think of how you shot Jared then shot him again then shot him again until his head split down the middle and that ghostly thing came flying out of him. Think of how he's frozen solid right now under a heap of Glad trash bags back at the Pack-N-Go, just a few yards away from poor George Farmer, who'd fared even worse. Not much left of poor George Farmer, who used to hand out the really big candy bars every Halloween, do you remember? You remember, don't you, Shawnie? Of course you do. My little Shawnie . . .

Somehow, she made it to the stairwell. Looking up was like staring into a mineshaft. It would take an eternity plus two extra days to hoof it all the way to the top. Glancing down, she saw that she'd shed a lot of blood on the concrete floor in her trek across the basement. As she looked at the bloody smears, she felt her bladder let go and warm urine traced down her inner thighs, soaking the sweatpants.

Don't lose focus now. You've done so good this far. You can make it farther. Just one foot in front of the other. One step at a time. Wasn't there a television program or a song called "One Step at a Time" or something like that? That's good—think of that, think of good things. Don't think of your leg and how every time you put pressure down on it you feel like a burlap sack that's about to get torn down the middle. Whatever you do, don't think of that.

"Stop it." The words came out breathy and not quite a whisper. "Please. Stop it."

I'll stop it if you promise to keep moving.

"Deal."

She lifted her good leg and took the first step. It wasn't too difficult, and this realization gave her instant hope. But then the second step came, and it was a doozey—sending shocks of electric fire soaring through her soul. Thankfully the stairwell was equipped with a sturdy handrail; she hooked onto it and threw all her support against it, the rifle now slung back over her shoulder where it belonged. Old Blue.

Holding her breath, she managed to take on two more stairs. She was really moving now. Another step . . . and her left knee weakened. If it hadn't been for the handrail, she would have toppled backward, probably smashing her head on the cinderblock wall at the foot of the stairwell.

This was impossible.

No, Shawnie. Nothing's impossible. Listen up—I'll make you a promise. You make it to the top of those stairs and the second you swing that basement door open, this'll all be over. Just like snapping your fingers and waking from a dream, this will all be over. How does that sound? One foot in front of the other and let's just see how bad you want to wake up from this nightmare, Shawnie. Let's see how bad you want it, girl.

Bad. She wanted it bad.

Gripping the handrail tighter, Shawna pulled herself up another step . . . then another . . . then another. Several more steps ahead of her the basement door was closed. She could make out the faint crack of daylight at the bottom of the door. It would be good to see daylight again. It seemed like centuries since she'd seen daylight.

Somehow she made it to the top. Steadying herself against the wall, she reached down and twisted the doorknob in her sweat-sticky hand. Already her mind was wandering through a blessed valley, free of this nightmare. When she swung the door open, she was already wearing a wan smile.

The upstairs hallway was choked full of people.

Townspeople—all of them crowded together in the hallway, their heads slightly bowed, their eyes shut. They were packed together like stowaways in the cargo hold of a steamship. The sound of their joined slumber was like a thousand bees buzzing.

Shawna stumbled and fell backward down the basement stairs. She cracked her head smartly against the wall halfway down, but that was quickly eclipsed by the shock of searing pain she felt race like fire up her leg. The rifle came loose of its shoulder strap and clattered down the stairs on its own where, upon striking the wall, fired a single round into a section of drywall.

Shawna struck the basement floor at the foot of the stairs, the back of her head up against the cinderblock wall. Her vision briefly blurred . . . but when her sight returned, all she could see were the countless eyes—the open eyes—of the townspeople standing in the rectangular frame of the basement doorway directly above her.

She managed to turn her head just enough to see Old Blue on the last step. Close . . . but too far out of reach. Anyway, she couldn't move.

Couldn't—

There rose a shrill cry in unison as the townspeople poured through the doorway and fought over one another to get down the stairs. To get at *her*.

Shawna screamed and somehow managed to launch herself forward. Two of her fingertips actually grazed the hilt of the rifle before the townsfolk were upon her, clawing and tearing and biting and ripping. They got into her leg wound and tore her calf open like a bag of frozen peas.

—make a promise to you make a promise if you make it to the top of those stairs you can wake up wake up wake up you can wake up if you make it to the top to the top of the—

Blessedly, she didn't live long enough to suffer the worst of it.

CHAPTER EIGHTEEN

A man in a gray wool cap with earflaps and a camouflaged winter coat rimmed in rabbit fur stepped out of the nearest doorway behind Kate. He was hefting what Todd at first thought was some sort of long-barreled gun, but on closer inspection proved to be a butane torch connected to a hose that ran up under the man's coat.

Kate turned around and didn't make a sound. She stepped coolly over to Todd, who still had the gun aimed in at the stranger.

The stranger eyed them through narrow slits beneath a rough, crenellated brow. His chin and neck was heavy with dark stubble and there was a slick of snot drooling from one nostril like an exclamation. His dark eyes fixated on Todd's handgun.

"You ain't from Woodson," said the man. He had the voice of a rumbling old washing machine.

Todd's hands shook; the gun rattled. "No."

"Where'd you come from?"

"We were driving out from O'Hare," Todd said. "Our rental broke—"

"What town's that?"

Todd raised an eyebrow. "Town?"

"O'Hare." Though Todd would have believed it impossible, the man's eyes actually grew narrower. "Never heard of the place."

"It's an airport," Todd said. "In Chicago."

The man lowered his weapon. "I heard of Chicago."

Unsure if the man was joking or not, Todd kept the gun trained on him. He did not believe this man to be one of the possessed . . . but that didn't mean he wasn't dangerous.

"Is this your house?" Kate asked. "We didn't mean to break in."

"Ain't my house. I followed you here."

Sweat trickled down Todd's brow. "Followed us?"

The man sauntered into the kitchen and glanced casually into the sink, which was loaded with unwashed dishes. "Saw the smoke from the church this morning so I figured I'd have a look. That's when I saw the two of you coming out of that amb'lance."

"Who are you?" Todd asked the man.

"Name's Tully. Up until a week ago I lived over on Acre Drive. I'm down at the sheriff's station now, which is across town. It's been safe so far; they don't know we're there." Tully's eyes flicked toward Todd's handgun. "You can put that peashooter down now, son."

Embarrassed, Todd lowered the gun.

"How long you two been tromping around town, anyway?"

"Since last night," Kate said. "Our Jeep broke down on the highway. We walked through the woods and found the town . . . found the town like this." She paused then added, "There were more of us."

Tully spat something green into the sink. "There were more of us, too. Whole town's worth."

Again, Todd couldn't tell if this stranger was attempting humor—albeit morbid—or if he'd been living up here in the middle of nowhere for too long. Todd couldn't read him. "What's that thing you got there?" he asked Tully.

"Little homemade flamethrower." He unzipped his coat to expose a series of fuel canisters strapped to his belt with duct tape. "Can get almost twelve feet out of her if there's no wind."

"So fire kills those things," Kate said. "Or does it just hurt them?"

"Oh," said Tully, zipping his coat back up, "it kills 'em, all right." He leaned over the counter and peered out one of the windows. Outside, the sky looked like the color of old dishwater. "The skin-suits need rest. They sleep during the day, but they sleep light. But those tornado monsters or snowstorm things or whatever they are—they're still out there and they're still plenty pissed off."

"Skin-suits?" Todd said.

Tully raised his elbows and dangling his hands like limp rags, miming a marionette. "People puppets. Whatever you call 'em."

"I don't call them anything," Todd said. "This is all new to me."

"You think it's old hat to me, partner?" Tully stared at him hard, his eyes rheumy. He reached up and began opening cupboards, peering inside. "Like

I said—a week ago I had a nice little place over on Acre. Worked days at the plant in Bicklerville and played pool down at the Blue Shue every other night." He bent down and went through the cupboards beneath the sink. "You think I been doing this my whole life? Running around Woodson with a flamethrower strapped to my hips?"

"No, sir," Kate said. She sounded like someone being reprimanded by a schoolteacher.

"Damn straight," said Tully. He stood and went over to the refrigerator. Standing on his toes, he managed to peek into the cabinets over the fridge, but they were empty. "Those things came and ate the town. They blew all the power out and then our cars wouldn't start. Phones went dead. They've got us quarantined."

"How many are left?"

Tully spat a second ball of phlegm into the sink then tromped in his heavy boots over to a new wall of cabinets. The first one he opened elicited a wry smile from his otherwise hardened features: the liquor cabinet. "How many what?" he said.

"How many people," Todd clarified. "How many of you are still alive?"

"There's six of us down at the station." He was collecting the liquor bottles and loading them into a child's Superman backpack he'd found beside the refrigerator. "I suppose you two make eight."

"So we're going with you," Kate said. It was not a question. She was watching Tully like someone who'd paid a good price to step foot into a freak show.

"Keep running around out here, you're both liable to get yourselves killed. That's a fact. See how easy I followed you both up from the amb'lance and right into this house? Them things out there are ten times sneakier and a hundred times more dangerous. It's a fool's game, wandering around out there in the snow."

"What about getting out of town?" Todd said. "Is there any way?"

Tully stacked the last of the bottles in the Superman backpack then turned to the refrigerator. He pulled the door open and reached into one of the compartments, worked his fingers around. "Told you," he said. "Cars don't start. Can't call anybody to come and get us. Molly has one of them little handheld doohickeys—BlackBerry, she calls it. Tried to send out an email but the screen went all funny. Kept spitting out random math equations or some shit." As an afterthought, he added, "Molly's from town. One of the survivors back at the station. You'll meet her."

"That sounds just like what happened with the cell phones," Kate said, picking the flip phone up off the counter. "No numbers, no letters. Just nonsense."

"My guess is they're jamming us," said Tully. He paused to glance at Kate appraisingly from over his shoulder. "That angry-looking cloud out by the church this morning—well, where the church used to be, I guess—see, I think it's sending bad signals down to all our electrical appliances. Anything that runs on batteries that they couldn't knock out with the power—anything from cars to cell phones—they wind up jamming with astro-nonsense."

"What's that?" Kate asked.

"Garbage from space."

"So that's where you think these things are from?" Todd asked.

"Mister," Tully said, "I ain't got a fucking *clue* where these things are from."

"They're that smart?" Kate sounded dejected. "To scramble signals like that?" She tossed the cell phone back down on the counter and folded her arms over her chest.

"Smart," said Tully, "or just driven by some otherworldly instinct. Who the hell knows?"

"Scrambling signals and cutting off power doesn't explain why the cars won't start," Todd said.

"Cars got about a billion little microchips and whatnot in 'em," Tully explained.

"So there's no way out of here," Todd said again.

"Figured we'd sit tight until the power company came out here to see what happened to their line," said Tully.

"It's been a week," Todd said. "I would have thought they'd come out here by now."

"Maybe. Maybe not." Tully seemed disinterested. His hand returned from within the refrigerator with a handful of black olives. He popped them into his mouth like medication then pushed the refrigerator door closed with the sole of his boot. "We should get out of here."

They followed Tully back out into the yard. Instead of crossing back to the front and down to the street, Tully led them between properties enclosed by trees.

"Wait," Todd said, surveying the area. "You said we're going to the sheriff's station? Isn't it on the other side of town?"

"That's right," said Tully.

"We're going in the opposite direction. We should cut through the town square and head up the road."

"You don't want to go cutting through the square, friend." Tully was working something out of his teeth with his tongue while he spoke. "That's their nest. They've claimed it. For whatever reason, they all congregate there during the day. You head that way now, you won't make it out alive."

Without waiting for their response, Tully turned and continued pushing through the heavy snow. A beat later, Todd and Kate followed.

They cut between narrow fencing and through overgrown holly bushes, Tully leading the charge like a general about to overtake a hill. Aside from his camouflage coat and wool hat, he wore mud-streaked BDUs (every pocket bulged) and a bandolier of large rounds across his flannel shirt. Although he moved lithely through the snow, he jangled like a slot machine: aside from the fuel canisters at his waist and the clanking bottles in the backpack over his shoulders, his belt was overburdened with countless sets of keys. He looked comically like a janitor gone commando.

"Shhhhh," Tully said at one point, sinking down low to the ground. Todd and Kate followed suit. Peering through dense evergreen shrubs, Tully jerked his chin at something down in the street. "There's one now."

Todd maneuvered so he could see through the bushes. Down between two houses, the street sloped close to a muddy ravine beside which rose the leafless branches of ancient gray trees. At first Todd couldn't see what Tully was talking about . . . but then he happened to catch sight of a slight *wrongness* up in one of the trees. He squinted and leaned closer on the balls of his feet. Midway up in one tree, the air looked slightly discolored, almost brownish, and the tree branches in that particular spot seemed less defined than those around them. It was up there in the tree, perhaps fifteen feet wide, unfurled and just barely visible. The closest thing Todd's mind could compare it to was a stingray, with those triangular fins and an ill-defined underside.

"Where?" Kate whispered, crawling closer to him. "I don't see anything."

"There." He pointed and spread the bushes just a bit farther apart. "See?"

"I don't—*oh* . . ." Her hand closed around his arm. "I *see* it. My God, what *is* it?"

"That, my dear lady," said Tully, rising back to his full height, "is a question for the ages."

Tully led them the long way, but claimed it to be safer. They stayed mostly hidden between shops and houses or behind curtains of trees. The only time they crossed out in the open was when Tully led them up the snowy hillside that led to the old church. "It'll be safest to travel by the church because last night's fire would have frightened them off." There was a hint of accusation in Tully's tone that suggested he knew Todd and Kate, these two outsiders to his town, were somehow responsible for burning down the church. "Yeah . . . they'll steer clear of this spot for awhile, is my guess," Tully repeated, his heavy boots smashing craters in the hardening snow. Even with his backpack full of liquor he moved at a quick pace; Todd and Kate had a strenuous time keeping up with him.

"The whole thing burned." Kate was in awe. She paused to stare at the smoldering black teepee that, only the night before, had been a church. Smoke still poured up into the false sky where it spread out along the low cloud cover as if the clouds themselves were solid, tangible things. As a teenager, Todd had once tried to light a fire in his mother's fireplace without thinking to see if the flue was open. The result sent billowing columns of black smoke straight to the ceiling where they seemed to collect like helium balloons. Looking at the way the smoke from the church collected at the base of the clouds, Todd was reminded of that day, and how his mother had never been able to get the stink of smoke out of the sofa.

There was something that resembled an enormous scythe blade jutting up from the center of the smoldering rubble, charred black and brittle-looking. Todd's eyes hung on it for a very long time.

"That funky opening in the sky is gone now," Kate noticed, examining the sky above her head. The clouds were the color of soot and the air itself had a tallow tinge to it.

"Nope," said Tully, pointing out over the hill and over at a distant ridge. The sky over the ridge was a circle of midnight in which multicolored lights strobed. "It just moved."

Kate staggered and came to a standstill. She stared out across the valley with her mouth hanging open in disbelief. Todd thumped her back as he passed, waking her from her daze.

"We're starting to learn something about these things," Tully said as he walked. "They're mostly air, just thin air. Can't hurt you, can't do a damn thing except maybe blow your skirt up. But at certain times it seems they're able to concentrate and focus their energy just long enough to make those two sword-shaped arms of theirs grow solid. You can tell when they're getting ready to do it because that thread of light floating in their middles gets brighter."

"Yes," Todd said, "I've seen it."

"They can't stay solid for very long. That's where the skin-suits come in. They grab some poor soul, jab 'em in the shoulders, and slide into 'em like a diver climbin' into a wetsuit."

Todd was thinking of what happened to Chris, the crazed zealot, back at the church—the way that thing had broken through the ceiling and swooped down, to crawl inside the boy's body in order to attack them.

"They do it so they can feed," Tully was saying. "And they feed off us." He paused, looking out over the town he'd probably grown up in—a town he'd never feel the same about. There was a melancholic twinkle to his eye. "If you shoot one of the skin-suits, they come flying right out. They're not killed but it makes 'em real weak. You'll see—they just spout off into the sky, probably to tend to their wounds. Or their hurt feelings or whatever." Chuckling, Tully shook his head and continued walking.

"We've seen it," Kate said. "Our friend shot one down in the square. The man died but the thing flew right out of him."

"If you can set 'em on fire just as they're vacating a skin-suit, you're in good shape. That's the best way to do it."

"I saw a little girl," Todd said. He felt Kate look at him. "She had no face."

Still walking, Tully turned his head so that Todd could make out the man's sharp profile. He had a nose like a bathtub faucet. "Something about mixin' them with little kids doesn't take. Like the kids' bodies can't handle it or something. They lose their features. Most of the little kids around Woodson who changed ran off into the woods. They're all mad now. Down by the fire hall and the sheriff's station you can hear them rustling around in the trees. They ain't got no mouths so they can't make a sound, but you can hear 'em movin' around sure as the day is long."

"Stop it," Kate said. Her eyes were on her shoes now. "Please. No more about this."

Tully shrugged, the bottles jangling in the Superman backpack, and lit a cigarette. He didn't offer one to either of them.

CHAPTER NINETEEN

Todd had glimpsed the sheriff's station from the church bell tower last night: it was a squat, square building made of brick with very few windows at the end of a winding, icy road. It sat between the fire hall and a rundown gas station that had probably looked just as rundown before any of this madness had come to the town of Woodson. Partially concealed by black firs, it was hidden from the main road from three of its four sides, making it a good place to set up camp.

Tully led them to the large double doors—the kind of doors one would find on a gymnasium—that stood beneath an alcove of slatted wood. Metal trashcans stood like guards on either side of the doors; they were empty but reeked of kerosene. There was a shield fixed to the bricks which read WOOD-SON SHERIFF'S DEPARTMENT. Tully paused just before the doors and consulted the collection of keys dangling like gypsy charms from his belt. He quickly found the one he was looking for and shoved it in the lock, turned it. Then he looked over his shoulder at Todd and Kate while one hand unzipped his camouflage coat.

"They're gonna want your shirts off," he told them. "Sorry, ma'am."

Inside, the place was as dark and as quiet as the surface of the moon. A tiled hallway stretched off into the distance, the tiles alternately black and white like a checkerboard. There was a bulletin board on the wall in the entrance-way crammed with papers that fluttered in the wind. Tully shut the doors and wove a heavy chain around the handles. He clamped it shut with a padlock then pulled off his wool cap. Tight black curls sprouted from his head.

A light came on farther down the hall, from one of the offices. Tully made a whippoorwill noise and the silhouette of a head appeared out of the lighted doorway.

"That's Brendan," Tully grumbled, pulling his coat off. The tone of his voice suggested a distasteful attitude toward Brendan.

The man called Brendan exited the room and hustled quickly down the hallway toward them. He carried the light with him in the form of a halogen lantern. Halfway down the hall, Brendan called, "Who you got there, Tully?"

"Mickey Mouse and Donald Duck," Tully retorted.

"Don't fuck with me," said Brendan. "I want to see your shoulders."

Tully removed his bandolier and unbuttoned his shirt. The grim look he gave Todd and Kate suggested they follow his lead. Todd immediately began tugging off his shirt while Kate moved a bit more reluctantly.

As Brendan drew closer, Todd could make out his features—pale, gaunt, vaguely studded with beard. His hair was a mop of unruly black coils and his eyes swam behind the lenses of thick glasses. He stopped a few feet in front of Todd and Kate, the lantern held up close to their faces for examination. Brendan licked his lips like a reptile.

"Let's see," said Brendan, shifting his gaze to Tully. Tully bared him his exposed shoulders, which were loaded with pimples but otherwise normal, then climbed back into his shirt. Brendan turned back to Todd and Kate. "Both of you, too."

Todd removed his shirts and turned around so that Brendan could exam-ine his back.

"And the lady," Brendan said, addressing Todd for some strange reason. For the first time, Todd noticed a revolver poking out of Brendan's narrow waistband.

"Better do it," Todd told her.

Kate turned around and lifted her sweater over her head. Brendan held the lantern closer to her, illuminating the cuts and scrapes along her back. He reached out and hesitantly touched a particularly angry cut just below her right shoulder.

"She's obviously fine," Todd said, his tone suggesting Brendan remove his hand sooner than later.

Brendan's hand snapped back and he clutched the lantern in both hands. He had a nervous, bouncy quality that made Todd want to strap him to a chair. "Where'd you two come from?" he wanted to know. "Ain't from town."

"Their car broke down outside of town last night," Tully answered for them. "Their friends were killed."

"Oh. Shoot." Brendan's voice wavered. "I'm Brendan Parker."

Todd and Kate introduced themselves.

"Where are the others?" Tully asked Brendan as he continued down the hallway. Todd and Kate followed while Brendan skirted ahead of them to keep up with Tully.

"Bruce is still fucking with those laptops," Brendan said, "and Molly and the kids are downstairs in the basement. Did you find out what that fire was last night?"

"The church burned down," Tully said.

"St. John's? No shit? Damn." Brendan eyeballed the Superman backpack still flung over Tully's shoulder. "What'd you get?"

"Make yourself useful and get these two some warm clothes," Tully said, ignoring the question. "And give me the lantern."

"You got it," Brendan said, handing over the lantern to Tully. Brendan nearly collided with Kate as he spun away and took off down the corridor.

"Jumpy little beanpole," Todd commented.

Tully offered something that approximated a chuckle. "A week ago I wouldn't have said two words to that squirmy little weasel."

"Do you smell something?" Kate muttered to Todd.

"Yes. Smells like . . ."

"Hotdogs," Kate finished. Grinned.

They walked past a large room filled with desks and empty holding cells. Todd could see that the windows had been boarded up and all cracks and creases secured with industrial gaffing tape. Tully kept moving, not stopping until he came to a second set of doors bathed in shadow at the end of the hall. Again, he produced a new key and unlocked the deadbolt. A resounding *clang!* echoed through the corridor.

The door was opened and Tully maneuvered himself down a narrow flight of stairs. Calling back over his shoulder, he said, "Watch out. Handrail's gone." Then Tully sank down into the murky depths of the stairwell like a man wading out into the middle of a lake.

Todd went next, Kate's hand suddenly appearing on his right shoulder. Beneath him, the stairwell swayed and creaked and threatened to collapse under his feet. He wondered just how far down they were going. All of a sudden, he was overly aware of the handgun at the small of his back. If this was some sort of trap, he'd have to be ready. For Kate's sake, if not his own.

His shoes touched down on warped floorboards. Behind him, Kate almost stumbled but squeezed his shoulder for support before falling on him. Todd reached out and grabbed one of her hands.

"Thank you."

He couldn't see her face but she sounded extremely relieved.

Illuminated by the halogen lamp, Tully's bright orange face hovered in the darkness before them like a harvest moon. "Hold this," Tully said, handing Todd the lamp.

Bit by bit, the basement of the sheriff's headquarters took on appearance: slatted wooden bookshelves drooping at angles over wood-paneled walls; a potbellied stove in the center of the room around which someone had set a bunch of folding chairs; rows upon rows of rifles standing in a large shelving unit. There were unlit Chinese lanterns on bits of wire hanging from the exposed ceiling rafters and a card table was erected in one corner, playing cards scattered about it. Toward the far end of the room, an enormous hulking furnace stood—dark and defunct.

Tully's eyes looked like rat's eyes in the lamplight. "Listen," he grumbled. "You two wait here. Molly and the kids are still a bit jumpy. Let me tell them you're here before you storm in on them. Otherwise, you're liable to get your heads blown to bits."

"Waiting here sounds like a good idea, yeah," Kate agreed.

Tully clumped toward the back of the room where he knocked against a section of wall. Todd could hear faint murmuring coming from behind it. Then there was a sound like someone uncorking a bottle of champagne and the section of wall cracked open on a set of hinges. White light spilled out, briefly spotlighting Tully before Tully slipped into the room and shut the door behind him.

With only the lamplight between them, Todd and Kate stepped closer together.

"What if he's another psychopath, like that kid at the church?" Kate whispered. "What if being trapped like rats in this town all week has turned all the survivors into raving lunatics?"

"What other choice do we have?" he countered.

Behind the wall, someone's voice rose up in what sounded like concern. It sounded like a woman's voice. How many had Tully said were with him? Six, including Tully himself? Todd couldn't remember. Then Tully's head popped back out of the opening and he motioned Todd and Kate inside.

A woman with a very pregnant belly sat on a cot with a bottle of water in her lap. She looked to be in her early thirties, but the exhaustion and fear that had plagued her over the past week had multiplied her age so that she looked old enough to remember the Kennedy Administration. Reddish-brown hair curtained her face, and Todd could make out the vague hint of large, staring dark eyes. Her shoes were off, her feet clad in layers of socks.

Two kids curled together in another corner, an ancient-looking board game with wooden pieces laid out between them. They looked to be twins of the opposite sex, roughly around the ages of nine or ten. Their faces looked slim and sallow, with chapped lips splitting from the cold, but they were wearing so many layers of clothing they looked like two plump cherubs.

Tully pointed at each one as he made the introduction. "That's Molly Sanderson. The boy here is Charlie Dobbins and that's his sister, Cody."

"Hi," Todd said, feeling like a circus performer the way Molly and the kids stared at him. "My name's Todd Curry. I'm from New York."

"And I'm Kate Jansen."

"New York's far away," the boy—Charlie—said.

"Are you married?" Cody wanted to know.

"Yes, New York's far away," Todd said, "and no, we're not married."

Cody pointed at them. "You're holding hands."

Self-consciously, Todd and Kate released each other. "We're just good friends," Kate said.

"Did you check their backs, Tully?" Molly wanted to know. She had pulled her hair back to reveal a heart-shaped face with delicate features. She looked terribly mournful.

"Of course." Tully set the backpack down on a rickety old desk and the two kids stood up. The room itself was small and cramped, a few cots pushed up against a brick wall. There was a desk and a rolling cart stacked high with blankets, as well as a few towers of paperback novels piled high in one corner. The ceiling was a concavity of exposed joists networked with cables and wires.

"What'd you bring us?" Cody asked, both her and her brother saddling up beside the desk in anticipation of what was inside the Superman backpack.

"This stuff here's for us grownups," Tully told them, taking the liquor bottles out and setting them on the desk one at a time.

"Is that beer?" Cody wanted to know. Decidedly the more inquisitive of the two children, she pressed her nose against one of the bottle's labels.

"Not exactly," Tully said.

"Then what is it?"

"Medication," he said—another suspiciously dry Tully joke. "Hooch."

"Hooch," Cody parroted, pleased with the word.

"What about us?" Charlie said. His jaw was set firmly as he looked up at Tully. "Don't we get something?"

"Sure do." Tully reached into his coat pocket and produced two giant Snickers bars, which he held up in a V. The kids cheered and Tully dispensed the candy like a backwoods Santa Clause.

From her cot, Molly Sanderson was still scrutinizing Todd and Kate with uncertainty. "Have they met Bruce yet?" she asked Tully.

"Not yet."

"You should take them to meet Bruce."

"They're fine, Molly." For the first time, Tully grinned at Todd and Kate. His teeth were atrocious and the grin came across more as a grimace, as if he'd been sucking on lemons. "Ain't you?"

"Fine as paint," said Kate.

"Although I suppose I should take you to meet Bruce," Tully said, pausing to examine the way he'd set up the bottles on the desk. He picked one up, sniffed at the label, then set it down to select another.

Todd asked who Bruce was.

"Big Bruce the Moose. After Joe bit it, he took over."

"And who's Joe?" Kate said.

Tully unscrewed the bottle of bourbon and chugged it while the kids watched. A stream of gingery liquid trickled down the corner of his mouth. "I keep forgetting you two don't know nobody," he said after he'd wiped his mouth of his sleeve. He set the bottle back on the desk and the two kids stared at it as if in amazement. "Joe Farnsworth. He was the sheriff up until two days ago."

"What happened two days ago?" Kate said. Todd gave her a sideways glance that suggested he had a pretty good guess.

"Don't talk about it in here, Tully," Molly said before Tully could open his mouth. "You feel like telling your horrible stories, you go on upstairs."

"Good idea," Tully said, turning toward the door and taking the bottle of bourbon with him. He nodded for Todd and Kate to follow him then turned to the kids. "You two don't eat all them candy bars in one sitting, you hear? Save some for later."

Back upstairs in the hallway, Todd and Kate followed Tully and his bottle of hooch while Tully explained what happened to Sheriff Farnsworth.

"We were trying to get a signal out through the airwaves," Tully said. "Course, the phone lines are dead and the electricity's out, so we figured we might be able to rig some sort of broadcast antenna to the roof of the fire hall next door. The fire hall's taller than the station, so it made sense to go next door. Joe and Bruce—Bruce was one of Joe's deputies, see—they thought they could rig up their handheld radios to the antenna somehow. The plan was to try to reach Bicklerville, which is the nearest town, about sixty miles west.

"I volunteered to go up on the roof and set up the antenna but Joe trumped me. He said he was still the sheriff and he was going to do it. And he did—he got up there and got it set up." Tully took another swig of the bourbon then said, "They came out of nowhere and took him right off the roof."

Todd imagined what it must have looked like watching the man being carried off into the night by one of those things. The thought caused him to think back to Nan Wilkinson, who'd come crashing down through the stained glass windows in the roof of the church.

"That's horrible," Kate said.

"Joe was a good son of a bitch. We went to high school together."

"Did you guys try the radios?" Todd asked. "Did it work?"

"No. Apparently those clouds hanging low over the town are blocking any signals through the air. Nothing gets in, nothing gets out. That's what me and Bruce think, anyway."

They arrived outside a closed office door with a drawn shade in the glass. A dull blue light, like the light from a television set, radiated through the slats in the shade. Tully knocked twice then opened the door and the three of them stepped inside.

The office was a zoo of metal shelves cluttered with computer equipment. The bluish television light radiated from a laptop screen on a desktop; a man of sturdy build and a shaved head perched forward in a chair at eyelevel with the screen, his deputy's uniform doused in a sickly azure light.

The man did not acknowledge them as they filed into the room. "Hey, Bruce," Tully said, clearing his throat, "this is Todd and Kate. Their car wrecked outside of town last night. I found them this morning wandering around."

Bruce looked quickly at them then returned his stare back to the laptop. Columns of numbers rained down the laptop's screen like digital snow. "Hey," Bruce said.

"Brought you some go-go juice," Tully said, setting the bottle of bourbon down next to the laptop. Bruce hardly noticed.

"How's that laptop running?" Kate asked. She came around the other side of Bruce's chair and looked at the screen from over his shoulder.

"Battery powered," Bruce said, "but I'm getting ready to shut it down before I drain the damn thing." He reclined in his chair and folded his hands behind his head. "Not that it matters. It ain't working."

"It looks like the cell phones," Kate said.

Bruce bounced his foot on the floor. "I've got a whole wall of computers behind me. Not a single one's worked."

"I told them about the jamming signal," Tully said. "About the cloud cover, too . . . and what happened to Joe."

"It's like they've got us trapped inside a bowl with a lid on it," Bruce said. When he turned slightly in his chair, Todd could see what looked like a splatter of dried blood down the front of his uniform. "Those aren't normal clouds. They look almost metallic, like there's some sort of filaments threaded through them. We had the walkies working hand-to-hand down here on the ground but that was about as much as we could get out of them. The antenna on the roof of the fire hall didn't do shit. 'Cept get Joe killed."

"Even if you got one of these laptops to work," Todd said, "what good will it do you?"

Bruce reached out and wrapped a big hand around the neck of the liquor bottle. "If we were anyplace else in town, it wouldn't do shit," he said, bringing the bottle down into his lap. "But the station here was outfitted with fiber optic cables earlier in the year. Supposed to make our computers work faster when we're on the internet. The cables run underground and they go out past the highway and halfway down to Bicklerville where the transformer station is. The cables themselves are unaffected by the power outage." He thumped a hand against a small black box that looked like a DVD player. "If I can get one of the computers to work, I can hook this modem up to a battery and power it up, then run the modem to the computer. With a little bit of luck, I could log onto the internet, get in touch with neighboring PDs."

"Get in touch with the fucking military," Tully suggested.

"But none of that matters because every single one of these computers is fucked. Whatever they're doing—sending blocking signals down from the clouds or using some science fiction goddamned mind control—they're making the computers go haywire." Disgusted, Bruce chugged down some bourbon. Then he turned off the laptop to conserve the battery pack. It whined and the room fell dark, except for the halogen lamp Tully carried with him.

"I don't think that's totally accurate," Todd said.

Bruce took another swallow of bourbon then handed the bottle to Kate. She just stared at it, cradling it in both hands. "What's that?" Bruce said.

"About those things sending signals or whatever down from the clouds and screwing with the computers. I don't think that's what they're doing."

"Then what are they doing?"

"See, I think maybe they *did* send some sort of signal," Todd said, digging around in his pocket, "but my guess is it was probably a single pulse sent out earlier in the week. Just one initial jolt that's kept everything screwed up."

"Why do you say that?" said Bruce.

"Because of this," Todd said, producing his cell phone. He powered it on and handed it to the deputy. "I've got no signal but it isn't scrambled. The two other cell phones we found in one of the houses in town looked just like your computer screen—a jumble of characters that made no sense. But my phone's fine."

"So was mine," Kate said, still holding the bottle of bourbon.

Bruce was staring hard at Todd's cell phone. After a moment of contemplative silence, he said, "So you think whatever was in town when the attack started was affected by the pulse or surge or signal or whatever it was, but anything new that's *brought* into town—"

"Is completely unaffected," Todd finished.

"Jesus," Tully muttered. He took a step closer toward Bruce so he could see Todd's cell phone more clearly. "Is there a way we can hook that phone up to the fiber optic cables?"

"Shit," said Bruce, "maybe some electrical engineer could, but I haven't got a clue."

"We're so close," Tully said to no one in particular. "There's gotta be something we can do. I can feel it."

Footsteps out in the hallway caused Todd to turn toward the door. Brendan materialized through the gloom, his arms laden with fresh, clean clothing. "Hey," he said, skidding to a stop. "Was wondering where you all went off to. I got you some clothes." He handed sweaters and pants out to Todd and Kate. "Also, I been heating up some hotdogs in the office down the hall with some candles. They're probably still cold on the inside, but hell, if you're hungry . . ."

"Todd's cell phone works," Tully said.

"No shit? You mean we can call for help?"

"Not exactly," Bruce said. "There's still no signal, but at least the screen ain't scrambled."

Sighing, Bruce handed Todd back his cell phone then rubbed his eyes with the heels of his hands. Smirking, he said, "Too bad you didn't bring a fucking computer with you, too. Then we'd be in business."

Almost grinning, Todd said, "I did."

CHAPTER TWENTY

Out in the hallway, one of the children screamed. Kate nearly dropped the bottle of bourbon on the floor. Tully and Todd went to the door as Bruce popped out of his chair, one hand already reaching for his service pistol.

"It's Cody," said Tully, rushing out into the hallway and taking all the light with him. Kate set the bottle and the new clothes down on the desk and hurried out after the men, her heartbeat already strumming in her ears.

The hallway was a black mineshaft. At the end of the hall, a shape flitted past one window. Something was outside.

Cody Dobbins came racing down the hallway toward them, her face pulled back in a mask of absolute terror. Tears streamed down her cheeks. She slammed against Tully, who hugged her awkwardly with one arm while adjusting one of the fuel canisters clinging to his hip. Behind Tully, Bruce had his pistol raised and was advancing down the hallway with his back against the wall.

"What did you see?" Tully asked the girl.

"There's someone outside!" Cody cried into his chest.

Todd pulled his own gun and crept along the wall opposite Bruce. They looked like mirror images of each other.

"How many?" Tully asked Cody.

"Just one. A girl. She's outside in the snow."

There were only a few windows of pebbled glass at the far end of the hallway, each one reinforced with wire. Bruce and Todd approached them cautiously and attempted to peer out, but the distortion of the glass made it impossible to see anything outside.

"Go back downstairs with Molly and Charlie," Tully told the girl. He withdrew himself from her embrace and produced the muzzle of the flamethrower out from under his coat. He moved down the center of the hallway like a firefighter approaching a burning building.

In the doorway of the office, Brendan stood like someone who'd just been startled out of a sound sleep. His eyes looked muddy behind the thick lenses of his glasses.

Kate took Cody's hand. The little girl looked up at her with wide, terrified eyes. "Come on, sweetheart. Let's get you downstairs with your brother."

"I see someone," Bruce said. He was leaning against the wall, his back flat against it. He held his service weapon down at his waist and gripped with two hands. He craned his neck to see out the pebbled windowpane, the milky issuance of daylight spilling across his features. Todd noted an angry-looking scar like a cleft in his chin. "Or something."

Breathing heavy and sweating through his clothes, Todd squeezed the hilt of his own weapon tighter. He kept leaning over to peer out one of the front windows but everything outside was blurred by the pebbled glass and wire meshing. "I can't make anything out," he told Bruce.

"A shape," said Bruce in a low voice, "just beyond the alcove."

"Are you sure there's only one?"

"Can't be positive, but it looks that way."

"Any chance it's someone from town? A survivor?"

The look Bruce gave him suggested such a thing was next to impossible.

His flamethrower in hand, Tully pressed himself against the wall beside Todd. Raising his voice just a bit so that Bruce could hear him on the other side of the window, Tully said, "I've got the keys to the door. I can unlock it and on the count of three, you two yank them open. I'll light up whatever's on the other side with the 'thrower."

Bruce appeared to chew this over. He kept trying to sneak a peek through the glass but was having difficulty making out any details. "Whatever it is, it's just standing there."

"Cody said it was a girl," Todd reminded them. "She must have gotten a better look."

"From where?" Tully said.

Bruce thought for a moment. He jerked his chin toward a glass-enclosed secretarial office behind Todd and Tully. "She goes in there sometimes and plays secretary. There's windows."

Todd and Tully went in. Slivers of light beamed through the blinds over the windows. The light held a greenish tint. Together, Todd and Tully squatted down before one of the windows. With the barrel of his gun, Todd lowered a section of blinds and they both peered out.

"It *is* a girl," Tully said.

Todd could say nothing. It was Meg, the girl from the church, who'd somehow followed them from the ambulance and stood now in the shade of the alcove in her dirty blouse, a look of disorientation on her face.

"She could be . . ." Tully began.

"No," Todd said. "I know this girl. She's one of them now."

"I wonder what scared Cody so much," Tully said. "She looks normal enough. I mean, what do you think—"

He cut himself off just as Meg turned her head and stared straight at their window. The girl's eyes looked muddy in her skull, as if they'd been painted on by a careless artist. As they watched, Meg's mouth came unhinged, as grotesquely wide as a python's, and a shrill but distant keening vibrated the bones in Todd's ears. Around them, the windows rattled in their frames.

Tully shuddered and jammed a finger into one of his ears. "What is she doing?"

"Calling for the others," Todd said, rushing to his feet and back out into the hallway. By the front door, Bruce was wiping condensation off one of the windows. "It's one girl," Todd said. "She's one of them now. That noise we're hearing—I think she's trying to tell the others that we're here."

"Fuck this," Tully said, zipping around Todd and nearly throwing himself into the double doors. He fumbled with the wreath of keys at his waist. After selecting the appropriate key, he jammed it into the padlock and turned it. The chain fell away to the floor.

Bruce came over and grabbed one of the door handles while Todd reached out and snatched the other. Out in the cold, queer afternoon, the high-pitched wailing stopped suddenly.

"Do it now!" Bruce shouted, and he and Todd yanked the doors open.

Tully charged out into the snow, a tongue of fire already spouting from the nozzle of the flamethrower. Guns at the ready, Todd and Bruce rushed out after him.

"She's gone," Tully said, looking around.

Bruce sniffed at the air. "Careful, gentlemen . . ."

"No footprints in the snow," Todd said. "How could—"

In a blur, the girl dropped down from the roof of the awning and landed squarely on Tully's shoulders. Her mouth so wide she nearly split her head in two, the Meg-thing drove her teeth into the soft flesh of Tully's neck. Tully screamed—a horrible gurgling wail—and sent an arc of flame spouting toward the underside of the awning.

Todd was elbowed aside by Bruce, who fired a shot at the thing on Tully's back. The round tore a chunk of grayish flesh from Meg's exposed forearm. Snow blew out as if by compressed air and trailed from the arm like smoke from a burning car racing down a hillside. It reminded Todd of the time he'd helped move Brianna's stuff across town to his apartment in a friend's borrowed pickup truck; unbeknownst to both of them at the time, Bree's beanbag chair had sprung a leak, and when Todd had glanced up at the rearview mirror, the bed of the pickup was domed in a blizzard of white Styrofoam balls . . .

Tully dropped the flamethrower in the snow, its cable still hitched to one of the canisters at Tully's hip. Blood gushed from Tully's mouth as the Meg-thing tore deeper into his neck.

Todd snapped from his stupor. He ran up behind Tully and grabbed a fistful of the Meg-thing's hair. With a solid tug, he wrenched the girl's teeth out of Tully's neck. The Meg-thing made a sound like truck brakes squealing. Todd pressed the pistol against the girl's temple and pulled the trigger. The gun bucked in his hand.

The Meg-thing's head rocked and went unnaturally back on its neck. She sloughed off Tully's back just as Tully dropped to his knees in the snow.

Todd staggered backward, the pistol smoking in his hand. At his feet, Meg's lifeless body began shuddering, one leg kicking out and carving a swath in the snow.

Bruce ran over to Tully and clamped a hand to the jagged tear in Tully's neck. Tully uttered something wet and unintelligible then slumped forward against Bruce, frighteningly still. "Todd!" Bruce yelled, but Todd could barely hear him. Bruce could have been calling to him from underwater, from a distant planet . . .

Still staring down at Meg's body, Todd watched as a slurry of snow came funneling out of the exit wound at the side of Meg's head.

Reality rushed back to slap him in the face.

"Better get him inside quick!" Todd shouted, rushing over to help Bruce drag Tully inside. The front of Tully's coat was black with blood and more came spurting between the fingers Bruce had pressed over the neck wound.

"No," Bruce said. "The legs, the legs! Grab his legs!"

Todd fumbled with Tully's legs while Bruce grabbed Tully and hoisted him from beneath his armpits.

A blast of icy wind struck Todd's back. He whirled around in time to see a massive clot of snow rising up like a pillar before him. Twin wing-like appendages unfolded from the mass just as a thread of steel-colored light intensified at the center of the thing.

Todd cried out, rolling over on his side in the snow. The pistol went sliding out of his hands. Above Todd, the wing-like appendages crystallized into twin blades of curved ice the color of smoke. The creature reared up like a horse, the blades cleaving the air. It emitted an ear-piercing whine. Todd scrambled away on his buttocks, his boots struggling for purchase in the snow.

The scythes chopped down, slicing through the air with a sound like a passing jetliner. The scythes knifed into Tully's slumped shoulders. Tully shook as if he'd been zapped with an electrical current. The glowing silver thread suspended at the center of the clot of snow dulled and turned the color of bronze as it passed through Tully's camouflage coat. Blackish blood was already saturating the coat, and rivulets as dark as India ink ran from the serrations at his shoulders.

Bruce released Tully just as Tully's head snapped around to glare at Todd. His eyes blazed like torches. His lips and chin were smeared with Tully's own blood.

"... *odd* ..." the Tully-thing croaked—a voice like a creaking floorboard.

Bruce brought his service weapon up to Tully's head but Tully's arm shot up lightning-quick and knocked the gun out of Bruce's hand. Tully never took his eyes from Todd the whole time.

"... *ook* ... *odd* ..." the Tully-thing growled through lips frothing with blood. The thing inside him managed a hideous smile that seemed too wide for the man's face. Tully had about a hundred tiny teeth crowded into his mouth.

Bruce administered a roundhouse kick to the side of Tully's head. Tully's eyes shook like the last two gumballs in a gumball machine. Then the Tully-thing spun around with animal ferocity and launched itself at Bruce. Bruce just barely dodged the thing, and took off running around the side of the building.

Todd scrambled over to the pistol, grabbed it, and rolled over into a seated position with the pistol clenched in both hands. Without pausing to aim, he fired shot after shot, praying he wouldn't accidentally strike Bruce in all the mayhem.

One round must have struck one of the fuel canisters on Tully's belt, because there sounded a dull *plink!* less than a second before the Tully-thing burst into flames. It began screaming, a flaming comet continuing forward in its momentum, its arms flailing. The heat ignited the other fuel canisters, setting off a series of explosions that launched bits of flaming flesh and articles of clothing across the macadam until they eventually landed, smoldering, in the snow.

The burning man-thing began running toward Todd. It had no discernable shape—just a writhing conflagration with legs. Tully's steel-toed boots left steaming divots in the snow. Its anguished cries were like the trumpeting of an elephant.

Todd pulled himself to his feet and ran for the double doors, but the thing was bounding toward him at an impossible pace. A mere couple yards from Todd, the fiery Tully-thing fell down into the snow, the stink of burning flesh and chemical fuel poisoning the air. The flaming heap bucked and roiled in the snow in a mockery of life . . . until the creature itself burst from Tully's body and leapfrogged into the snow. It too was on fire, its usually translucent form made nightmarishly visible by the heat of the flames. A lion-shaped skull pivoted wildly on a thin stalk of neck as it burned, its eyes like bottomless black pits. As Todd watched from the doorway, the thing dragged itself through the snow by the carved blades of its arms. Smoldering black scales were left behind in the path it carved through the snow, reminding Todd of fireplace soot.

Bruce appeared around the corner of the building. He froze in astonishment as he saw Tully's body smoldering in the snow and the burning creature dragging itself out from under the station awning.

The creature was heading toward Meg's body. It needed an uncorrupted vessel, even a dead one: the fire was killing it.

A hooked arm rose up out of the flames and planted itself squarely into Meg's chest. A moment later, Meg's body jerked. One of the dead girl's arms swiped in a semicircle through the snow. But as the thing climbed on top of her, the girl's body also burst into flames. That arm continued to swipe back and forth in the snow, back and forth, until the inferno overtook it and all went still.

Bruce practically tackled Todd, driving him backward into the sheriff's station. Together they slammed the doors shut and leaned against them, breathing laboriously.

"Jesus," Todd panted. Even with the doors closed, the acrid stink of the fiery massacre burned the hairs in his nose. "Did you see? It couldn't . . . couldn't get inside her . . . because the fire kept . . . kept it solid . . ."

"I lost my gun," Bruce gasped.

"Do you think . . . more will come?"

"I don't know."

A dark shape ambled toward them from the opposite end of the hallway. Todd aimed his gun at the darkness.

It was Brendan, shaking with fear. In all the commotion, Todd had forgotten about Brendan.

"Did you kill it?" Brendan's voice trembled. "Where's Tully?"

"Tully's dead," said Bruce. "We should probably put the fires out and bury the bodies before any more of those things comes sniffing around."

"Fires?" Brendan warbled. It sounded like his tongue had grown too big for his mouth.

"Brendan," Bruce said, still out of breath. "Get a shotgun from the gun locker, will you?"

Stupidly, Brendan nodded then retreated back into the darkness. Todd listened to his footfalls pad down the floor tiles.

"Come with me," Bruce said. "There are shovels in the sally port. We'll have to be quick before those things show up and figure out we're in here."

Less than three minutes later, they were back outside. Most of the flames had died, leaving charred and steaming corpses sizzling in gray snow. Tully's and Meg's bodies still resembled something vaguely human, but the third corpse—the creature—was unidentifiable. It was large—perhaps twelve to fifteen feet in length—and something about the fibrous twists of its multi-sectional body suggested something serpent-like. Again, Todd thought of the fleshy, arrow-shaped wings of a stingray. One of the thing's hooked arms was still buried in the smoldering black flesh of Meg's corpse.

"I can't do this," Todd said, feeling like someone was tickling the back of his throat with a feather. "I'm going to throw up."

"Then throw up and let's get on with it," Bruce said, his bald pate glistening with sweat.

While Brendan stood guard with a shotgun, Todd and Bruce donned work gloves and tossed handfuls of snow onto the corpses to cool them. When Todd bent and, turning his face to the side, grabbed hold of Tully's ankles and pulled, he heard a sickening crunch and felt the bones surrender. Tully's feet came loose in Todd's hands. Sickened, Todd dropped them and staggered several paces away where he vomited into the snow. Behind him, he heard Brendan moan.

"Fuck," Bruce said once Todd returned, feeling hollowed and jittery. "We'll never be able to move them. Let's just cover them with snow right here. Give us a hand, Brendan."

The work was grueling and took longer than Todd would have thought. The men took turns vomiting in the snow while they worked. The worst moment came when Bruce dug the ball of keys from Tully's belt; they came away with bits of flesh seared to them, and the sound was like ripping up old carpeting.

Once they finished, there were three mounds of snow beneath the awning of the sheriff's station—one much larger than the other two.

* * *

Perched like some predatory bird on her cot, Molly kept stealing glances at Kate when she thought Kate wasn't looking—but Kate could feel the pregnant woman's stare like hot embers against her flesh.

They were back down in the basement room, where they counted down the minutes in what felt like eternal silence. Still shaken by what she'd seen outside, Cody clung to Kate, who'd taken up one of the empty cots across the room from Molly. Looking bored, Charlie sat on the floor before the board game, crushing little wooden game pieces beneath his shoe while chewing absently on his Snickers bar.

"Come here, Cody," Molly called to the girl—the first thing that had been said since Kate had taken Cody down here—though Molly maintained her gaze on Kate.

Cody didn't move—she had her face buried against Kate's chest, her spindly little legs folded up under her. In Kate's arms, the girl felt almost nonexistent.

"When are you due?" Kate asked once the silence had become overbearing.

"Next month. But Brendan says I should be prepared for the worst. He said the particles or pulses or whatever from those clouds could have caused . . . maybe caused . . ." Molly's voice trailed off.

"Brendan shouldn't talk about things he knows nothing about," Kate told her. "He doesn't know any more about what's going on than we do. He shouldn't have scared you."

"He didn't scare me." Molly's eyes were lucid.

"Do you know the sex?"

"No. We wanted to wait, to be surprised. Brendan says if it's a girl, the electrical pulses in the air may have, uh, compromised her reproductive capacity. Those were his exact words, just how he said them—'compromised her reproductive capacity.' Brendan's very smart."

"Sounds like he's been thinking a lot about things." Then a notion came to her. "Brendan's the father?"

"We're not married," Molly said defensively. "Not yet, anyway. We will be, though. We agreed the baby needs both parents. It's important to have both parents be a part of a child's life."

Above their heads, doors slammed.

"Do you think they're okay?" Charlie wanted to know.

"I'm sure they're fine," Kate said when Molly wouldn't answer.

"What if one of those things gets in here?"

"Nothing is going to get in here, Charlie."

"But what if one *does*."

"Then we kill it," Kate said.

"They didn't know we were here until you and your boyfriend showed up," Molly said.

So that's what this is about, Kate thought. "We were careful coming here," she promised Molly. "No one followed us."

"You can't know that."

"It wasn't even our idea to come here. It was Tully's idea. We came with him, followed him."

"Well what do you expect? Tully's a good man. Did you think he'd just leave the two of you out there to die?"

"Of course not. I just don't know what you want me to say."

"And now you've brought these things to us," Molly went on, ignoring Kate now.

Kate knew there was nothing she could say to this woman. Molly had made up her mind to dislike and distrust her and there would be no convincing her otherwise. "If I did," Kate said evenly, "then I'm sorry. It wasn't deliberate."

Visibly disgusted, Molly turned away.

There were footsteps on the other side of the door, along with the sound of muffled talking. Molly produced a revolver from under her pillow, surprising Kate. The pregnant woman held the gun in a shaking hand against the swell of her abdomen. Both Cody and Charlie looked up at the door, frightened.

The door opened. Todd, Bruce, and Brendan came in, their shirts half off to bare their shoulders. Molly relaxed and stashed the gun back beneath the pillow.

"What was it?" Kate asked, sitting up straighter.

"One of the skin-suits was outside by the front doors," Bruce said, peeling his shirt off the rest of the way. It was wet with blood. He balled it up and stuffed it in the Superman backpack. He went over to a pile of clothes and blankets on a rolling cart where he began hunting around for a fresh shirt. "We killed it."

Todd sat beside Kate on the cot while Brendan, looking pale and out of sorts, leaned a shotgun against the desk. Then he stared down at his hands in near disbelief, watching as they vibrated like a pair of tuning forks.

"Where's Tully?" Molly asked. She looked from Bruce to Brendan. "What happened to Tully?"

"The Tull-man," Brendan said forlornly, his eyes distant and unfocused.

"He's dead," said Bruce, pulling on a clean shirt. There were dark smudges under his eyes.

Cody's grip around Kate tightened. Kate rocked her gently, telling her that everything was going to be all right—such feeble, futile promises.

"This is *their* fault," Molly said. That sharp look was back in her eyes. "Those things didn't know we were here until they showed up."

"Relax, Molly," Bruce said.

Molly shook her head. "No. We should have never let them in here."

Brendan sat beside Molly on the cot. He placed one hand on her knee but looked too preoccupied to offer her any worthwhile comfort.

"There was only one," Todd assured her, "and we killed it."

"You don't know that! There could be more right outside, watching and waiting. There could be a whole goddamn army of them."

Against Kate's chest, Cody sobbed. "Stop it," Kate told Molly.

"We're okay for right now," Bruce said. He went to the liquor bottles on the desk and selected some tequila.

"But what about later?" Molly protested. "Those things will come back, Bruce. You know they will."

"And if they do, we'll fight them off again, Molly." Bruce leaned against the desk and unscrewed the tequila, took a swallow. "There's nothing more we can do about that."

"There is," Molly said. "We can send them both back out there, let them fend for themselves."

"Molly," Brendan said, seemingly returned from his stupor. He rubbed her thigh.

But Molly could not be consoled. "We could send them out and make them lead those things away from us."

"No one is going out there," Bruce said. "We're in this together now."

"They brought those things—"

"They didn't do anything!" Bruce yelled back. Again, Cody shuddered and Charlie gaped up at the sheriff's deputy, a combination of fear and awe on the boy's face. More calmly, Bruce said, "No one did anything, Molly. This—whatever this is—just happened. And now we've got to survive it. Together. We're not doing anyone any good fighting amongst ourselves."

"You're not the law anymore, Bruce," Molly grumbled. She placed both hands flat against her distended stomach. "There *is* no law anymore. Not in Woodson."

Cody sat up. Her face was red from crying. "Please stop yelling," she said.

Bruce looked down at the bottle in his hands while Molly, her eyes welling with tears, looked away from him and at the wall.

"Hey," said Brendan, clapping his hands together and startling them all. Some color had returned to his face. "Who wants hotdogs?"

"I do!" Charlie boomed.

"I do," Cody echoed, less enthusiastic.

Brendan stood, forcing a goofy grin. "Then let's go, gang. Train's pulling out of the station. All aboard!"

Charlie hopped up and Cody climbed down off the cot. Still grinning, Brendan opened the door and saluted Charlie, who giggled and saluted him back.

"Brendan," Todd said, and handed him the pistol.

Brendan nodded almost imperceptibly, stuffing the pistol into his waistband at the small of his back. Then he barked at the kids: "Let's go, soldiers! Left! Right! Left! Right! Forward—march!"

A smile beginning to overtake Cody's delicate face, Brendan led the kids out into the hallway. Their footsteps receded into the darkness.

Bruce grunted his approval. Rubbing a hand along his bald pate, he took some more tequila from the bottle before handing it over to Todd. "I want to hear about this computer you mentioned," Bruce said.

Todd chugged a mouthful of tequila, winced, and handed the bottle to Kate. "I had a laptop with me when we came into town," Todd said. "If I'm right about what's going on—about why my phone works while everything else in this town is going haywire—then my laptop should boot up and work fine, too. If you can hook it up to that modem of yours, Bruce, we can get online, maybe even make a phone call out."

"Theoretically," Bruce said.

Kate took a swallow of the tequila. It burned all the way down her throat before exploding in her stomach.

"Wait a minute," Molly said. "Are you saying we've got a working computer?"

Still want to kick us out? Kate thought, smiling wryly to herself.

"Sort of," said Bruce. Turning back to Todd, he said, "Where is it, exactly?"

Todd took the bottle back from Kate. He looked instantly miserable. "I think," he said, drawing out his words, "I think it's back at the town square."

CHAPTER TWENTY-ONE

A look of total resignation overcame Bruce's face. His whole body appeared to deflate. On her cot, Molly's eyes darted back and forth between Bruce and Todd.

"The *square?*" Molly said. Defeated, she slumped back against the wall.

"We'll just have to go back and get it," Todd said.

"But Tully said—" Molly began, before Bruce spoke over her.

"The square is like ground zero, Todd. That's where they've all been congregating. Not to mention I caught sight of that electrical eye in the clouds while we were out front, burying the bodies. That eye is seated directly over the square right now."

Kate frowned. "So what does that mean?"

"It seems to attract them, gives them strength," Bruce said.

"Just like last night, back at the church," Todd said. Too clearly, he could recall last night's escape from the church, and how one of those things had gotten inside Chris while, unbeknownst to the rest of them, another had gotten inside poor Meg. And once they'd exited the church, there had been all those townspeople—what Tully had succinctly dubbed "skin-suits"—standing there as if awaiting instruction.

Instruction from that glowing eye in the sky, Todd thought now.

"Where exactly in the square is this computer of yours?" Bruce asked.

"If it's still where I left it, it's inside the Pack-N-Go."

"If the Pack-N-Go is still there, too," Kate added, attracting an impatient glare from Molly.

Bruce sighed. The halogen lamps gleamed off his scalp. "Well, then, I guess we don't have much of a choice."

"We can make torches," Kate suggested. "They kept away from the torches last night. And when one of those snow-things rose up out of the ground, I think I burned it."

Bruce was shaking his head. "A torch might scare one off, or even injure it unless you really nail 'em, but chances are it'll get away and will only come back with friends. When they're in groups, they swoop down over you and generate enough wind to extinguish any small flames."

"We've learned that the hard way," Molly added.

"So what do we do?" Kate said.

"We travel as incognito as possible," Bruce said. "Same way Tully got you both here, I'm sure. Far as I can tell, they don't have any extraordinary senses. No amplified sense of sight or smell—not like a dog or a wolf or anything—so it's our best bet just to lay low."

"All those guns out there against the wall," Todd said. "I assume you've got more than enough ammo?"

"Yes. And Tully had another flamethrower. It's upstairs in one of the offices. We can take that, too."

"We should probably go sooner than later," Kate said. "No sense waiting around till nightfall."

"Kate," Bruce said. "We're gonna need you to stay here."

"No. I can help."

"You can help here."

"No."

"Kate." Todd put a hand on her shoulder. "He's right. Someone needs to stay here with Molly and the kids."

"Brendan can stay."

"Brendan knows the town. It makes no sense leaving him here when he could be more helpful to us out there."

"Brendan's not going anywhere," Molly said. "He's staying right here with me."

"See?" Kate said. "Brendan's not going to want to leave her."

As if summoned by the repeated mention of his name, Brendan appeared in the doorway. "What about me?" he said, popping the last of a hotdog into his mouth. Charlie and Cody scampered into the room looking more contented than they had when they'd left.

"They're talking crazy, Brendan," Molly said. "They're talking about sending you out there!"

Around a mouthful of hotdog, Brendan cocked an eyebrow and said, "Huh?"

"Todd's computer," Bruce explained. "It's back at the Pack-N-Go, Brendan. The three of us have to go get it."

"Out there? At the Pack-N-Go? But Tully said the square—"

"I know what Tully said," Bruce barked, "and he was nowhere near the square when he died an hour ago. If Todd's computer actually still works, we can use it to contact the outside world."

"It's our only chance of getting out of here," Todd added.

"But what if it *doesn't* work?" Molly demanded. "The three of you will be going out there and risking your lives for nothing."

"Come on, Molly," Bruce said. "It's our only shot."

Molly looked pleadingly at Brendan. "Bren . . ."

"It makes sense, Molly." But Brendan didn't sound too confident.

"We're gonna need the guns," Bruce told Brendan. "And Tully's extra 'thrower, too."

"Like, now? We're going now?"

"Brendan!" Molly cried, cradling her belly in case Brendan had somehow forgotten about the state she was in.

"We should go soon," said Bruce. "But first I want us all to go upstairs so I can show everyone here what to do with the computer once we bring it back."

"Why won't you just do it yourself, Bruce?" Brendan asked . . . but then turned his eyes down toward the floor when he realized the motive behind Bruce's suggestion.

"All right," Bruce said, adjusting his gear belt. "Everyone upstairs. You, too, Molly."

"It's simple, really," said Bruce. They were all crowded around the desk in the computer room while Bruce held up a rectangular black box. "This is the modem. I assume we all know at least the fundamentals about computers and how the internet works?"

"Not me," said Cody. Some tired laughter circulated around the group. Cody smiled uncertainly, embarrassed.

"Look." Bruce pointed to a thick white cable that trailed from the rear of the black box and into the wall behind the desk. "The modem's already hooked up to the fiber optics. It can also be connected to a power source—a battery—to give it juice. Watch." He plugged a brick-sized battery into the modem. Lights lit up on the modem's faceplate. "See those lights? That means you're in business. If you've got no lights, you've got no power.

"When we've got the computer, we hook that to another power source"—he waved one arm at the shelves across the room, laden with, among other things, portable batteries—"then connect the computer to the modem with another cable. Okay, watch again—I'll show you." He demonstrated with the laptop that was already on the desk. "From there, with any luck, it'll be no different than logging onto the internet from your home computer. Any questions?"

"Seems too good to be true," said Brendan.

Bruce rolled his heavy shoulders. "As long as we're able to get the computer back here, plugging it in and dialing it out should be a piece of cake."

"Yummy," Cody said. Kate smiled and rubbed the girl's head.

"Just one more thing," Todd said. They all looked at him. "The operating system on my laptop is password-protected."

"Good thinking," Bruce said. "What is it?"

"Turbodogs," Todd said. He offered them all a meager grin. "It's my son's favorite cartoon. About a bunch of dogs who race cars."

Young Charlie nodded and quite matter-of-factly said, "Yeah, that's a good show."

Todd's grin widened. "So I've been told."

"Anyway, Kate was right," Bruce said. "No sense sitting around here wasting time. You two good to go?"

"Good to go," Todd said.

"Good to go," Brendan said, too. Yet his eyes, which never left Molly's, told a different truth.

CHAPTER TWENTY-TWO

In the gloom of the hallway outside the computer room, Todd sat on the floor with his back against the wall, loading fresh rounds into magazines. He could hear the others talking in hushed tones farther down the hall in one of the offices.

Setting the gun down, he managed to wrangle his wallet from his pants without having to stand up. He opened it. The folded racing form was still inside—the racing form that was stained with his blood.

It was a winning ticket, the one that had ended his unfathomable losing streak. That one race was his last chance, knowing that it would be all or nothing, and that he had no other choice. He'd bet to win, the name of the horse—Justin Case—almost prophetic in its allusion to his son. And it seemed God was smiling down on him that sunny afternoon, because the motherfucker had *won*, had come in *first*. Todd had not only won enough money to pay back Andre Kantos but would also have some left over for the next few months' rent. Needless to say, Todd was flying high when he left the Atlantic City Race Course.

Kantos and his men picked him up in the parking lot of the track. They were leaning against his car, four or five of them, each only uglier and angrier than the next. He'd already had a few run-ins with Kantos's men, the most recent one outside a Manhattan bistro where two of them smacked him around a little bit—a run-in that had hurt his pride and his conscience more than his face and ribs. But he knew Andre Kantos meant business; he wasn't going to be able to put him off for too much longer.

He'd paused in the parking lot when he saw Kantos and his men leaning against his car. The sun was already setting, the sky the color of ripening fruit on the horizon, and his shadow was stretched out long and skinny on the gravel before him.

"This is where I find you," Kantos said, peeling himself off Todd's car. He was stocky with large meathook hands and a face like a patchwork quilt. His thinning hair was the color of steel wool, greased back off his Neanderthal brow. A diamond stud earring winked at Todd, catching what remained of the sunlight. "You owe me a shitload of money, Curry, and this is where I find you?"

"I was gonna call you tonight, Andre," he said.

"Well, shit." Kantos smiled—a grim Halloween pumpkin smile. "I must be a fuckin' psychic, huh?"

"I've got your money." He'd produced the cashier's check with the race-track logo in the corner. One of Kantos's men came over to him, plucked the check from his fingers, and nearly pressed his beaky nose to it as he examined it. Todd also showed him the racing form. "See? I've got it."

Kantos came over to look at the check and the racing form. His beady little eyes glittered. When he turned back to Todd, there was a dispassionate sneer tugging at the corner of his pocked face. "You know, Curry," Kantos said. "I take it back what I said to you last time we met, about how you're one unlucky son of a bitch. Maybe I had you pegged wrong. Maybe you *are* lucky. What are the odds, right?"

Some of Kantos's men grumbled with laughter.

Andre Kantos took the cashier's check and folded it nicely into the front pocket of Todd's shirt. He did the same with the racing form. His face so close to Todd's, every nick and pore and crosshatched pockmark was clearly visible. The man's ruinous little eyes glittered like polished jewels.

"So I guess I'll see you first thing tomorrow morning with my money, huh?"

"Yes."

"All right." Kantos turned and lit a cigarette. "I hate motherfuckers like you who get lucky when the cards are down. Luck is for slouches and losers, Curry. People too afraid to cut their own way rely on luck. I ain't had a day of good luck in my life, you know that?" He turned to one of his men—a beast-like guy with a mug like an old catcher's mitt. "Show Mr. Curry how much I hate slouches and losers."

They showed him.

He'd slept off the worst of the pain in the backseat of his car, too defeated to attempt to drive. Later, he'd had to pull over on the Black Horse Pike where he vomited blood into the bushes at the shoulder of the road. The next morning his face looked like a Halloween mask and he was certain his nose was broken, along with a couple ribs and the knuckles of his right hand. (He'd been right on all accounts—it seemed his luck *had* turned around after all.)

But the worst was not the pain. It was not the doctor visits or the bandages or the harness he wore to bed for weeks until his ribs managed to mend themselves. The worst was that he could not let his son see him like this, that he could not tell Brianna that he had sunk so low. He'd canceled the boy's visit. And wept like a child himself that night.

Those thoughts washed through him now, a tidal wave of emotion. He felt something heavy in his chest.

"Hey." It was Kate. In his recollection, he hadn't heard her approach.

Stuffing the racing form back into his wallet, he looked up at her and tried to summon his best smile. He wondered if she could see through it to the misery and torment that was boiling just beneath the surface. "Didn't hear you sneak up."

"Am I interrupting anything? Did you want to be alone?"

"Not at all. Have a seat."

She sank down beside him, her back against the wall. "You feeling okay? You look a little . . . disconsolate."

He raised an eyebrow. "Disconsolate?"

"It means sad, pensive, melancholy."

Grinning, he shook his head and put his wallet back in his pocket. "I know what the word means. I just never heard anyone actually say it in a sentence before."

"But am I totally off the mark?"

"I guess I'm just thinking about things. Giving myself time to let my life flash before my eyes. Just in case there isn't time for it later."

"Don't say that. Todd, you're gonna find that computer, bring it back here, and help us call the police." She leaned closer to him. "*All* of us. You're all coming back to save the day."

He just kept grinning like an idiot. He couldn't help himself. "What's this big change in you, anyway?"

"What do you mean?"

"Well, you're certainly not the same woman I met last night at the airport bar."

"Jesus," she said. "Last night? It seems like a year ago." She looked at him. "What do you mean by that?"

"You're not the hard-edged, the-world-can-kiss-my-ass firecracker you were last night."

Kate laughed. "Oh, brother, believe me—after all this, the world can certainly still kiss my ass."

"I guess I'm just wondering if this is the real you."

"I don't open up to a lot of people, Todd."

"What about me? You think if we were in a different place and under different circumstances, you would have let me in?"

"No." There was no humor to her voice. "My parents fucked me up pretty good and now I'm fucking myself up every chance I get. I doubt I would have sat still long enough to see who you really were, had the situation been different."

"What if I would have asked you out right there in the bar? Forgetting for the moment, of course, that you're engaged."

She put her hand on the side of his face. Kissed him. Softly.

"This is a map of the whole town," Bruce said, pointing to the printout on the desk in the computer room. It was just Todd, Bruce, and Brendan in the glow of the halogen lamp, their weapons already secured on their belts. Each one was armed with a handgun and extra magazines, a shotgun and extra shells, and several rounds of loose ammunition packed into their pockets. Bruce had strapped Tully's extra flamethrower to his back, the fuel canisters at his waist, while he'd given both Todd and Brendan portable butane torches. Only for use in extreme emergencies, Bruce had warned them, wary about drawing unwanted attention to themselves while out in the open. "This is the sheriff's station here," he said, pointing with one steady finger, "and this is the town square here. The whole bird's eye view. We're talking just over a mile to the square then, of course, just over a mile

back. You both look to be in pretty good shape, but it can get pretty treacherous moving through the snowdrifts."

"It's not the snowdrifts I'm afraid of," Todd said.

"My plan is to cut straight through the trees here, bypassing the road. It's
a straighter shot but it'll get a bit dicey going through the woods. It slopes
down to a small stream that we'll have to cross, then climb up the embankment on the other side. From there we'll have no choice other than to cut
straight through Vermont Street and over onto Fairmont. That's when we'll
be the most visible."

Bruce traced his finger up the map toward the center of town.

"Crossing Fairmont will bring us up to the back end of the shops in the
square. Most of them are connected but there are narrow alleyways between
some of them. That's our ticket into the square itself—take one of those alleys
down to the street on the other side. We'll come out roughly about here"—Bruce
pointed—"and the Pack-N-Go is three or four shops down this way to the left."

"Three," said Brendan. "Three shops down."

"What's this thing look like, in case we wind up having to search for it?"

"It's in a black nylon carrying case," Todd said. "Pretty standard. It's got a
tag with my name and address on it."

"All right," Bruce said. "We'll establish rendezvous points as we go. In the
event any of us get separated, we backtrack to the last rendezvous point and
wait for the others. And if all hell breaks loose and we've got the computer . . .
well, let's just remember what our goal is here. Priority one is to get that laptop
back here to the station. That means it's a priority over your life"—he pointed
to Todd—"and your life"—he pointed to Brendan—"and my life. We've got
two kids downstairs who need to grow up."

"And an unborn baby," seconded Brendan.

Bruce nodded. "Right." He rolled up the map and handed it to Todd. "You
take it in case you get lost and turned around. Brendan and I grew up here;
we can find our way back blindfolded."

Todd folded the map and tucked it into the pocket of the police coat Bruce
had given him. "Good idea."

"And these," Bruce added, sliding two walkie-talkies across the desk.
"We've only got two batteries that still have any juice, and they're both about
half full, so we can't waste 'em. And whatever is blocking your cell phone
signal, Todd, it's also interfering with the handhelds, although not as strongly
since we're down here on the ground. The frequencies stay pretty low, geo-
graphically speaking."

Todd picked one up. It was about the size and weight of a brick.

"You take one," Bruce said to Todd, "since you'll be the one who'll probably get hands-on with the laptop. If we're not in earshot when you grab the

computer, give us a chirp on the handheld and let us know we need to beat a retreat."

"Sounds good," Todd said, clipping the handheld to his belt.

"All right," Bruce said. He was piling a few extra articles of clothes into a backpack. "Are we ready?"

Both Todd and Brendan said, "Yes."

Outside, the world was silent. The sky radiated with a sickly green hue and the low-hanging clouds looked like brownish chunks of clay. There was no breeze; the bare branches of the nearby trees remained motionless, climbing up into the false-looking atmosphere like countless medieval spires. Kate, Molly, and the two kids stood by the double doors as the men waded out into the snow. Before leaving, Bruce handed Kate one of two keys that unlocked the front doors. "The minute we start walking, Kate, you lock this door behind us," he told her. "And when we get back here, you demand we show you our shoulders."

"Roger," Kate said, nodding. Bruce had also showed her where the shotguns and shotgun shells were kept in case of an emergency. He'd showed her how to load and charge the weapon.

Brendan and Molly hugged. Bruce tousled the kids' hair. From the doorway, Kate smiled at Todd. He winked at her and said, "Don't look so disconsolate," and Kate laughed and covered her mouth with one hand as tears welled up in her eyes.

They left.

CHAPTER TWENTY-THREE

By the time they reached the entrance of the woods, a light snow had begun to fall. The three men cast wary glances toward the heavens and held their breath, each one wondering if they were about to be attacked. But the snow just fell, covering their tracks and powdering their clothes.

Their gear weighed them down. It hadn't been too difficult walking along the culvert from the sheriff's station down to the main road, but by the time they reached the edge of the woods, they were sweating and breathing heavy. Todd's muscles ached and the wound on his injured leg throbbed with a dullness that was almost nauseating. They paused only once, leaning against trees while Bruce distributed cigarettes to each of them. They smoked and kept their eyes peeled for movement in the road above. They saw nothing, saw no one.

The climb down into the woods was steeper than Todd would have imagined. Bruce untangled a length of rope from his belt and tied one end around the bole of a sturdy tree. "We'll go down like mountain climbers rappelling down the face of a cliff," Bruce said.

Brendan went first, inching his way backwards down the steep and icy decline, a flag of vapor smoldering from his lips. As cautious as he was, it took him a good seven or eight minutes to reach level ground. Exhausted, he collapsed against a tree to catch his breath.

Todd went next, descending in a similar fashion. Hand over hand, he fed the rope up and out while his booted feet were careful not to trip over each other. Halfway down, his heel struck a partially buried tree stump and he lost his grip on the rope. He fell backward but managed to spin halfway around in the air, so that he struck the sloping ground on his right side. The wind was knocked out of him as he started sliding toward the valley floor. Below, Brendan scrambled to his feet and stood like the goalie of an ice hockey team, his legs far apart and bent at the hips, as if to catch Todd on his way down. Luckily, though, Todd managed to snag a tree root and arrest his descent. His breath whistling from his throat and his nose running into his mouth, he glanced up at Bruce, who stood peering over the precipice seemingly a million miles above him, and smiled weakly.

Bruce must have seen the smile, because he raised a hand in return.

At the bottom of the incline, Todd approached Brendan while making sure all his gear was still secured to him. Brendan clapped him on the back, his cheeks aflame from the cold. As Todd watched Bruce begin his descent, tears streamed from the corners of his eyes and froze midway down his cheeks.

When Bruce finally joined them on level ground, the sheriff's deputy was panting like a bloodhound. The top of his head had gone a bright crimson.

They continued into the heart of the woods, crunching through previously undisturbed snow. "Have you noticed?" Brendan said at one point. "Not a single squirrel or bird, not even a deer. Listen." They all stopped to listen. "Everything is totally quiet. I mean, I don't think I've ever heard anything this quiet before."

"Maybe they got to the animals first," Todd suggested. The thought troubled him in ways he couldn't quite understand—herds of zombie-like deer galloping along a snowy countryside, attacking their brethren in fitful rages, impaling other animals and possibly people with their antlers.

"Haven't seen any animals," Bruce said as they continued on through the woods. "Maybe they sensed this all coming and they skedaddled before the shit hit the fan. Like how farm animals always know when a tornado's approaching."

For some reason, that thought didn't make Todd feel any better.

Ahead of them, Brendan stopped suddenly. Todd nearly walked into him, catching himself at the last minute. He began to say something but Brendan quickly shushed him. Then Brendan pointed off into the distance, where the trees crowded together like soldiers trying to keep warm on a cold winter's night.

"What is it?" Todd said, whispering now. "What are you pointing at?"

"*There.*"

It took him a few seconds for his eyes to adapt and relate to his brain what he was seeing: two children dressed in tattered, soiled clothing, the hair on their heads beaded with frozen clumps of ice.

They had no faces.

"Jesus," Bruce said from behind Todd. "Jesus, will you look at that?"

Todd's hands clenched. "What do we do?"

"Just stand tight for a minute," Bruce told him. "I don't think they see us."

"I don't think they *can* see us," Brendan said. "My God, how in the world do you think—"

Behind the two children the trees seemed to disassemble themselves until Todd realized that much of what he'd *thought* were trees were really just more faceless children, their skin the color and texture of bark, their clothes muddy and earthen in hue. They seemed to float right out of the trees like battle-field ghosts, each one's face a blank bulb of flesh-colored putty. Todd counted twelve, thirteen of them . . .

What if they attack? Todd thought. *What if they all charge us at once? Could we possibly defend ourselves against so many of them? And how many more are out there that we haven't spotted yet?*

"They're rejects," Bruce said, pushing between Todd and Brendan. "Freaks. When the creatures get inside little children—like, preadolescents—they corrupt them and break them and turn them into those things."

Brendan was trembling. Kate had told Todd that Brendan was the father of Molly's baby; now, Todd wondered if Brendan was thinking of his unborn child while staring across the forest floor at these sad misfits.

"Pay them no mind," Bruce told them, walking ahead of them. "Just keep moving."

They continued deeper into the woods. At one point, Todd looked over his shoulder to where the children had been standing, and was surprised and a bit unnerved to find that they had vanished. He imagined packs of feral children, disfigured in their featurelessness, roaming the forested hillsides of the state for years and years to come.

* * *

In the basement of the sheriff's station, Kate attempted to keep Charlie and Cody occupied by playing board games with them. They'd gotten through one full game of Monopoly and were halfway through Life when Cody began to whimper. The little girl climbed up onto one of the empty cots and curled into a fetal position. Worried, Kate got up and sat down on the edge of the girl's cot.

"What's wrong, honey?"

Cody just rubbed her eyes with her fist.

Kate pressed the back of her hand to the girl's forehead. "She's warm."

Seated cross-legged on her own cot across the room, Molly grunted and began stacking pillows around her. "Are you a nurse or something?"

Kate ignored her. She stood and searched randomly around the desktop for anything that was not a bottle of liquor. In one of the desk drawers she located some bottled water. She opened one of the bottles and gave it to Cody. The girl took a few hesitant sips then lay back down on the cot.

"I think your sister's got a fever," she said to Charlie.

"She gets headaches," Charlie informed her.

"Does she? What kind?"

Charlie shrugged. He was picking at the rubber sole of one of his sneakers. "I don't know. She used to take medicine."

Oh please, you're fucking with me, kid, Kate thought. "What kind of medicine, Charlie?"

"I don't know."

"Was it special medicine or just aspirin?"

"What's a ass-prin?" he said. "I don't know what that means."

Molly snickered.

"Something funny?" Kate said, looking at her from the corner of her eyes while she unfolded a blanket and placed it over Cody. The little girl was shivering now.

"You're trying to be that little girl's mother," Molly said.

"No," Kate corrected, "I'm trying to take care of her because no one else is here to do that."

"Do you have any kids of your own?"

"No." She hated answering Molly's questions, humoring the bitch like that, but she couldn't help herself.

"Are you unable?"

"Excuse me?" She felt some of the old Kate Jansen return to her—the Kate Jansen who would have gotten up, swaggered over to snide little potbellied Molly, and cracked her across the jaw. Lord knows she'd done similar things in the past to nicer people.

"I'm just saying," Molly crooned, continuing to fluff her pillows. "It's just, you've been fawning all over those two ever since you got here. It's like you're trying to make up for something."

"Are we seriously having this conversation?"

"It's just talk," Molly said, as if her comments thus far had been completely innocent. "I'm just passing the time."

"Well you can pass it by telling me where I could find some aspirin."

Molly shrugged and looked bored. She picked up one of the paperback novels that were stacked beside her cot and absently thumbed through the pages. "This is a police station," she intoned, no longer looking up at Kate. "I'm sure there's Tylenol or something around here somewhere."

Kate tucked the blanket up under Cody's arms and legs then stood, running her fingers through her hair. Part of her was holding onto Gerald, and how worried he must be by now that he hadn't heard from her . . . but a larger part was out there with Todd. Standing in the doorway of the sheriff's station as they headed down to the road, she had the sinking feeling that she would never see him again.

"I'm going to find some aspirin," Kate announced, and left.

They reached the river and found it frozen. It was about twenty feet wide and couldn't possibly be very deep; nonetheless, Todd did not like the idea of plowing through the ice even up to his shins. It was cold enough out here that his feet would freeze instantly. And there would be no turning back until after they'd completed their task. He would just have to be careful.

"You can use these overhangs for handholds," Brendan said, inching his way out onto the ice while he gripped overhanging tree limbs like monkey bars. "They don't go all the way across but it's better than nothing."

"We should probably go one at a time," Todd said, bending down to survey the thickness of the ice. He thumped a gloved knuckle against it and it seemed sturdy enough.

When his handholds ran out, Brendan stretched his arms out like airplane wings. He took miniscule steps and looked like a tightrope walker overcautious of his balance. On the other side of the streambed, the scraggly twists of overhanging limbs dropped back down; Brendan's long arms rose and he gripped the limbs. A number of branches snapped away and shattered like glass on the surface of the frozen stream.

With two ungraceful bounds, Brendan made it to the other side of the stream. He executed an awkward bow that nearly sent him tumbling back onto the frozen stream before seating himself into the Y of a nearby tree. He lit a cigarette and looked like someone waiting for a bus.

Bruce eased himself out onto the ice next. As Brendan had done before him, he utilized the overhanging limbs to facilitate his way out to the center of the frozen stream. Releasing the last of the limbs, the deputy sheriff crossed the center of the stream much quicker than Brendan, his balance more aligned and steady. He didn't even bother grabbing for the overhanging branches on the far end of the streambed; he simply continued across at a steady pace, half-sliding, half-galloping.

When Bruce made it to the other side, Brendan handed him his cigarette and Bruce sucked the life out of it.

Todd slid out onto the ice, one hand groping for the branches above his head. He grabbed a sturdy one and inched out further onto the ice. Beneath him, the ice felt solid. Thankfully, blessedly solid. As Brendan and Bruce had done, he used the overhead branches as support until he got to the center of the stream. But then he took an overzealous step and heard something that sounded like a bone breaking.

He looked down and saw a hairline fracture in the ice. It ran perpendicular underneath his right foot. Holding his breath, he lifted his boot and took one easy step backward. His heart was suddenly racing.

Something clutched at his hair.

Todd uttered a cry and jerked down, feeling something claw-like scrape his scalp. His knees gave out, sending him backwards toward the ice. The world spun.

"Shit—"

He struck the ice with the center of his back—a solid punch that knocked the wind from his lungs. Instantly, he became aware of a bizarre sense of *give,* of *surrender,* and freezing water was suddenly infiltrating his clothes. He struggled to sit up but couldn't; the small of his back had crashed through the ice, trapping him like a turtle that has been turned on its back.

Bruce and Brendan snapped to their feet on the far side of the stream. "Rope!" Bruce yelled. "Todd! Hey, Todd!"

Todd's legs pumped at the air. The heavy police coat was becoming saturated and heavy. The back of his head was against a shelf of ice . . . but he soon heard that beginning to crack and break, too.

If that goes, he thought, *I'm going under. For all I know, this little stream could be twenty feet deep . . .*

Something flitted in front of his eyes. He felt something sting the side of his face: Bruce's rope whipping across his cheek. Blindly, Todd groped for it. He found it and wrapped the rope around both his hands just as the shelf of ice at the back of his head broke apart. He felt his head snap back on his neck followed by the heart-stopping sting of the freezing waters that engulfed him. His whole face went under, his arms pinwheeling, his legs bicycling in the air.

The rope tightened around his hands. He felt his arms nearly pop out of their sockets at the force of the pull. He was still holding his breath, his eyes clenched shut, when he realized he had been pulled clear of the water. He gasped, the force of which hurt his lungs, and he lunged forward until he was flat on his stomach atop the ice. On the other side of the stream, Bruce and Brendan were tugging the rope, dragging Todd toward them.

They managed to drag him up into the snowy embankment. Gasping, his skin stinging from the cold waters, Todd lay on his back, shaking violently.

"Help me get the coat off him," Bruce instructed, and Todd was quickly manhandled like a rag doll. They stripped him of the police coat and then his shirt, too. His skin began to harden and crystallize. "Here." Bruce thrust a fresh shirt at him, which he'd dug out of the backpack he had slung over his shoulders. "Lift your arms and we'll help you put this on."

Teeth chattering like typewriter keys, Todd obeyed.

Upstairs, the hallway looked slanted in the darkness. Gloomy half-light bled through the pebbled windows at the end of the hall where it pooled in murky white puddles on the tiled floor. Rubbing her forearms for warmth, Kate traced down the hall, stopping in every office she passed on the way. She searched the desks, the shelves, the file cabinets. There was no aspirin anywhere.

Opening a set of massive metal doors, she peered into the sally port. Her breath was visible right before her eyes. She saw the dark, hulking shapes of two police cruisers. The air smelled like radiator fluid.

Continuing farther down the hall, she became overly conscious of every noise that surrounded her—the ticking of a battery-powered wall clock, the rattle of old pipes deep in the walls, the sudden arrival of wind bellowing through the eaves. At the end of the hall she saw a secretarial office enclosed in stenciled glass. The door was unlocked. She entered and tiptoed around a desk, knowing with near certainty that every secretary in the good old U.S. of A. kept a bottle of aspirin in their desk drawer.

She pulled out a chair and began sifting through the drawers. It didn't take her long to locate the pills.

"Bingo."

She stuffed them into her pocket and, shaking like a maraca, darted back around the desk toward the office door.

However, she paused as she passed before one of the shaded windows. Peeling away the shade, she looked out into a milky haze of greenish daylight . . . and at the heavy snow that was falling.

Fear gripped her.

Down by the edge of the road, human-like shapes shuffled into view. Kate could make out no details but held her breath, hoping it was Todd and the others. Had something gone wrong? Were they coming back so soon?

But no—it wasn't Todd and the others. She counted five distinct shapes in the shadows of the looming trees. The snow refracted the greenish light from the sky, forcing her to question what exactly she was seeing. It was a trick of the light reflected off the snow.

"I hope," she whispered, and hurried back downstairs.

CHAPTER TWENTY-FOUR

In a fresh, warm shirt and sweater, Todd tried his best not to let both his shivering and his embarrassment show as they scaled the embankment and climbed back out of the woods. The clawing he'd felt at the back of his head had been from one of the overhanging branches. After Bruce and Brendan had pulled him up onto dry land and peeled off his soaking wet clothes in exchange for dry ones, they had all shared a good laugh and a few more cigarettes. But there was a greater nervousness among them now—unspoken, like a child's worst fear.

Vermont Street was a ghost town. The houses were dark and there was no movement—thankfully—in any of the windows. Heads down and with a purpose, the three of them trucked up Vermont without pausing. Once, the sounds of tree limbs crackling rose up from a nearby yard, but none of them turned to look in that direction. They kept moving, not once looking back.

Vermont Street ran parallel to Fairmont. With Bruce in the lead now, they crossed through two yards then hunkered down between two houses while Bruce attempted to survey the street ahead.

"There's something making noise down over there," Bruce said, trying to peer around the corner of the house to see what it was.

"I hear it, too," Todd said. "It's a downed power line. Probably still kicking up sparks."

"Where are all the skin-suits?" Brendan asked from the rear of the queue.

"Tully said they go into the houses every once in awhile," Bruce said. "I guess those snow monsters can do whatever they like when they're floating around on their own, but maybe they can't stay out all day and night in the skin-suits. Maybe the bodies start to freeze." He sighed and added, "They're just people, after all."

Todd put a hand on Bruce's back. "Let's keep going."

They hurried down the slope of the yard toward the street. The snow was coming down hard now, limiting their visibility. Beyond a veil of pines were the brick storefronts that lined the western edge of the town square. So close. Directly above the square, the swirling eyelet in the clouds pulsed with a sickly green light. Todd thought he could feel a change in the air, like how just before a storm the atmosphere would become charged with electricity. It became more difficult to breathe, too; each inhalation was becoming more and more restrictive.

They followed Bruce across the street, where cars were parked on a slant in the shoulder's ditch and where others had been turned completely on their sides. Todd could see windshields caked with blood and bloody streaks in the snow as the vehicles' occupants had been dragged away.

The town square sat in a bowl ridged with trees. Bruce led them through the trees, past the bare branches of deciduous flora to where the evergreens clotted together for better concealment. On their hands and knees, the three men crawled beneath the trees and through the prickling swats of bristly, cold branches. The smell of sap was very strong. They paused only when they'd reached the end of the copse, each of the men pulling aside bristling boughs to peer down into the town square.

"Oh," said Todd, "you gotta be kidding me."

There were perhaps thirty townspeople gathered in the center of the town square, and perhaps another dozen or so lingering in the shaded alleyways between some storefronts. They all affected the same slump-shouldered, loose-limbed stance, their faces, from what Todd could make out at this distance, a mask of catatonic nonattendance. Despite the skin-suits, there was nothing remotely human about their appearance. That empty, vacuous glaze over their upturned faces made them look like wax dummies.

"What are they doing?" asked Brendan.

"They look like they're . . . listening," Todd said. He pointed at the glower crater carved into the clouds, the crater's epicenter a storm of electrical current and brilliant, dazzling lights. "Like they're getting subliminal instructions from that thing in the sky."

"Like they're getting *something*," Bruce muttered.

Todd could see the Pack-N-Go across the square, its front windows busted out, the interior dark. The icy sidewalk in front of the store was littered with arrowheads of triangular glass as well as boxes of cereal, packets of Ramen noodles, burst soda bottles, and fluttery rolls of paper towels.

"How the hell are we supposed to get into the Pack-N-Go then back out again without those things seeing us?" Brendan said. He was drumming his fingers against his knees—a nervous habit.

"Maybe they're in a trance," Todd suggested. "Maybe it won't be as hard as it looks."

"You willing to bet your life on it?" Bruce jerked his chin farther up the square, where the main street led back up an incline and through the town.

It was the direction Todd and the others had come last night as they walked into the square, looking for signs of life. Now, a grayish slurry of snow slowly rotated like a tornado in slow motion. At first glance, it appeared camouflaged by the snowfall itself . . . but on closer scrutiny, Todd could make out the subtle density to it and the distinction of its shape—the funnel of twisting snowflakes trapped in a vacuum that never touched the ground. It was large enough to block the entire street—the street that led out of town.

This is insane, Todd thought. *This is a nightmare. I should just curl up in a ball and sit here until I wake up.*

Something akin to a giggle bubbled up from deep within Brendan. Both Todd and Bruce looked at him, matching expressions of puzzlement on their faces. Brendan's fingers continued to drum restlessly on his knees. "You know," he said, a grin tugging at one corner of his mouth, "I think I've got a plan."

"Okay," Kate said, shaking the bottle of aspirin, "this should help with the headache, sweetheart." She froze in the doorway. "Where's Charlie?"

"He went to find me my medicine," Cody intoned, not lifting her head from the pillow.

Kate glared at Molly, who feigned interest in her book. "Why'd you let him go?"

Molly sneered and refolded her legs beneath her. "I'm not that boy's mother."

Fuming, Kate dropped to her knees before Cody's cot. She popped the cap on the aspirin and shook a bunch of tablets into her palm. Then she read the directions on the bottle, realizing she'd never in her life administered medication to a child before.

"How old are you, sweetie?"

"Eight and three quarters," Cody said.

Kate poured all but one tablet back into the bottle. "This will make you feel better," she told the girl.

Still cradling the water bottle like a baby doll, Cody raised her head off the pillow. Her hair was damp with sweat and her face looked as red and as hot as a smoked ham.

Kate put the aspirin in Cody's mouth. At her back, she could feel Molly's eyes boring into her. "You have to swallow it whole," Kate told her. "No chewing."

The girl nodded. She drank from the water bottle and grimaced as the pill went down.

Kate stood and set the aspirin bottle down on the desk next to the collection of liquor bottles. The shotgun still leaned against the desk. "You shouldn't have let Charlie go," she said to Molly. Then, without another word,

Kate snatched up the shotgun and one of the halogen lamps, and hurried out of the room.

"It just came to me," Brendan said. He was talking fast, moving his hands about a lot. "But I'm gonna need help. Like, Bruce, man—we can *do* this."

"Do what?" Bruce asked, skeptical.

Ignoring him, Brendan leaned over and grabbed a fistful of Todd's sweater. "You just sneak on down there, get as close to the Pack-N-Go as you can without actually setting foot into the square where those things can see you. Just sit tight and wait for the distraction."

"What distraction?" Todd asked.

Still chuckling like a madman, Brendan sprung to his feet and pushed through the trees.

Todd and Bruce exchanged a look. "Just be careful," Bruce said before rising and following Brendan through the trees.

Todd turned back to face the square. That spiraling aperture of light was slowly revolving, carving away the brownish, dirty-looking clouds as it turned. Looking at it caused something uncomfortable to turn over in Todd's stomach. He blew into his gloved hands for warmth. Suddenly, his fingers felt numb, useless.

Then he was up and hustling through the pine boughs. The crust of snow crunched beneath his heavy boots while he toed fallen pinecones out of his way. When he finally came out of the trees, he was facing the rear of the shops along the town square, which sat maybe twenty yards ahead of him and at the bottom of a slight decline. Todd counted the number of shops over from the alleyway until he was certain he was looking at the back of the Pack-N-Go. Whatever Brendan had planned, he'd said for Todd to get as close as possible to the Pack-N-Go. Todd meant to do just that.

He crouched in the snow, adjusting the gear at his belt. The butane torch was at his right hip beside the handheld radio, the handgun wedged into the rear of his waistband. He had the shotgun's strap slung around his chest, restricting his breathing.

He could sneak down there and cut through the alley between the two closest buildings . . .

An icy wind chilled his bones and froze the tears to the sides of his face. Taking a deep breath, he poised himself . . . then ran down the slope and ditched into the alley. The butt of the shotgun scraped against the bricks—a sound like the grinding gears of a garbage compactor. He had the pistol in his hand now, though he couldn't remember drawing it. He held his breath as he scaled the brick alley wall. Snow funneled through the narrow brick canyon; the sky directly above was the color of rotting vegetation.

He paused at the mouth of the alley, hiding in the shadows, his left shoulder against the wall for stability. The pistol weighed a thousand pounds in his hand. Across the darkening town square, he could see a number of Tully's skin-suits staged around the bronze horse statue at the square's center. They all had their heads craned up at the eyelet in the sky, their skin cast with an ungodly hue, their eyes black orbs in the pasty dough of their skulls.

What have you got planned, Brendan? Just what exactly am I waiting for?

Hunkering down into the dirty snow of the alley, Todd waited for a sign. For several moments, his heartbeat was all he could hear, somehow amplified in the freight train roar of the wind tunneling down between the buildings.

How long do I sit here? How much time do I give them? What if they get killed? I can't waste time sitting here until nightfall.

He decided to count silently to one hundred. If nothing happened by then . . .

He had reached ninety-eight, his grip tightening on the pistol, when he heard a sound like a locomotive come squealing into a train station. Leaning his head out the mouth of the alley, he saw something large come creeping down the declining street at the far end of the square. The street sloped down toward the square and as the thing approached, it began to gather speed. Todd could make out the vague suggestion of a slouching, mouth-like grill and two lantern eyes, dark and defunct and blind.

It was a car—a muddy brown Oldsmobile with a dented hood and a windshield networked with cracks. It came streaming down the street, collecting momentum, its hubcaps blurring with speed.

Todd's heartbeat quickened.

"Charlie?"

Kate came to a stop in a storage room at the far end of the sheriff's station. She held the shotgun in both hands, the barrel angled toward the floor. The halogen lamp hooked onto her belt, it thumped against her thigh with every step. She'd searched the other rooms and offices for the boy, as well as the chemical-smelling sally port, with no luck. Now, the storage room stretched out before her like a cave, its walls surrendering shelving, its floor littered with heaping boxes and wooden crates. The light fixtures in the ceiling were a column of sightless eyes dangling from thin metal stalks.

A slight shape stood out in the darkness at the far end of the room. Kate brought up the shotgun.

"Charlie?"

The shape shifted, melding with the shadows.

Kate approached, wending around the landmines of boxes and crates, her feet hardly coming up off the floor. The shotgun rattled and shook in her hands.

There was a smell—a severe decaying smell—that seemed to permeate her senses and infiltrate every nuance of her body. When she was a young girl she had played hide and seek with some of the neighborhood kids. Tired of getting caught all the time, she decided to outwit them all by climbing inside a dumpster behind the supermarket. Five minutes later, alerted by the sound of her cries when she couldn't open the hatch to climb out, her friends found her at the bottom of the dumpster—filthy, reeking, petrified, and painted with greasy swill.

All that rushed back to her now in a wave of memories. The smell, the claustrophobia . . .

The dark.

"Charlie," she said, lowering the shotgun. Startled, the boy spun around, his eyes wide, as if he'd just been awakened from a nap. She rushed to him, the lamp banging against her thigh and causing the shadows to jounce and dance as if in firelight. She gripped him by his shoulder, shook him. "Didn't you hear me calling you? What are you doing back here?"

"I was . . . uh, Cody was sick . . . I was trying to find her medicine . . ." Then he turned his head to look back at whatever had been so attractive to him while Kate had been calling out his name only a moment ago: the circular opening of a pipe jutting from the wall.

Kate unhooked the lamp from her belt and brought the light closer to the pipe's opening. She sucked in her breath, the light shaking in her grasp.

Snow was billowing out of the pipe and sprinkling to the cement floor.

Kate pulled Charlie behind her. "Get away from it." There was an oil rag on top of a stack of boxes to her right. She snatched up the rag and stuffed it into the mouth of the pipe.

"Is that . . ." Charlie began, his voice small. He couldn't finish the question.

Kate held her breath. She took a single step away from the pipe, bumping against Charlie in the process. She was thinking of those five people-shapes she'd glimpsed across the street from the station, watching the building. Had they been discovered?

Bending to one knee, Kate brought the halogen lamp to the spot on the floor where the snowflakes had fallen. Sour breath escaped her. Instead of melting to water, where the snowflakes had fallen there was now ink-colored droplets of a bloodlike substance on the concrete floor. There was almost a functional formation to the spatter . . . and the longer Kate stared at it, the more it reminded her of celestial bodies sparkling brightly in a country sky.

"We need to get back with your sister and Molly," Kate said, jumping back up to her feet.

The Oldsmobile came careening down the street toward the town square, chunks of ice snapping under its tires. There was no driver behind the wheel and, of course, the car wasn't actually *running*—it had been pushed from the top of the hill and was now beginning to swerve out of control.

Any doubt as to the consciousness of the townspeople scattered about the square was instantly eradicated as, in unison, they all swung their heads in the direction of the speeding automobile. Todd's grip tightened on the handgun. He watched as the vehicle entered the square, moving at a quick clip, jouncing over the rutted snow packed hard as cement atop the street. With no one behind the car's steering wheel to control it, the vehicle struck a sizeable chunk of snow and hopped a curb. The undercarriage shuddered. Sparks flew from beneath it and one of its hubcaps took off in a different direction. The passenger door flung open, struck a parking meter, and instantly slammed shut again.

With shark-like eyes, the townspeople followed the course of the runaway Oldsmobile, their heads turning on their necks like wooden puppets.

Todd saw it coming before it actually happened: the Oldsmobile smashed into the front of the hardware store, sending a shockwave across the square and a display of shimmering fragments of glass into the air. An exhalation of debris wrapped in black dust showered the sidewalk.

A deep-octave moan rose up among the townspeople. Like robots programmed to do so, they pivoted in unison and faced the destroyed façade of the hardware store. The front windows were still smoking, the tail end of the Olds cocked at an angle in the center of the store like a sneer.

Then, as if someone had fired a starter's pistol, the townspeople took off toward the hardware store. They didn't shamble or stagger like the puppeted skin-suits they were—rather, they loped like gazelles, the width of their strides astounding. Their fierce agility and speed shocked Todd into temporary immobility; even his mind seemed to shut down. He could only watch as they attacked the hardware store, spilling into the busted front windows and swarming over the Oldsmobile like ants.

Great bursts of snow exploded from the ground as vaporous tornados of shimmering snow-dust corkscrewed up into the air. Todd counted four . . . five of them. They rippled through the air as they soared toward the hardware store.

Taking a deep breath, Todd dashed out onto the sidewalk and ran toward the Pack-N-Go.

From the top of the hill, Brendan cheered as he watched the Oldsmobile smash through the front of the hardware store. Without someone inside the car to steer it, he'd had his doubts how far the car would actually get before it ran off the road, most likely colliding with a tree. As it turned out, he couldn't have planned a better outcome.

"I was fired from that hardware store when I was in high school," Brendan said, grinning. "Fuck 'em, I say."

They watched as the skin-suits turned their heads and emitted a resounding wail. It sounded like an orchestra warming up. When the skin-suits began loping toward the hardware store, Brendan clapped his hands then clapped Bruce on the back.

"Come on," Brendan said, beaming. "We're not done yet, *compadre*."

Charlie in tow, Kate skidded to a halt halfway down the hallway. Molly stood facing Kate, the pregnant woman's face a testament to some indescribable horror.

"They're outside," Molly cried. "There's so many of them! They know we're here!"

Kate ran past her and into the secretarial office. Peering through the blinds on the windows, she could see the shapes had crept closer to the building. There were at least a dozen of them now, all staring at the police station. Skin-suits, as Tully had termed them. Their clothing matted with blood, their eyes as vacuous as muddy pools, they were like creatures that had shuffled right out of a nightmare.

Trembling, Molly appeared in the office doorway. "They know we're here, don't they?"

Kate examined the empty faces of the townspeople. "I can't tell."

"Of course they do!" Molly shouted. "You brought them here! And now we're going to die!"

"Shut up," Kate barked. She doused the halogen lamp, bathing them in darkness. "No one's going to die. Get back downstairs with Cody."

"She's asleep."

"I said go!"

Startled, beginning to cry again, Molly retreated down the hallway. Charlie now occupied the doorway in her place, a terrified expression on his pale face. He was visibly quaking.

Kate turned back to the window. Something beneath the snow moved and caught her attention—a mound rose then sank, rose then sank, as if the snow itself was breathing. The surface of the snow began to ripple, as if something were vibrating underground. Then, like one of those old Bugs Bunny cartoons where Bugs tunnels under the ground on his way to Pismo Beach, something beneath the snow—or perhaps the snow itself—began tunneling across the front lawn of the police station, leaving in its wake disturbed mounds of upturned powdery snow.

Whatever it was, it was snaking closer to the building, heading for the front doors.

Whatever it was, it was *big*.

They're surrounding us like the fucking Cavalry, Kate thought, terrified.

One of the skin-suits—a middle-aged balding man with a beer gut, wearing sweatpants and a Chicago Bears sweatshirt—began walking up to the front doors of the station. He had that same off-kilter look in his eyes that strange Eddie Clement had when they'd stopped to pick him up last night on the side of the road.

"What do we do?" Charlie said from the doorway.

Kate racked the shotgun and discharged a shell. She held it up to the boy so that he could see what it looked like. "I need you to go to the room with all the guns, Charlie, and bring me more of these. They're in boxes on the shelves. Do you know what I'm talking about?"

Without expression, Charlie nodded.

"Good," she said. "Now go. Hurry."

The interior of the Pack-N-Go smelled like death. Todd hurried inside, crunching on shattered glass and bits of cereal. The damage was unfathomable, the sights atrocious. The plastic trash bags he had used to cover the two dead bodies had blown away, revealing purpled, crystallized mummies in the aisles of the convenience store. The parts of them that still looked human— a twisted and frozen hand or the teepee bend of a leg—were somehow the hardest things to look at.

Also, there was now a third body, fresher than the other two but more horribly disfigured in death, draped over a section of fallen shelving. The head was opened up like a piñata, trailing ropy crimson goop over cereal boxes, rendering the person unidentifiable. Yet Todd recognized the clothing and knew without doubt that this was what remained of Fred Wilkinson.

As the townspeople tore into the hardware store across the square, Todd ran over to the refrigerated section of the convenience store where the ventilation grate lay on the floor beside the stepladder he and Kate had used to climb through the ductwork and into the gun shop next door. Blood had been sprayed along one of the glass freezer doors, frozen to gelatinous syrup. Spilled cola had made the floor tacky.

Todd spied his duffle bag on the floor and dove for it. Unzipping it, he rifled through the items inside until he located the laptop's nylon carrying case. Relief coursed through him. With trembling hands, he fumbled the walkie-talkie off his belt.

"It's Todd," he shouted into the radio. "I've got the laptop and now I'm getting the fuck outta here."

CHAPTER TWENTY-FIVE

B rendan and Bruce ran down Fairmont, parallel to the town square. They both planted themselves against the side of a pickup truck parked askew along the shoulder, the both of them breathing heavily. On the next street over, they could hear the commotion of the skin-suits tearing the Oldsmobile apart.

Bruce's walkie-talkie squawked to life: "It's Todd. I've got the laptop and now I'm getting the fuck outta here."

"He's got it," Bruce said, turning to Brendan.

But Brendan hadn't heard him. He was busy removing the gas cap from the side of the pickup truck.

Kate peeled the blind away from the windowpane and reached up, unlocking the window. She slid the window open just enough so that she could address it with the business end of the shotgun. Cold, blustery air filtered in, freezing the sweat on her brow. The man in the Chicago Bears sweatshirt was standing directly beneath the station's awning now, looking at the front doors. Kate charged the shotgun, the sound of which caused the man in the Bears sweatshirt to whirl his head around in her direction. His head sat cocked at an unnatural angle. Fresh perspiration burst from Kate's pores.

She aimed in.

Pulled the trigger.

The sound was deafening.

The man in the Bears sweatshirt slammed against the double doors as his right leg vanished into a spray of buckshot and misted black blood. He howled—as inhuman a sound as the distant, haunting moan of a sperm whale—and propped himself up against the door with one hand. Around him, the snow rippled in half a dozen places, as if alive. Overhead, the sky was briefly blotted out by a swiftly passing shadow.

Kate charged the shotgun again and pulled the trigger.

A large swipe of the Bears sweatshirt was eradicated. Blood spattered the double doors. The man shrieked and shuddered as something large and the color of smoke withdrew from his body; the smoke-colored thing spiraled up where it got caught in the net of the awning. The man's body dropped life-lessly to the ground. Trapped beneath the awning, the swirling mass of vapor and snow briefly glowed at its center with a brilliant silver light.

Again, Kate racked the shotgun and aimed this time for the awning. She fired, the butt of the gun slamming against her shoulder, and blew a hole in the top of the awning. The vaporous phantom swirled toward the hole and escaped.

She turned, startled by Charlie, who stood at her side. He was holding several boxes of shotgun shells.

Just as Todd was about to slip out of the Pack-N-Go and back out onto the street, the laptop case over one shoulder, a brilliant flash of light mushroomed up over the storefronts at the opposite end of the square. Shocked into immobility, Todd stared at the rising inferno that blossomed up into the clouds.

Something had exploded.

The townspeople poured back out of the hardware store as fiery debris rained down around them. Some caught fire and began shrieking and flailing their arms. When the entities inside them vacated their bodies, the skin-suits slumped lifeless to the sidewalk where they burned like funeral pyres.

Clutching the laptop case to his chest, Todd ran.

The explosion shook the sheriff's station. Kate dropped a shotgun shell as she sat reloading the weapon in her lap. She twisted around back toward the window in time to see a fireball rise up over the distant trees.

"Jesus," she breathed.

"What was that?" Charlie said, sitting down beside her.

"I don't know, honey." The things beneath the snow cut sharply to the right and began tunneling toward the street down below. Likewise, the remaining townspeople turned and looked at the flower of flame rising up above the treetops. They began moving in the direction of the fire, slowly at first . . . then graduating to a deer-like run, their feet cleaving the snow like knife blades.

"They're leaving," Charlie said, peering out the window over Kate's shoulder.

"For the moment," Kate said.

After Brendan had unscrewed the pickup's gas cap, they'd emptied some of the extra fuel canisters down the side of the truck and, backing up through the snow, left a trail of fuel from the pickup to the opposite side of the street. Bruce had launched a blast of flame from the flamethrower to the fuel that was soaking into the snow. The fuel ignited and traced across the street where it climbed up the side of the pickup truck and vanished into the throat of the gas tank.

The truck had exploded.

Now, the two men ran like bandits up Fairmont Street. White faces appeared in the windows of the surrounding houses. Behind them, the flames from the explosion burned like a holocaust at their backs.

On the front porches of the houses along Fairmont, the skin-suits emptied out of the doors and watched them run. On the lawns, the snow rippled and appeared to breathe. Whirlwinds of snow funneled up from the ground and speared into the sky. Around them, there was a whole invisible world awaking from its slumber.

"Run!" Bruce shouted, slightly ahead of Brendan. "Don't look back!"

But Brendan did just that—he staggered and glanced over one shoulder in time to see the skin-suits come streaming off the porches, giving chase. Brendan lost his footing and crashed to the snow. His tongue exploded with a sharp and sudden pain as his mouth filled with the taste of copper.

Ahead of him, Bruce skidded to a stop and began running back toward Brendan, who was already struggling to his feet. The ground vibrated with the pounding of countless feet closing the distance. Brendan propelled himself forward, managing to just barely duck out of the way as Bruce's flamethrower belched out a stream of dazzling white fire toward the oncoming mob.

Blood seeping from his mouth, Brendan continued to run until the ground rolled and undulated beneath him. It shook him to the ground. Rolling over, he managed to swing the shotgun's strap over one shoulder and rack the weapon. Behind him, the skin-suits cried out in agony as Bruce hosed them with fire . . . but they were still closing in, hungry to get at them both.

Directly in front of him, the ground seemed to rise up—a white, formless monolith as tall as a school bus standing on end . . .

Screaming, Brendan fired the shotgun at the rising crest of snow. The blast was ineffectual: it rendered a hole in the center of the mass that quickly refilled with fresh snow. Brendan attempted to chamber another round but the shotgun jammed. He threw it to the ground and, on his hands and knees, crawled away from the looming snow-beast just as it began to take definite shape.

To Todd's ears, it sounded like World War III had erupted on the other side of the town square. Smoke blackened the sky and some of the trees behind the rows of shops at the opposite end of the square were on fire. An acrid stench simmered in the air.

The laptop secured against his chest with both hands, Todd raced back up the incline behind the storefronts and crashing through needling pine boughs. When he emptied out into the street on the other side of the trees, he could see the insanity and confusion that was working its way up Fairmont toward the intersection: there were townspeople on fire and dropping like uprooted fence posts in the middle of the street. There was what looked like a burning automobile on the shoulder of the road. And Todd caught the glimpse of some rising pillar of snow driving straight up from the ground, maybe three stories tall . . .

He didn't allow himself more than that initial, cursory glance before his pumping legs carried him through the intersection and across the snow laden lawns of apocalypse-dark houses.

Beneath him, the ground erupted. He was thrown into the air, his fingers digging into the fabric of the laptop's carrying case. When he struck the ground, the force squeezed the air from his lungs and his head snapped back on his neck, striking the frozen pavement of the street. He felt the wound at his leg reopen.

Something big was crawling up out of the ground. Todd blinked, clearing the blurriness from his eyes while scooting backward on his hands and feet like a crab. The thing rose and blotted out the sky, a shaggy white behemoth with the body of a worm capped with a multi-tooth maw that reminded Todd of lawnmower blades. Its sturdiness was questionable, as its body was comprised solely of snow, and as it towered over him, its shadow like the shadow of a skyscraper, bits of itself avalanched down its cylindrical hide.

Paralyzed with fear, Todd could only stare up at it. He went instantly deaf, unable to hear any sound other than his own blood rushing through his veins—a sound like an old washing machine.

Above him, the thing swayed, unsteady. Todd could see the sheath of its snakelike belly threaded with thin silvery filaments of light. *It's legion,* he had time to think. *It's a bunch of those snow phantoms smashed together to make this monstrous beast.*

The thing roared and Todd's hearing returned, his eardrums nearly bursting.

Something clambered at Todd's side and Todd cried out. It was Brendan, his face an O of terror as his eyes locked on the monster.

Todd managed to jump up. He faded in one direction then took off in another, carving a swath of zigzagging footprints in the snow. There was a narrow pass between two houses; he shoved his head down and charged for it, hoping that the creature would prove too big to follow him through.

If I could just—

Something snagged his ankles, tackling him to the ground. Yowling, he rolled over on his side to see something black and snakelike, perhaps the thickness of a boa constrictor, come untangled at his ankles and bow up into the air. His first thought was, *Tentacles! They have tentacles!* But then he saw it for what it really was: the fallen power line.

The line swung and spat blue-white fire from its frayed end. Todd covered his face with his arms and rolled farther down the lawn, feeling every bump and crenellation in the snow through the threadbare fabric of the sweater. When he came to rest, he sat up on his knees, the entire world spinning on its axis.

The power line whipped against the ground until it swung around and connected with the base of the giant snow creature. Despite the creature's appearance, its hide was made of something other than snow: the moment the electrical teeth of the power line bit into it, the snow turned black like burning paper, and Todd could then see the segmented plates that made up its belly. It caught fire and mewled with thunderous aplomb. It only managed to put the fire out by collapsing in on itself, showering the blaze in an avalanche of snow.

A second later, and it was like the thing had never existed.

Across the yard, Brendan jabbed a finger at him. There was a wild, feral look in his eyes. "You!" he screamed, rupturing his throat by the sheer force of his excitement. "Get the hell out of here!"

That was the only invitation Todd needed. Again, he was on his feet and running to beat the devil. He did not dare look behind him to see what became of Bruce and Brendan, who were still fighting off the encroaching horde of townspeople; nor did he want to know if that giant snow-beast had rematerialized out of nothingness.

Up ahead he could see the woods they'd crossed earlier, and he knew he was halfway back to the station.

CHAPTER TWENTY-SIX

In her urgency, Kate had ushered Charlie and Cody into the sally port. She opened the back door on one of the cruisers and instructed the children to get inside. They were both trembling, with Cody clinging to her brother and whimpering audibly, and although Kate's heart went out to them, she knew she couldn't afford to slow down.

Before slamming the door shut, Kate bent down and peered inside. Both siblings were clutching each other and trembling with fear. Tears had carved clean slicks down their grimy faces. "No matter what you two hear," she told them, "you both stay in here and don't come out until I come get you. Do you understand?"

They both nodded.

Kate left them.

In the basement, Molly was petrified. She refused to leave her cot, having unconsciously barricaded herself with pillows and paperback novels. Kate had little hope that down feathers and John Grisham would be enough to keep those things at bay, if any actually happened to get in here.

"What happened to those things outside?" Molly wanted to know.

Kate set her shotgun against one wall and began stuffing extra clothes into a plastic bag to take back to the kids. "I don't know," she said. "They took off."

Molly was inconsolable. "Took *off*? What the fuck does *that* mean? Where'd they go?"

"*I don't know!*" Kate's own temper was incontrollable; she felt it burst through her from the wellspring of her fury. "There was some kind of explosion down the road. It must have scared them off."

"What explosion?" Molly pulled a pillow into her lap. Her eyes looked sloppy in their sockets. "My God, what if something happened to them?"

Kate knotted the bag of clothing then tossed it on her cot. She went straight to the desk and began rummaging through its drawers for a lighter, a book of matches—anything that would catch fire. Blessedly, she located a Zippo with the Marines insignia on the side, and she silently thanked a God that she wasn't so sure she believed in at the moment. She slipped the lighter into her pocket.

"What if they're dead?" Molly wouldn't shut the fuck up.

Kate reeled around to her. "Listen—if those things *do* come back here, I don't think it's a good idea that you stay down here."

"It's *safe* down here."

"No," Kate said. "It's not. There's only one door. If they come to it, where are you gonna go?"

"Are they inside?"

"No." But she wondered. "I don't think so. Not yet."

"Oh, my God . . ."

"I took the kids to the sally port—it's where they keep the cars—"

"The cars don't *work*," Molly moaned. She wasn't listening anymore.

"It's safer there. They're hiding in the cars. I think you should go there, too. If anything gets inside, there's more than one way out from the sally port. Plus, it's made of concrete, like a garage." She drummed her knuckles against the drywall. "Not like this sheetrock shit."

"You're talking too fast."

Kate squatted down in front of the woman. "Molly, I think you should come with me to the sally port. Do you understand?"

But Molly was shaking her head. "Fuck you. I'm not going anywhere."

For one instant, Kate considered snatching her by the hair and dragging her upstairs. Had she not been pregnant, she might have done just that. But despite her terror, Molly had fight enough left in her; dragging her up the stairs might prove dangerous, even lethal, for one or both of them.

Smirking, Kate stood. "No," she said. "Fuck *you*."

Back upstairs, she gathered some food from the commissary—bags of pretzels and potato chips, a six-pack of Mountain Dew, granola bars, an uneaten Italian sub wrapped in tinfoil in the fridge—and, burdened with the halogen lamp, bag of clothes, and the shotgun over one shoulder by its strap, she carried the stuff back to the sally port.

She expected the kids to still be whimpering in the backseat of the cruiser, but when she opened the door she was startled to find them sitting stock still, their heads slightly cocked in the direction of the open door.

"Jesus," Kate said, dumping the food and clothes into the foot well. She reached out and grabbed the collar of Charlie's shirt, pulled him toward her. "Come here." Slipping a hand down his collar, she felt around the smooth flesh of his shoulder blades.

"Stop it," he whined. "Your hand's cold."

"I'm sorry." She withdrew her hand, uncomfortable.

"We're just tired," Charlie said. Eerily, he sounded much older than he was.

"Here," Kate said, opening the bag and pulling out the various articles of clothes. "I grabbed whatever was there. Put these on and stay warm. It's cold in here. Just keep warm, okay?" She looked over to Cody. "How's your headache?"

"Hurts."

"Okay, okay. Todd and the others will be back soon, okay?"

"And then what?" Charlie said.

Kate did not have an answer for him. "And here," she continued, filling their laps with the junk food and sodas. "Eat if you're hungry, but don't get sick." She slipped back out of the car.

"Where are you going?" Cody said.

"I need to go back out into the hall, sweetheart. I need to check things out."

"With the gun?" Cody sounded so small.

Kate nodded. "Yeah. With the gun." She looked at Charlie. "Keep your sister warm."

In the hall, she went around to every window she could find, peering out. The pebbled glass made it difficult to see what exactly was going on out there. At the double doors, she checked and rechecked the lock on the inside of the doors even though she hadn't unlocked it since Todd and the others left.

Get the fuck back here, Todd.

Nonetheless, she managed to drag one of the secretary desks out into the foyer and prop it up in front of the door. It might not stop the possessed townspeople from breaking in but it might slow them down. Enough to take a few down then reload the shotgun, anyway.

She hoped.

Returning to the darkened storage room, she began looking around for things with which to board up the windows. There were more than enough wooden crates and the slats seemed sturdy enough; it was locating a hammer and nails that proved difficult. Eventually, though, she found some in a tool chest under an old poker table. Quickly, she set to work prying apart the crates, working like a demon and sweating through the layers of her clothes.

She stopped only when she felt a cold breeze at her back.

Holding the hammer up by her face as a weapon, she spun around and faced the darkness. Only stacked boxes caroused in the shadows, leaning into one another like deteriorating architecture. She bent and groped for the shotgun that she'd set on the floor, walking her fingers across its girth before snatching it up and propping the hilt beneath her right armpit.

I'm just scared and jumpy. I'm alone. There's no one here.

But *was* she? *Was* she alone?

One of those things had been trying to come in through that pipe, she recalled. *Had Charlie not seen it . . . had I not plugged it up . . .*

She went to the wall to see if the oil rag was still jammed into the mouth of the exposed pipe. It was.

But there could be more.

The thought caused goose bumps to break out along her arms.

Frantically, she searched all the walls, and even moved heavy boxes out of the way to make sure there weren't any more exposed pipes. Satisfied that there wasn't—and exhausted from the exercise—she paused to give herself a few moments to catch her breath.

Something was moving across the floor.

Her hand vibrating like a seismograph, she lifted the halogen lamp to better illuminate the room.

At first she didn't see it—a dark patch in a world of dark patches; a slick of spilled oil on the concrete—but then it *moved,* betraying all sense of the inanimate, and Kate uttered a sharp cry. The halogen lamp fell from her hand and struck the floor. There was a shattering sound and the room went pitch black.

Oh my God oh my God oh my God what was that thing?

She'd caught only the vaguest glimpse of it, yet its image resonated like the afterimage of a flashbulb in her mind—a meaty twist of fibrous tissue, perhaps as long and as thick as an infant's arm, that arched like an overgrown inchworm along the floor while trailing a slick of glistening mucus behind it . . .

And now it was somewhere in here with her.

In the dark.

Oh my God oh my God oh my God what was that THING?

Trying not to panic, she began patting down her pockets until she felt the bulge of the Zippo lighter in her hip pocket. She tweezed it out with two fingers, flipped open the lid, and rolled the flint wheel. A narrow white flame issued out of the lighter, illuminating a circle around her roughly three feet in diameter.

Then she *heard* it—a sandpapery *shhhh* as it dragged itself across the floor, followed by the tacky peel of the sticky mucus. The sound was like an old man smacking his lips in his sleep.

Kate squatted and brought the flame closer to the floor. She could see it, less than a foot away from her, *coming toward her.* Disgusted, she thought of dried meats hanging from deli ceilings, the phallic protrusion of cured, uncut salami. Acid burned at the back of her throat.

It was heading toward her, yes, but it was also moving *away* from its spot of origin: the place on the floor directly beneath the jutting pipe which was now clogged with a balled-up oil rag. The inky drops of syrup were no longer patterned on the floor. With mounting horror, Kate realized that the thing before her was what had become of those gooey drops of bloodlike milk— that they had melded together to form this eel-like obscenity, this creeping phallus.

She realized she still held the hammer in her left hand. Steeling herself, she drew the hammer down on top of the atrocity. Its head was flattened and emitted a yellow pus-like substance that stank like sulfur. Its rear still wriggled, side to side now as if in pain, and she brought the hammer down again and again and again until the thing stopped moving. When she'd finished, on the floor before her was a gnarled fibrous abortion in a puddle of yellowish glue.

Kate leaned over and vomited on the floor. And she might have even passed out had she not been pulled from her half-swoon by sudden pounding at the far end of the station.

At the front doors.

She dropped the hammer and wended her way through the darkness while holding the shotgun now in both hands. She hit the hallway like a bullet and paused, wondering if the banging she'd heard had come from someplace else. Listening, all seemed quiet. Perhaps one of the—

The banging echoed again down the long, hollowed corridor . . . and this time it came with such ferocity that the doors were shaking in their frames. The chains through the door handles rattled and the desk she'd moved in front of the doors squealed across the tiled floor as it was, inch by inch, pushed away from the doors.

Kate charged a fresh round into the shotgun and held it up at eye level. She proceeded to march down the hallway, one eye closed, aiming the barrel of the gun straight at the center part of the two doors. If anything came bursting through there, it was going to get one motherfucker of a surprise.

Then a voice: *"Kate! Kate, open the fucking doors!"*

Confusion shook her. Then reality reached out and cracked her across the face. She lowered the shotgun and closed the distance to the double doors in a sprint. Before he left, Bruce had given her the key to the deadbolt. For one traumatizing moment, she forgot where she'd put it.

Oh God oh God oh—

But then she remembered, and dug it out of the rear pocket of her pants. It suddenly seemed so tiny, so useless, in her overlarge hand.

"Kate!"

"I hear you!" she shouted back, though the pounding of his fists were louder than her voice. She managed to shove the desk out of the way and, after three or four nervous jabs that missed the keyhole completely, she lucked out and jammed the key into the lock and turned it. The rolling of the tumblers was as loud as a truck starting in the dead of night.

Todd burst through the door, clutching a black nylon case to his chest. His hair was matted with snow and his skin looked an unhealthy shade of light blue. Blood trailed from one nostril. "Shut it! Shut it!"

Kate had been holding the door open in anticipation of Bruce and Brendan coming through . . . but when she saw no one else outside, she slammed the double doors and refastened the chain and padlock. Behind her, she could hear Todd's boots squelching wetly down the hallway as he took off toward the computer room. Kate gripped the shotgun in both hands and raced after him. By the time she reached the computer room, he was fumbling around in the dark with the cables on the desk.

"Here," Kate said, and clicked on the Zippo.

Todd nodded his appreciation and began digging the laptop out of its carrying case.

"What happened to the others? Are they dead?"

"I don't know. They're still out there."

"Stop." She touched his right forearm lightly, the shotgun inching up at him. "Let me see your back."

He paused, the laptop halfway out of its case. He set it on the desk then pulled his sweater and the shirt underneath over his head. His skin was pale, goose-pimpled, his frame wiry. But his shoulders were clean.

Kate lowered the shotgun. "Those aren't the clothes you went out in."

"There was an accident. Hold the light closer."

She brought the flame down close to the laptop as Todd plugged in the battery source then ran a cable from the back of the laptop to the modem. He plugged the modem into the battery source, too, and watched as the row of green lights blinked in succession on the face of the rectangular black box—just as Bruce had demonstrated.

"Where's everyone else?" he asked, still breathing heavy from his trek back and forth across the town.

"Molly's still downstairs but I put the kids in one of the police cars in the garage. After you guys left, those things started surrounding the station. They knew we were in here. I didn't want them to get trapped downstairs without a way out."

Todd flipped open the laptop screen then squatted down to get a better view of it. Kate held the lighter's flame closer to it.

"Oh," Todd said. "Oh, shit."

"What's wrong?" Panic ringing in her ears.

"Shit." He sounded dejected. "The fucking screen's cracked."

Bending down beside him, Kate could see it: the crack from the upper right corner to the lower left, bisecting the screen. "Will it still work?"

"It better." He depressed the power button and held his breath.

The laptop lay motionless.

Then it beeped and the tiny lights along the front panel illuminated. The screen blinked then came on—the crack a disturbance but not one that would hinder the laptop's ability to perform.

"Jesus Christ," she whispered, very close to Todd's face. Her cheek brushed his bare forearm; he hadn't put his shirts back on. "This could really work, couldn't it?"

"Let's hope so." The Windows prompt appeared, requesting his password. Todd typed in TURBODOGS and hit ENTER. The screen faded black then opened on his desktop—the wallpaper depicting a remote island in the middle of some undisturbed Caribbean waters, clear as lucid thought, the skies unmarred by clouds and about as blue as a newborn baby's dreams of the womb.

"I would give my right arm to be on that island right now," Kate said, looking longingly at the screen's wallpaper.

It took less than a minute for the programs to load. Todd danced his fingers over the keyboard and summoned the Internet Explorer box.

"Where are you going?" Kate asked.

"I'm going to contact the Bicklerville Police Department," Todd said. "It's the next town over and the closest police station to Woodson." The Internet Explorer page was still loading, the screen blank. "Come on, come on . . ." He looked behind the laptop and saw the row of green lights blinking on the faceplate of the modem. "This should work. Come on, baby. Come on."

The webpage died without loading.

"Fuck," Kate said, the word nearly sticking to her throat.

Todd slammed a fist down on the desktop. He closed out the box on the screen and attempted it over again. A new box appeared as the Internet Explorer began to load. "Come on . . . let's make this happen . . ."

"If this doesn't work, we're dead. Those things will come back. They know we're in here and they'll come back. And they'll find a way in." She was thinking of the horrid wormlike thing she'd smashed to death with the hammer. She shuddered.

"It'll work."

The page was still loading . . .

"It's our last chance, Todd."

"It'll work," he repeated. Digging around in the front pocket of his pants, he pulled out a single dollar bill. He slammed it down on the table then turned to her, grinning. "I'll bet you a buck it works."

Kate laughed and felt tears trace down her cheeks. "I don't have any money, Todd."

"It's okay," he said. "I know you're good for it. Take the bet."

She looked at the computer screen.

The page was still loading.

"Go on," he urged. "Take the bet."

Still loading . . .

"Okay," she said. "You're on."

Still—

"Hot damn!" he howled, slapping his hands together. The Yahoo! homepage opened, the Yahoo! icon header outfitted in a Christmas theme with snowmen and an ornamented tree. "We're in business!"

Laughing through her tears, Kate clicked the lighter shut and said, "I guess I owe you a buck!"

In the search box, Todd typed BICKLERVILLE IOWA POLICE DEPART-MENT and hit the search button.

Back out in the hallway, someone else began pounding on the front doors. "Oh, shit!" Kate cried, hopping up and banking the barrel of the shotgun against the lip of the desktop. She ran out of the office and down the long hallway, the dreary light coming in from the pebbled windowpanes making the hallway look as though it was submerged underwater. She struck the doors with such force she felt a twinge in her funny bone, and quickly unlocked the padlock again.

Brendan slouched through the doorway, bleeding from a gash at the side of his neck. He hooked onto Kate for support and Kate fought off a scream, the shotgun protruding up toward the ceiling between them. One hand pressed to the wound at his neck, Brendan opened his mouth to speak— *"Mawwwh"*—just as blood as black as squids' ink spilled from his mouth and dribbled down the front of Kate's shirt.

"Shut . . ." Brendan managed, ". . . doors . . ."

Still clinging to Brendan, Kate kicked the double doors shut then shouted for Todd. "It's Brendan! He's hurt!" Black shapes began flitting behind the pebbled glass. "Jesus, Brendan, did you bring them *back* here?"

Brendan collapsed in her arms; it took all Kate's strength to hold him up.

Todd came up behind her. He seemed to do a double-take at the horrific amount of blood. "We need bandages," he said, sliding both hands beneath Brendan's armpits. "Lock the doors!"

Kate rushed to the doors while Todd dragged Brendan's twitching body down the hall toward the bank of offices. Just as she pushed them closed, an arm slipped through the gap, firing like a piston and clawing at her. Kate screamed and began pounding at the arm with the butt of the shotgun. The thing on the other side of the door hissed like a snake just as a *second* arm appeared, this one stained with blood the color of mercurochrome. The thing shoved itself against the doors, its strength too much for Kate. Instead of fighting against it, she jumped back several feet and allowed them to swing open.

The thing that stood on the other side of the threshold had, at one time, certainly been human—but what had happened to it over the past week or so had twisted it, broken it, carved away any sense of humanity it once had, leaving only a fiery, razor-eyed husk in its place. Its head tipped so far back on its neck, Kate was certain its Adam's apple would burst through the taut flesh of its throat . . . then, opening its mouth, it released a deafening wail that shook the windowpanes and caused snow to shake off the front awning.

"Cocksucker," Kate muttered, and fired a round at the thing's head.

The blast tore through the upper torso of the thing, its chest opening up like some rare undersea plant. Blood splattered everywhere. The thing's body shook, trembled, then folded almost neatly to the ground as something whitish and forceful as a windstorm funneled out of it. The whitish cloud took off like a shot out across the front yard and vanished into the veil of trees at the other end of the street.

Covered in blood herself, Kate rushed forward and slammed both doors shut. She padlocked them and felt the world tilt as if to shake her off into space.

When she turned around, she was startled by Molly, who stood just a few feet ahead of her but cloaked in shadows. She had both hands resting on the swell of her belly, her feet clad in fluffy pink socks. "Did they come back?" Her voice sounded like someone had her around the neck. "Where's Brendan?"

Kate pointed down the hall. "Todd took him down there. Molly!"

But Molly was off running. Kate shouldered the shotgun and went after her, suddenly conscious of all the blood that had slapped across her face and chest after shooting the thing on the front steps.

Todd had placed Brendan down on the floor in the computer room, one of Todd's shirts wrapped as a loose bandage against the man's throat. Blood pumped steadily from the wound and spread out in a growing puddle on the floor. Brendan bucked and kicked his legs and blinked his eyes in rapid succession. He was struggling to keep focus and stay alive.

Molly stood in the doorway, gaping down at him, the only light coming from the bluish hue radiating from the laptop's screen. Kate rushed up behind her and nearly crashed right into her.

"Oh." Molly's voice was small—the voice of a dormouse. "Oh. Bren . . ."

Todd was tearing strips of cloth from a T-shirt, his bare chest smeared with Brendan's blood. He caught Kate's eyes and thrust the T-shirt at her. "Tighten the bandage on his neck," he told her, then spun back around to the computer.

Kate bent before Brendan, ripping strips of fabric from the shirt. One knee went right into the spreading pool of blood. Brendan offered her a wan smile. His eyes looked like they were rapidly losing focus.

"Get away from him," Molly said from the doorway.

"He needs help," Kate said, ignoring her. She began to tie one of the loose strips of cloth around Brendan's neck. He winced as Kate slid it beneath his head, soaking her hands and sleeves in his blood.

"Leave him alone," Molly continued. "You people have done enough." Her voice softened. "Bren, honey, are you okay? Brendan?"

Brendan made a gurgling sound deep down in his throat.

"I think," Kate stammered. "Todd, I think he's choking on his blood!"

Todd dropped to her side and wrapped two hands around Brendan's right forearm. He gave Brendan a tug, propping him up on his side. Brendan shuddered and a steady stream of thick lifeblood oozed from his lips and puddle at Todd's knees.

"I said leave him alone!" Molly screamed. She looked instantly like a spoiled child, balled fists and all. "You're killing him!"

"We're trying to *save* him," Todd said. He tightened the bandage around Brendan's neck, and that seemed to slow the flow of blood. Some semblance of normalcy returned to Brendan's eyes.

"They . . . cut," Brendan managed. His voice still sounded wet, gurgling.

"We just need to stop the bleeding," Todd told him. He kept looking from Brendan to the laptop. A message box was in the center of the screen. Looking back to Brendan, Todd asked about Bruce.

"He was . . . right behind me . . . setting fires," Brendan wheezed. "Whole town . . . burning."

"I want to take him downstairs," Molly said. There was a pleading quality to her voice now that sounded very unlike her. "It's not safe to be up here, and he should have never gone out with you two." She glared at Todd. "Help me take him down. He should rest."

Todd nodded. "That's probably a good idea." He looked at Kate. "Help me lift him, will you?"

They stood and each one slung one of Brendan's arms over their shoulders. As Molly looked on, Kate and Todd carried Brendan back out into the hall and down the basement steps. Going down the stairs elicited soft little cries from Brendan as he struggled to combat the pain. In the backroom, they set him down on the cot beside Molly's and Todd rechecked the bandage at Brendan's neck. Blood was still seeping through and the bandage was coming loose from jostling him down the stairs.

"Goddamn it," Todd said. He unwound the bandage while Kate brought the halogen lamp closer. The wound was a gaping black maw in the left side of Brendan's neck. To Kate, it looked grotesquely vaginal, and she fought hard not to lose it and throw up all over the place again. "One of those hooked claws?" Todd asked Brendan, curling two fingers in a pantomime of the creatures' scythe-blades.

Weakly, Brendan said, "Yeah . . ."

Todd spun around and snatched a bottle of whiskey off the desk behind him. He unscrewed the cap and hovered over Brendan again like a guardian angel. "This is probably gonna sting like hell."

"Already stings like hell," Brendan offered, and there was a second appearance from that wan smile. His lips frothed blood.

Todd doused the wound in whiskey and Brendan screamed at the ceiling. Thick cords stood out on the poor man's neck. Todd used up a third of the bottle cleaning the wound, soaking the cot and the nearby blankets in the process, then redressed it with the torn-away sleeves of a fresh shirt.

Eyes wide as ping pong balls, Molly stepped across the room and eased herself down on her own cot. She looked like she wanted to touch Brendan— either to comfort him or just confirm his existence—but she forced her hands to remain in her lap beneath the push of her pregnant stomach. Her fuzzy pink socks were black with blood; she'd left footprints on the floor.

Todd pulled on a fresh shirt from the pile on the rolling cart. As he buttoned it, he surveyed Brendan, who stared at the ceiling with a disquieting serenity. Todd looked to Molly. "You'll keep an eye on him?"

Scowling, Molly turned away and stared at the liquor bottles lining the desktop. She didn't give him an answer.

CHAPTER TWENTY-SEVEN

I t's getting dark again," Kate said. She was with Todd in the computer room, looking out the single window against the far wall. The glass wasn't pebbled like the windows out in front hall, but it was double-paned, its center cloudy with condensation. The sun blazed like a greenish bruise behind the nearby trees. Above, the sky looked like tarpaper stretched across the face of the planet.

Todd was rapidly hammering away at the keyboard. He'd been sending out instant messages to various police departments' emergency hotline connections throughout Iowa and Illinois, each one professing the same message:

Please help! We are hostages under attack by terrorists in Woodson, Iowa. Send heavy firepower—the military and national guard. No phones/power/radio/heat. Send help soon!

It had been Kate's idea to mention a terrorist threat. Had they spoke the truth—had they mentioned what was truly going on in Woodson—they risked having their messages instantly deleted and probably laughed at by the neighboring police departments.

Not that it mattered: it had been fifteen minutes and no one had responded to a single message.

Kate sat down in one of the rolling chairs by the desk. She, too, had changed her shirt again, anxious to rid herself of the creature's blood. She watched Todd type frantically in the lamp light. "Maybe none of the messages have gone through," she suggested after the silence had grown too thick. "Maybe it's not making a strong enough connection to the internet to transmit."

Todd shook his head. "No. We're getting web pages without a problem."

"Then . . ." But she caught herself.

"What?" Todd said, looking at her from over his shoulder. Half his face was blue from the light of the computer screen. "Tell me. It's probably what I'm thinking, too."

For whatever reason, it bothered her to hear him say that. "It's just . . . what if this thing isn't isolated to Woodson? What if it spread to the next town? What if they're dealing with the same crap we are?"

The look on Todd's face betrayed his thoughts. Kate knew he'd been thinking the exact same thing.

Then something chimed on the computer screen.

Both Todd and Kate locked eyes for a heartbeat. Then Kate launched herself out of the chair and crowded around the laptop with Todd, staring at the screen. An instant message box had appeared in the center of the screen, one word blaring up and filling them both with insurmountable hope:

help is on the way

It had worked.

It had worked.

Kate sprung up and threw her arms around Todd's neck. She kissed him, hard and quick the first time around . . . then slower and with more passion the second time. On the desk, the laptop began to chime over and over again as similar responses to their S.O.S. came through.

A dark shape flashed by the window. Then two more. Then two more. Kate's smile drained from her face. Todd turned to see what had frightened her just as more shapes flitted by outside.

"Christ," Kate uttered. "They've come back."

"Get the kids," Todd told her. He grabbed his shotgun off the desk. "We should stay together."

Holding her own shotgun to her chest, Kate nodded then took off down the hallway.

In the basement, surrounding by the slowly diminishing light of a single dying lamp, Molly watched as Brendan—the father of her unborn baby— took his last breath before expiring in front of her eyes.

At first she didn't realize he had died. She stared at him, aware that his chest had stopped rising and falling, aware that the ungodly gurgle of his respiration had ceased deep down in his throat, but the full realization of what she was seeing did not dawn on her until many long minutes had passed.

Then, soundlessly, she wept into her hands.

What was going to happen to her child? She was alone in the world now, pregnant and alone. She had no parents—they'd both died a year ago in an automobile accident out on Highway 28, her old man drunk as a skunk behind the wheel of the family Plymouth, the son of a bitch—and now God had seen it fit to take Brendan away from her, too. Brendan, who had always cheered her up with raunchy jokes and funny faces. Brendan, who had shunned her the first few days after she'd told him she was pregnant . . . but who eventually came around, because he was a good guy and was going to be a good father, too. He'd said so—Molly, I'm going to be a good father. Just like that. A promise. Brendan had had a shitty old man, too (although the son of a bitch was still alive and living in Vegas somewhere, allegedly with a showgirl with fake tits, although Molly never completely bought into that one). Brendan was going to make up for his own shitty father and for Molly's shitty father, too.

The world, it seemed, was full of shitty fathers.

Then, for whatever reason, she felt anger well up inside her. Eyes bleary with tears, she looked back at Brendan's silent and still body. For the first time, his stillness actually struck her, and the thought ripped through her like lights on a Broadway marquee—HE'S DEAD HE'S DEAD HE'S DEAD. She looked down and found that her hands were immeasurably calm. She turned them over and examined the pink, puffy palms. As she looked, tears spilled from her eyes and landed in her cupped palms. And for whatever reason, this made her angrier.

For a long time, Molly sat with her legs folded beneath her on the cot as the lamplight slowly died all around her.

Armed with a shotgun and pistol, Todd stormed into the secretarial office and crawled to the nearest window—oddly enough, the one Kate had been perched out of earlier that day, although Todd had no way of knowing this at the time. The blinds were cockeyed and partially raised. He slid down beneath the window and reloaded shells into the shotgun. His fingers shook. Above his head, dark shapes moved around outside. He was too terrified to sit up and look out.

But he did anyway.

He counted six of the skin-suits staged at the end of the driveway, standing motionless as mannequins. Two more stood closer, at the far corner of the building. They stood so close together their heads nearly touched. Outside, the strong wind rustled the distant trees and flapped the clothes of the townspeople.

Also, something was breathing beneath the snow. Todd thought of the massive creature that had lunged at him back on Fairmont Street—the way it shuttled up from the ground and towered over him, as unfathomable as an Egyptian god. How many more of those things were out there? And how many other things, stranger and each more dangerous than the next, waiting to attack?

Todd thought of the old H.G. Wells story, *The War of the Worlds,* and how he'd read it a long time ago to Justin. The boy had grown tired of the standard children's storybooks and professed an interest in things beyond the appropriateness of his age—aliens and monsters being the two frontrunners. Of course, Brianna had objected. She didn't want the kid sitting up in bed all night because of scary bedtime stories. Moreover, she said it wasn't appropriate to tell stories to a boy of Justin's age that dealt with ghouls and goblins and strange fruitlike creatures from outer space that descended on the unsuspecting populace to terrorize, torture, and inevitably kill. Yet despite Bree's protestations, Todd had snagged a handful of books from the local library—books he, too, had enjoyed as a child (although he'd had no father around to read them to him)—and every night before Justin went to bed, they would read a chapter. Or sometimes two or three chapters, if the story was really cooking. If the creatures from those books ever gave Justin nightmares, the boy never let on. And although Brianna, who was no dummy, eventually learned that Todd had ignored her wishes, she never said anything more about it. Todd thought that had probably been one of Brianna's best moments.

She put up with a lot from me, he thought. A pang resonated in his heart, and his mind added, *They both did.*

Bleakly, he wondered if he would die here, right here, right in this spot. Crouched on the floor beneath a window in a sheriff's station in the middle of godforsaken nowhere . . .

I wonder if Justin asked for me. When I didn't show up at the house, I wonder if he asked Bree where I was.

But the idea that he had let his son down again was more torture than Todd could handle. He swiped at his eyes with his sleeve then sat up and looked back out the window.

He counted twelve this time.

Kate opened the door to the sally port, once again struck by how bitterly cold it was. Across the garage, she could see the twin nubs of the children's heads in the backseat of the first police car. She raised the lamp and waved at them. Then she climbed down the steps and went over to the car.

"Hey," she said, opening the car door.

The children turned their heads in Kate's directions.

Their faces were creaseless bulges of flesh—featureless.

Kate screamed and threw herself backward against the wall. Behind her, a shelf collapsed, raining empty paint cans and sheaves of paper down on her.

The two faceless children began climbing out of the back of the police car. They moved with the slow uncertainty of someone negotiating a room in absolute darkness.

Kate set the lamp down then leveled the shotgun at the first child—the one that had been Charlie. Her finger lingered on the trigger. Pulled it back slightly . . . pulled it . . .

She lowered the gun. "Fuck," she groaned, trembling. Across the room and midway up the wall, Kate caught sight of what appeared to be some sort of exhaust vent. Sparkling snow breathed out of the vent slats like confetti, swirling down to the floor.

Kate turned and ran out of the room, slamming the sally port's door shut behind her. There was a series of deadbolts on this side of the door. Kate turned them all.

* * *

There were so many out there now, Todd could not keep count. They all seemed planted at strategic spots, all awaiting some sort of instruction, or so it appeared. That thing beneath the snow continued to breath—the snow itself rising and falling, rising and falling—and Todd found himself thinking of hospital respirators.

Something moved out in the hallway, collecting his attention. Todd swung the shotgun at the office door as a finger rushed into the half-light. The figure moaned and called Todd's name.

He lowered the shotgun. "Kate? I'm here."

She rushed to him, her own gun held away from her body as if she wished nothing more than to be done with it, the lighted lantern swinging from her crooked elbow.

"The light," he beckoned to her. "Put it out."

She quickly doused it then crept up next to him against the wall. She was shaking.

"What happened?" he asked. "Where are the kids?"

She just shook her head very fast, not looking at him.

"Kate, what happened to the kids?"

"They're . . . they *changed*." She stared at him, her eyes frighteningly lucid. "No faces."

Todd felt his muscles clench. He turned back to the window. "They're all out there now."

Kate ran her fingers through her tangled hair. "God, what are they waiting for? Just let it happen already."

He squeezed her shoulder.

Her smile warmed him, though there was little effort in it. Then her eyes widened and she looked past him and out the window. "Todd, they're running."

He looked and saw them—all of them—charging toward the building at breakneck speed, their feet kicking up clouds of snow, their arms pumping like machine pistons.

"What—" he began, just as they simultaneously pummeled the side of the building. Blood went everywhere. Some of them fell backwards into the snow. But the ones who remained standing, which were most of them, slowly backed away from the building . . . only to rush at it again. This time, Todd heard a distant window shatter. Beneath the awning, the station's front doors appeared to buckle.

"They're smashing their way in," Kate said.

Todd pulled open the window, the cold quickly sinking its teeth into his flesh, and shoved the nose of the shotgun out. He fired at the closest townsperson, who went down in a gaudy display of radiating innards. One of the snow-beasts whirled out of him and spiraled off into the night.

Kate scrambled over to the next window and followed suit, poking the barrel of her shotgun out, charging a round, and firing.

On the floor between them lay a pile of shells. Not enough to fend them all off, but maybe enough to lessen the numbers.

There's no use in lessening numbers, Todd thought, continuing to fire the shotgun out the station's window; he was going deafer with each blast, his entire body vibrating from the recoil. *There's no use in doing any of this. There's a whole town's worth of things out there, ready to rip and tear and bite into us . . . not to mention that thing in the snow and whatever else awaits us . . .*

He chose to think of his son while he shot. The good times, like the Christmases and birthdays, the times they'd gone to Prospect Park or the Jersey Shore. He'd taught the boy to fly a kite in an open field where wildflowers burst like supernovas from the green grass, and the boy had cheered and shouted and beamed as the kite climbed higher and higher and higher. As a tiny baby, eyes all squinty and fists clenched and pink, he'd been nothing more than a mushy hump in his mother's arms. The way the sunlight bleached the nursery coming in through the side windows, and the one time the hornets' nest fell and got caught behind the shutter. All the hornets rasping against the windowpane. Laughing. That's not scary, is it? No, Daddy, it's not. I'm a big boy. Yes, you are. Yes! Yes! Fishing off Luck's Pier, hooking bass and, holy Jesus, a snapping turtle, would you look at that? Yes! I'm a big boy. I'm a big boy and I love you, Daddy.

I love you, Daddy.

The front doors caved in and the front awning collapsed. One of the creatures was shambling through an open window. The snow around the building pulsed with a lifelike current.

"Todd!" Kate shouted at his ear. She grabbed hold of his hair, shook his head. "Todd! Look!"

He looked . . . just as an arc of white flame shot out of the darkness. He couldn't tell what the hell he was looking at. As he watched, one of the skin-suits went up in a blazing inferno. A second skin-suit leapt at the quick-moving figure but was ignited just like his brethren.

It was Bruce. Bloodied and battered, but it was Bruce.

"Holy shit," Todd mouthed.

Bruce charged across the lawn, igniting every single one of the bastards that hazarded to block his path. Within seconds, the snowy front lawn of the sheriff's station was alight with burning people, screaming and running and falling on their faces in the snow. Some of the snow-beasts escaped in a whirl of white smoke, but this time they didn't dissipate into the ether: they swooped toward Bruce now, coming down low as he launched fire from his flamethrower.

"Jesus," Kate said, "they're trying to extinguish the flame."

Todd nodded. "Just like Tully said."

"Where's he going?"

Bruce continued across the lawn, his big booted feet leaving behind craters in the snow. He was heading for a thin fence of trees. And beyond the trees stood the decrepit little gas station.

"They're following him," Todd said. "I don't believe it."

The thing beneath the snow swirled like a whirlpool then began tunneling toward Bruce. It was moving too fast; Bruce would never reach cover before the thing was on him.

No, Todd thought suddenly. *I don't think Bruce has any intention of reaching cover. I think Bruce is here to end this thing, one way or the other.*

The skin-suit that had been squirming through the broken window dropped back out onto the snow. It was a heavyset female with a face like sagging dough. She began running after Bruce—just as they all did.

Todd grabbed Kate's wrist and yanked her to her feet. "It's not safe in here anymore."

Together they ran back to the computer room, Todd slamming the door shut behind them. On the desk, the computer continued to ding as all of Todd's messages were returned.

Kate hurried to the window, stared out. "He's luring them to . . ."

"To the gas station," Todd finished, coming up behind her.

Bruce had a sizeable lead on the pursuing skin-suits, but the thing tunneling through the snow was coming up on him fast. Moreover, the sky was alive with twisting tornados of snow, each one glowing silver at its center. As they watched, Bruce burst through the spindly trees and crossed the tarmac of the gas station. The pumps slouched like tired old men. Bruce turned and fired another blast from his flamethrower at the encroaching townspeople.

"There must be a hundred of them," Kate marveled.

The thing beneath the snow cut sharply to the right and ran the length of the gas station tarmac. The tarmac itself was shaded by a partial steel awning, which kept much of the snow from falling on the blacktop. It seemed the creature did not want to climb up out of the snow. Or maybe it *couldn't.*

Bruce dropped to his knees and began fiddling with something on the ground.

"Oh, shit," Kate said. "Did he drop the flamethrower?"

"It's hooked to a cable . . ."

"Is he . . . he fucking tying his *shoe?*"

But no—he wasn't tying his shoe and he hadn't dropped the flamethrower.

"He's unscrewing the fuel door," Todd said. "Where the trucks come and pump full under the gas station . . ."

"Oh," Kate said—almost childishly simple.

The townspeople swarmed onto the tarmac. Several of them struck the support beam of the steel awning, knocking the beam askew. The awning wavered from side to side, as if in contemplation, then crashed down onto a tow-truck that was parked on the far side of the gas station.

Bruce stood and looked like a ghost among phantoms.

Just before the townspeople clawed into him and tore him apart, Bruce fired one final blast from the flamethrower: directly down the mouth of the fuel door.

An instant later, it was like the apocalypse had come.

CHAPTER TWENTY-EIGHT

When Todd came to, he found himself sprawled on the floor and covered in bits of glass. He sat up, aware of the aches and pains throughout his body, as the glass tinkled to the floor all around him. The room was bitterly cold. The second his vision cleared up, he understood why: the force of the explosion had busted out the window.

Shaking glass out of his hair, he rolled over to Kate, who lay unconscious beside him, her face a patchwork of lacerations, cuts, and scrapes. Gently he shook her awake, brushing busted glass from her clothes, face, and hair.

Hesitantly, her eyes blinked open. "What happened?"

"Bruce blew up the gas station."

"Are we . . . where are we?"

He helped her to her feet. They both went to the window, shuddering at the cold. Across the field, the gas station burned. All around the station and like a photo from some Nazi concentration camp, charred bodies littered the snow. There were dozens of them, some still burning, others smoldering like bits of charcoal in the belly of a grill. The air reeked of scorched flesh and burning gasoline. Also among the carnage, Todd could make out a number of large, hulking shapes, almost amphibian in their appearance, like frozen black relics. Charred scythes stood motionless in the air. Others had melted to a tarry black gruel along the blacktop.

"The window," Kate said.

"Help me." He went and grabbed his laptop's carrying case from the desk and pressed it against the window sill. Kate located some masking tape and they taped it up over the window, making sure not to leave any cracks for anything to get in. Not even wind.

"Christ, how long were we out?"

"I'm not sure. I don't remember . . ." His voice trailed off. He was looking at the laptop's screen, which was black. The row of green lights on the modem's faceplate was dead, too. "I think our battery just died."

"But they got your message. Everyone did. They said help was coming."

Their arms around each other, they crept out into the hallway. Cold yellow moonlight pooled in the front hall, issuing in through the place where the double doors had been. The doors themselves now lay in concaved heaps on the floor.

Todd and Kate rushed to them, attempted to lift the doors back in place. They were too heavy. Kate yelped and fresh blood dripped down her palm. Todd took her hand anyway.

"Look," he said, pointing out into the night. The swirling eyelet of light had moved close to the police station; it now sat midway between the gas station and the police station, casting a shimmering artificial light down on the snow. The snow itself appeared to glow.

Things began moving—in the trees and shrubs, down in the ravine and out by the woods. Even beneath the snow. The sense of motion was all around them.

As they watched, bright twists of light spiraled up into the simmering eyelet. The lights seemed to come from all over the town, drawn to the central location of the eye in the sky like hounds to a scent. They sparkled like jewels, their appearances just barely glimpsed.

"It's easier to see them if you don't look directly at them," Todd said.

"Like stars," Kate said.

For close to five minutes, they watched the glittery snow lift off the ground, the houses, the trees, the roofs of nearby automobiles, and rise up into the eyelet. The eye itself appeared to undulate, as if viewed through heat waves rising off some desert blacktop. The swirl of colors at its center briefly reflected the world below—the treetops and rooftops, the wrecked cars in the ravines, the dark lampposts staggered like mile markers down the center of town. Yet Todd could make out faint differences in color and structure of the details . . . causing him to wonder if what he was seeing was indeed a reflection, or if he was actually glimpsing through a window of sorts into a whole other world, a whole other dimension. But then the glowing colors returned, masking the mirrored image, and both Todd and Kate could make out a distinct sucking sound—a vague and suggestive inhalation. The eyelet's light grew in intensity—a silvery light not unlike the silver threads in the snow creatures themselves—before the clouds swallowed it up completely.

A moment later, they were left staring at a natural night sky.

Todd put an arm around Kate, hugged her close to him. They were breathless and in awe. Squeezing her tightly about her shoulder, Todd could feel Kate's heartbeat strumming through her entire body.

"Look," Kate said suddenly. She pointed down into the valley of the town square. "Do you see?"

He did: down in the square, several pairs of headlights appeared. He thought he could hear the grinding of gears as the heavy vehicles crept slowly through the town square.

"That doesn't look like the cops," Kate said. "Those vehicles look military."

Todd's arm slipped down off Kate's shoulder. He grabbed her hand and urged her forward. "Come on."

Kate began laughing. She was about to run along with him until she heard something behind her. She managed to turn around in time to see Molly standing in the open doorway of the sheriff's station, her enormous belly protruding from beneath her too-small sweatshirt, her fuzzy pink socks planted firmly in the snow. There was a look of haunted desperation on the girl's face that caused Kate's blood to run cold.

Molly raised a handgun and fired a single shot.

CHAPTER TWENTY-NINE

He was aware of vagaries—the indecision of fragile consciousness. Faces peering down at him. A bright light shining directly in his eyes. The sensation of hands tugging and pulling at his body. Then blackness.

In his dreams, he was running along a snowy hillside that crested high above a model train village. Something chased him. Something hideous and malformed, the noises of its pursuit akin to the feral ululations of wildcats. He ran, his skin burning and his eyes tearing, knowing that he could not keep up the pace forever. It was only a matter of time before a sharp bladed talon pierced through the soft flesh of his back, bursting through his backbone and severing his spinal column . . .

At one point, Kate was looking down on him. She smiled warmly and smoothed the hair back from his forehead. Then he was in a truck or an ambulance or some such vehicle, with whirring buzzers and blinking lights all around him. Faceless people in white attended to him. At one point he sat bolt upright (or at least imagined he did) and shouted nonsense into the ether.

There was a room—puke-green walls, paisley curtains, water-stained acoustical ceiling tiles. There was a small television set bracketed to the wall and in the doorway, shapes blurred back and forth like memories of family members long forgotten.

Justin was there. His son. He stood for a moment in the doorway, his mournful dark eyes almost pleading with him. Todd felt himself wanting to say something, wanting to reach out and touch the boy, but he felt strapped down and helpless. *This isn't my body,* he thought. *And if it is, I am no longer in control of it.*

Which made him think of monsters. Monsters that took over people's bodies and marched them around like puppets on strings.

But no . . . no . . .

Later, the pain came.

Still somewhat groggy, he blinked his eyes open to find a large Hispanic female in a white jumpsuit of sorts drawing blood from his inner forearm. She looked down at him and smiled humorlessly.

"Where . . . am I?"

"Hospital," said the nurse. "You were shot."

"Shot?"

"Do you know your name?"

"Yes," he said. "What happened to my friend? A woman. Her name's Kate."

"There are people outside waiting for you," said the nurse. "You should rest but they seem very eager to see you. The doctor said it would be all right, if you are up for it."

"Yes," he said. "Please."

The nurse left and Todd attempted to prop himself up on the stack of pillows at his back. The movement caused a sharp pain to go shooting straight across his right shoulder were it pooled like lava along the right side of his ribs. Wincing, he gripped the bed sheets in both hands until the pain subsided.

Two men in black suits entered the hospital room.

"Mr. Curry," said the first suit—a well-built man in his late thirties sporting a buzz cut that turned silver at the temples. They both stopped at the foot of his bed, their hands folded in front of them. "I'm Carl Freed and this is Michael Shovanson. We're with the Department of Defense, Chicago field office."

"Am I under arrest or something?"

"Not at all," said Freed. Beside him, Shovanson—skin the color of ground coffee and a bald head reflecting the fluorescent ceiling lights—produced a notepad and pen from the inside pocket of his suit jacket. "We just need a statement from you about what happened."

Todd attempted to raise his right hand and drag his fingers through his hair, but just lifting it halfway caused the pain to explode in his shoulder again. He sucked air in through clenched teeth.

"You in pain?" asked Shovenson. He had a voice like a bassoon.

"A little."

"We'll just take that statement," said Freed, "then get out of your hair. Your girlfriend is outside waiting to see you," he added, as if hoping this would move things along quicker.

"I'm afraid you won't believe a word of what happened," Todd said. He tried on a smile but it felt false on his face. For one horrible moment he thought he might actually break down in tears in front of these two men.

"We just need to hear it from you, Mr. Curry," Freed said, unrelenting.

"A lot of people in that town are dead, Mr. Curry," Shovenson added.

Todd took a deep breath, then said, "There were things in the snow." He thought about this statement for several drawn out minutes—the agents did not press him at all as he thought—then finally added, "I think they *were* the snow."

"How did you get into town?" Freed asked.

Todd told them the whole story, starting with the flight cancellation to renting the vehicle to what happened when they picked up Eddie Clement in the middle of an otherwise deserted road. Shovenson took minimal notes and neither man ever raised an eyebrow. When Todd began telling them about the creatures in the snow and about the walking skin-suits, he did so with terribly forced levity, the words impossible to his own ears . . . but the men still did not balk.

When Todd finished, he sighed deeply—which also hurt his injured shoulder—and fixed both men with a frank stare. "You probably think I'm full of shit. Ask the woman outside—the one you called my girlfriend—and she'll corroborate everything I've just told you, word for word."

Shovenson flipped his notepad closed then stuffed it back into his suit jacket.

"This was just a formality," Freed said. He walked over to a nightstand and picked up the remote control for the television bracketed to the wall. "We have reports to write."

"Reports," echoed Shovenson, as if this was some part of a private joke the two men shared.

Freed clicked on the TV. After the picture came on, he began flipping through various channels. Most of the channels were news stations, each reporter looking grim and uncertain. Freed finally left the TV on one chan-nel where a female reporter was talking about the bizarre events that had occurred in a small town outside Minneapolis, resulting in the disappearance of half the town's population.

Todd blinked his eyes and just stared at the TV.

"So far," said Freed, "we're looking at twenty-nine separate incidents across the country. Several more were reported in Canada, and more reports are filtering in every hour. The folks who rescued you wound up rescuing another thirty-eight people from Woodson, many of them hidden in basements and armed like militiamen."

Todd studied the seriousness of Freed's face. "So . . . so this happened *all over?*"

"Twenty-nine different towns," Freed repeated. "Mostly relegated to the Midwest. By all accounts, it seems there was something in the storm."

"That wasn't just a storm," Todd said.

To this, neither Freed nor Shovenson felt the need to comment. They adjusted their ties and passed a look between them that suggested they wanted to go back to their hotel rooms and go to sleep.

"We left a card with a contact number with your girlfriend," Freed said as they both moved toward the door. "If you think of anything else, or just need to call and talk to someone about what happened, don't hesitate to use the number."

"Get well," said Shovenson, and the two men left.

When Kate came in, she looked much smaller and emptier than he had remembered her. She watched him for a few moments in the doorway before coming to his bedside and kissing him squarely on the forehead. Her eyes glittered with moisture.

"Are you hurt?" he asked her.

She shook her head. "I guess I was luckier than you, huh?"

"What exactly happened?"

"It was Molly. She shot you just as we were heading from the station down to the road."

"Molly . . ."

"Brendan died. She blamed you. After she shot you, she dropped the gun and just sat down in the snow sobbing until the guardsmen showed up. She's been taken into custody."

"Jesus . . ."

"There were more people, Todd. In Woodson. They were hiding in basements and attics and in different places throughout the town."

"Yeah, I heard. Those two federal agents or whatever they were just told me." He nodded toward the TV, which was still reporting about the inexplicable occurrences that had happened across North America over the past week. "Can you believe this?"

"It's like one big cloud came in and draped itself right over the middle of the country," Kate said. "But it didn't happen everywhere. Just quiet, remote towns. Just like Woodson."

"Because they're smart. Because to do what they needed to do, they had to be able to cut the towns off from the rest of society. They had to pick places where they could easily do that."

"And what exactly did they come here to do?"

"Feed," he said. "Change us, maybe. Did you see what it looked like when that cloud opened up at the end? Just as it started sucking those things back into it?"

"Like you could see through it to the other side," Kate responded. "Like there were other places up there, beyond our world."

The notion caused his head to throb. He rested back on his stack of pillows, his respiration labored.

"After it was all over, I went back for Charlie and Cody," she said. "I thought maybe if those things had left their bodies, maybe they'd . . . you know . . . maybe . . ."

"Were they alive?" he said.

Kate didn't answer, but Todd already knew what the answer would be. On the TV, the reporter was replaced by a computerized map of the U.S. alight with red "hot zones," as they were labeled, throughout the country. "This just in," the female reporter's voice carried over the scene of the map. "Eleven people were discovered alive in the small South Dakota town of East Fork, their stories no different than the hundreds of others we've been hearing for the past two days now, bringing the total number of Midwestern towns involved in this uncanny and unexplainable nationwide event up to—"

"Please shut that off," he said.

Kate clicked the TV off. "Gerald's down in the lobby. We've been here for a few hours. I didn't want to leave until I knew you were all right."

"Thank you."

"I took the liberty of putting my number in your cell phone," she said. "I hope you'll keep in touch."

"After all we've been through?"

She laughed. "I'm not your only visitor, by the way."

His own smile faltered.

Smoothing his hair to one side, she said, "I hope you don't mind. I found the number in your cell phone and I thought it was the right thing to do . . ."

Looking past Kate, Todd could suddenly see Justin standing in the doorway of the hospital room. The boy was wearing the same ski jacket and bright boots he'd been wearing in what Todd had assumed had been a dream. When the boy caught sight of his father's face, he closed the distance from the doorway to Todd's bed in no time at all. Justin hopped onto the bed and, despite the pain it caused his shoulder, Todd gripped the boy and squeezed him hard. He smelled Justin's hair, his skin, his clothes—taking every bit of the boy in.

"Daddy," Justin said against his cheek. "Are you hurt?"

"I think I'll be okay, sport."

The boy hugged him hard and painfully around the neck. Todd felt his throat tighten and his vision grow blurry.

Brianna appeared at the foot of the bed. She looked frail and thin in a coat that hugged her too tightly, her hair tucked beneath a white beret. She clutched her handbag before her with both hands, uncertain what to say or even how to look.

"I'll leave you guys alone," Kate said. She turned and rested a hand on Todd's shoulder. "Take care, Todd."

"You, too."

Kate did not look back at him as she walked quickly out of the room.

His arms still wrapped around his son, he offered Brianna a tired smile as he rested his chin atop Justin's head. He could feel the boy's heartbeat against his own, the child's body warm and good. There was no pain here. Not here, not now. Still smiling at Brianna, he could feel the silence between them in the room, interrupted only by the scuffing of shoes outside in the hallway.

After awhile, Brianna smiled back. "Merry Christmas, Todd."

"Merry Christmas, Bree."

She came and sat on the edge of his bed. Hesitantly, she rested a hand on his leg. After a few seconds, she began rubbing his leg . . . timidly at first, but gradually warming up to him.

Closing his eyes, Todd leaned back against the pillows and listened as his heartbeat strummed in synch with his son's.

EPILOGUE

Nineteen miles west of Bicklerville, a thirty-eight-year-old woman named Tracy Murphy stood beneath the lighted awning of a gas station, pumping fuel into her Mercedes while surveying the stars that hung low over the distant trees. Somewhat jumpy from the strange stories that had been on the news the past two days, Tracy now doubted her decision to drive from her folks' place in Iowa back home to Nebraska. She'd originally planned to stay with her parents until New Year's Day, but she should have known better— Cliff and Joan Murphy fought like two feral cats tied up together in a sack. Had it not been for the snowstorm, the drive would not have been a difficult one at all. But the roads hadn't been plowed and Chuck's goddamn Mercedes kept overheating. Last night, as her eyelids drooped lower and lower, she'd had no choice but to take refuge in a shitty roadside motel where the sheets stank of dirty feet and a bloated tampon floated like detritus from a barge in the toilet. And with all that weird shit on the radio about people disappearing from neighboring towns . . . well, the thought was unsettling to say the least.

A rust-colored pickup truck pulled into the gas station and shuddered to a stop beside one of the pumps. Tracy could make out two slumped shapes in the cab, one larger than the other. No one got out of the pickup right away; as Tracy watched, the two figures remained inside, although she did not think they were talking. It looked like they were both staring straight ahead out the windshield at the highway as it wound off into the distant pines.

Eventually, a man climbed out. He wore a checkered flannel jacket and a grim expression. Several days' growth shadowed the line of his jaw. The man cast an uneasy glance at Tracy, his skin looking sallow and almost dull green beneath the fluorescent lighting recessed up in the awning. Tracy felt a cold twinge at the base of her spine. Quickly, she turned away from the man and silently willed the fucking pump to go faster.

She heard the man's footsteps approaching. Waiting for the man's reflection to appear behind her in the smoked window of the Mercedes, she balled her fist around her keys, the ignition key jutting straight out between her index and middle fingers. She'd jab him right in the eye if he laid a hand on her . . .

But he moved right past her and into the store.

Relief washed over Tracy. When the pump clicked, she replaced the nozzle and screwed the gas cap back on. She looked back up and into the convenience store. The man stood looking at bags of junk food in one of the aisles, his back toward her. Tracy could make out unusual slashes in the fabric of his jacket, directly over the shoulder blades.

Something felt wrong. Tracy turned around and could more clearly see the second figure in the cab of the pickup truck: a young child in a pink ski jacket, the fur-trimmed hood up covering the child's face.

Something isn't right about this, Tracy thought. The kid just stared straight ahead through the windshield of the pickup, the child's profile hidden behind the hood. The hood itself looked smeared with what Tracy thought might be grease or motor oil.

Tracy approached the pickup truck. Stories of kidnappings filled her head. Years ago, she'd gone to elementary school with a little girl who'd been swiped from the schoolyard. No one had ever found her again. The girl's name had been Lizzie and everyone used to call her Lizzie the Lizard because she had terrible eczema. Now, approaching the pickup, Tracy wondered what had become of Lizzie the Lizard . . .

Tracy stopped beside the pickup's passenger door. Standing so close that her breath blossomed on the window, she reached out and tapped on the glass. Inside, the child did not flinch. The greasy substance on the child's hood looked like it could be blood.

"Can I help you with something?" came a voice from behind her.

Tracy jumped and spun around. The man in the checkered flannel jacket stood staring at her, a box of Band-Aids in one hand. "No, I'm sorry," she stammered. Thinking on her feet, she said, "I thought I recognized your . . ." But she didn't know if the child was a boy or a girl. She took a guess, based on the color of the child's coat. "Your daughter," she finished.

The man just chewed at his lower lip, his eyes roving over her.

"Is she okay?" Tracy said. The child had not turned once to look in her direction.

"Emily's shy," said the man.

"Is she hurt?"

"What do you mean?"

Tracy pointed to the box of Band-Aids.

"No," said the man. "These are for later."

Tracy's heart was suddenly zipping through her chest. She looked down and saw that her hands were trembling. Quickly, she stuffed them into the pockets of her coat.

"Excuse me," the man said, moving around her and around the front of the car until he climbed up into the cab. Tracy took a few steps backwards just as the pickup's gears squealed and the truck began to ease forward.

Just before it left, heading back out onto the road, Tracy thought she saw the child in the passenger seat turn and place a palm flat against the window.

Tracy tried to make out the girl's face but found it was impossible: the fluorescent lighting erased her features and threw glare on the window.

As the truck pulled out onto the road, Tracy recited the license plate to herself over and over again. Her goddamn cell phone had died—yet another luckless addition to this already lousy trip—but she would call the police when she got home later that night. She'd give them a description of the man and tell them what the girl was wearing, too, and how it looked like there was blood on the hood of her coat. About the Band-Aids, too, because that was just . . . well, that was just fucking weird.

She climbed inside the Mercedes with all the good intentions in the world, but by the time Tracy Murphy made it back home to Nebraska, she had forgotten all about the strange man, the box of Band-Aids, and the peculiar little girl whose face she had not seen.

About the Author

Ronald Malfi is an award-winning author of horror novels, mysteries, and thrillers. Known for his haunting literary style and memorable characters, he is the recipient of two Independent Publisher Book Awards, the Beverly Hills Book Award, the Vincent Preis International Horror Award, and the IBPA Benjamin Franklin Award, as well as a nominee for the Bram Stoker Award. Malfi was born in Brooklyn, New York, in 1977, and eventually relocated to the Chesapeake Bay area, where he currently resides with his wife and two daughters.

RONALD MALFI

FROM OPEN ROAD MEDIA

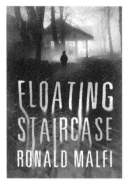